*Riv*

Where powerful pa

*Welcome to a rich and verdant land—where rugged, sexy men and bold, strong women flourish.
One powerful family has been living and loving here for generations. Watch as twelve passionate tales of old fortunes and new futures thrill this close community...*

Available now

White Lightning by **Sharon Brondos**—Lynn McKinney and Sam Russell have come together through chance. But now Sam wants some up-close and personal attention from Lynn...

Even the Nights are Better by **Margot Dalton**—Vernon Trent has held a torch for Carolyn Townsend since they were children. She's single again, so now's the perfect time to tell her...

About the author:

Margot Dalton grew up in Alberta, Canada, on a ranch that had been operated by her family since 1883. As she says, her home was 'where my great grandmother once traded flour and sugar to wandering Indian tribes in exchange for buffalo robes and beaded moccasins'.

Even the Nights are Better

MARGOT DALTON

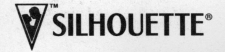

SILHOUETTE®

*First published in Great Britain 2000
Silhouette Books, Eton House, 18-24 Paradise Road,
Richmond, Surrey TW9 1SR*

© Harlequin Enterprises II B.V. 1993

Special thanks and acknowledgement to Margot Dalton for her
contribution to the RIVER DEEP series.

Special thanks and acknowledgement to Sutton Press Inc. for its
contribution to the concept for the River Deep series.
This series was originally called Crystal Creek

ISBN 0 373 82517 X

113-0009

*Printed and bound in Spain
by Litografía Rosés S.A., Barcelona*

River Deep™

A Note from the Author

Even the Nights are Better begins in the spring, and I soon realised that no matter how hard I tried, I just wasn't going to be able to describe the true miracle of April in Texas Hill Country. It's not only the green hills rolling off into the misty distance, the incredible blue of the sky and the miles and miles of wild-flowers. There's something even more magical in the air, something that goes far beyond words. I just hope that someday, everyone will have a chance to visit Texas in the spring and see it for themselves.

Margot Dalton

CHAPTER ONE

RAIN FELL over the hills of Central Texas during the night, carried by gray brooding clouds that had rolled in with the twilight and massed along the darkening skyline as soft and dense as piles of wood ash.

But it wasn't one of the torrential downpours that often lash the Hill Country in the spring, dropping two or three inches onto green wooded hillsides and gravelly creek beds in the space of a few hours.

This was a gentle sweet spring rain, pattering and rustling in the new green leaves, dancing on the silvered surface of the river, whispering through gullies and shallow draws in the midnight blackness. The moisture flowed like a blessing across the hills and valleys, and by dawn the world was made new, washed clean and bright as a freshly minted coin.

Just as the rain ended, a silver-gray Camaro came skimming along a country road in the early-morning freshness, its sleek sculptured sides catching and reflecting the rising sun's dazzling rays that broke into rainbows among the silent dripping trees.

This vehicle belonged to Vernon Trent and was

his one wry, half-joking concession to longing for vanished youth. On this glorious spring morning, Vernon Trent had just passed his forty-fifth birthday and was, on the whole, comfortable with himself and his life. He liked the maturity and confidence that came with middle age, enjoyed his friends and daily routines and didn't really miss the real or imagined crises of youth.

But he did have a stubborn boyish love for his shining, sporty Camaro, and never more than on a morning like this when he was alone at the wheel, the only living being in a world so fresh and lovely that it brought a lump to his throat.

His excuse for this drive was a scouting trip before office hours, a search for likely properties for a wealthy businessman from Dallas who fancied a retirement home here in the Hill Country. But this pretext was pure nonsense, of course, and Vernon was well aware of the fact.

After all, it wasn't as if he'd be likely to stumble across some new piece of land for sale out here. Vernon Trent knew every inch of these hills as intimately as he knew his own tidy kitchen back in the old stone house in Crystal Creek. There was nothing for sale along this road that he wasn't aware of already, and few that he hadn't listed personally.

It couldn't hurt, though, he reflected as he glanced appreciatively out the window. It couldn't hurt to drive for a spell out here anyhow. Maybe he'd get some ideas. And, he mused, smiling briefly into the smoky mirror, the morning was just so damned beautiful....

The rain-drenched scrub trees in the pastures, mostly cedar and mesquite, glittered damply in the sunlight as if they were fashioned from crystal and emeralds. Beneath the trees wildflowers were already blooming in shy profusion, bluebonnets and buttercups and Indian paintbrush, fluffy wild poppies and bright Indian blanket that carpeted the fields in vivid color.

Small animals, rabbits and coons and squirrels, frisked and played through the swaying grasses, rejoicing in life and springtime while a thousand trills of birdsong rose straight up to the clear blue heavens. Baby animals were everywhere, wobbly little calves and bony long-legged colts attesting to the enduring cycle of mating and renewal.

Vernon passed the high curved gates of the Double C Ranch, smiling as he thought about mating and renewal. There was a lot of that going on at the Double C these days, so much that the neighboring ranchers and townspeople were having all kinds of fun making jokes about the love affairs in the McKinney family.

They were affectionate jokes, though, because everybody liked and respected the McKinneys. In fact, there wasn't a soul Vernon knew of who wasn't tickled about what was going on out here, with J.T. finding himself a pretty young wife from Boston, and then all three of the McKinney youngsters unexpectedly following in their father's footsteps within a few months. Even that lovable wild man, young Cal McKinney, looked to be on the verge of settling down with a good woman. And *that,* Vernon thought fervently, was a real blessing for the whole family.

Just yesterday morning, during coffee time down at the Longhorn, Vernon had overheard Bubba Gibson joking loudly that the way everybody was behaving out at the Double C, somebody must have dumped a couple of barrels of love potion into the Claro River and let it drift downstream past the ranch.

At the time Vernon had laughed along with everybody else, but now it didn't seem so funny. Out here, surrounded by sunrise freshness and the beauty of springtime, it just seemed right and proper somehow that the people at the ranch should be fitting in with the cycle of nature, finding themselves some love and tenderness in a big lonely world.

A lot more fitting, Vernon thought with a sudden tightening of his jaw, than the way Bubba Gibson was acting these days.

No matter how many tons of love potion might be drifting down the Claro, there was no excuse for

Bubba's flagrant affair with Billie Jo Dumont, a girl younger than his own daughter. Bubba didn't even trouble to hide his infatuation, almost seemed to flaunt it, in fact. People felt sorry for Mary Gibson, who bore this public humiliation with quiet dignity and never said a word against her philandering husband…at least, nothing that anybody heard.

Vernon's wide pleasant mouth set in a hard line and he frowned again, gripping the wheel and surging around a bend in the road a little faster than was really necessary.

Like many confirmed bachelors, Vernon idealized women, liked them and enjoyed their company and had strong feelings about how they should be treated. Especially good women, wives like Mary Gibson who helped their husbands and stood by them through all the lean years, all the building and struggling and hard work. To Vernon's way of thinking, a woman like that deserved the very best her man could give.

If I had a wife who'd stood by me like that, Vernon thought, *there'd never be a minute that she couldn't trust me. I'd give her so much.…*

But just then his thoughts halted abruptly. Even his breathing was suspended for a moment as his car purred toward the gates of the Circle T, the ranch adjoining the McKinney place. Pain stabbed at him, as fresh and powerful as it had been all those years ago. Briefly, Vernon Trent's shining cheerful world turned gray and cloudly while he swept past the big stone gates.

He gripped the wheel again, wondering with a touch of desperation if he was ever going to get over those old feelings. Maybe it was all this thinking about love, about J.T.'s marriage and the young people finding partners for themselves, even the animals all happily paired out there in the thickets, playing and mating and nesting in secret places....

Vernon shook his head restlessly, staring down at the ditch beside the road. Something caught his eye and he hesitated, then braked, backed the low-slung powerful car around and drove slowly back toward the gates of the Circle T. He pulled over onto the shoulder and stopped, got out and walked around his car to peer down into the wet grassy ditch.

Vernon Trent was a good-looking man, even in the bright impartial light of the sunrise. He was a little above medium height, with broad shoulders and a stocky muscular frame, though he was probably carrying twenty pounds or so of excess weight these days. Vernon knew well enough that he'd been letting himself go and should be doing something about getting back into shape, but somehow he just never seemed to find the time or the incentive. In the meantime he disguised the extra pounds well enough with casual pleated corduroys and roomy worn tweed sport jackets like the one he wore this morning.

His face was blunt, square and full of good humor, and his brown eyes were shrewd, though they sometimes softened to a thoughtful faraway look that made people suspect that Vernon Trent might still be a bit of a dreamer.

His thick sandy hair was half-gray, but that was nothing recent. The same dusting of silver had been there for more than twenty years, ever since Vernon came home from Vietnam. He'd wandered into the lonely bus depot at Crystal Creek on a hot August morning with his duffel bag on his shoulder and a slight limp that only bothered him occasionally, in damp cold weather. But there'd also been a look in his eyes that even his best friends had never found the courage to inquire about, and that hair gone gray before its time....

Right now, though, none of this ancient history was on Vernon Trent's mind. His concerns were more immediate, focused on the small crumpled dark mass he'd sighted at the side of the road just where the shoulder straggled into a lush growth of weeds and grass.

He edged forward intently, heedless of the damp foliage brushing against his pant legs and the puddles of water that squelched up around his suede shoes. He knelt beside the little furry object.

"Hi, fella," he muttered huskily. "How are you? Pretty bad, aren't you? Poor little guy. Poor little guy."

His square tanned face was tender with sympathy, his brown eyes full of compassion as he touched the little dog's matted fur. The suffering animal lay shivering in the weeds, gazing piteously up at Vernon's face, blue-black liquid eyes glassy with pain. The dog was slick with dampness, one of those comical terrier types that look like brisk self-propelled mops when they're on their feet and in motion.

But this little dog wasn't likely to be in motion in the near future, Vernon suspected. There was no doubt that the animal had been hit by a passing car during the rain last night. It lay crumpled and twisted on the grass, its tongue lolling, one hind leg obviously broken, and a long gash in its side crusted with blood.

Vernon gazed down at the animal, then reached out again to touch one of the silky ears. The little dog lifted its jaw, pink tongue wavering painfully in a feeble attempt to lick the big man's fingers.

Vernon swallowed hard at this and dashed a hand impatiently across his eyes. After a moment's hesitation he got briskly to his feet and hurried back to his car, opening the trunk and taking out a battered old plaid blanket that had served many strange purposes over the years. Without pausing to think further, he rolled the little broken body into the soft fabric, set it gently on the seat beside him and pulled through the gates of the Circle T and up the long curving entry road.

Usually when Vernon Trent drove up this particular road, his heart was in his mouth and he had a hard time breathing normally, beset by all the crazy adolescent reactions that he never seemed to outgrow no matter how old he got. Today, though, wrung with concern for the pitiful little object on the seat beside him, Vernon wasn't bothered quite as much by his own emotions.

Still, when a slim woman came out of the barn at his approach and looked curiously over at his car, Vernon's throat tightened and his heart leaped with excitement, then settled into the old dull ache that had been part of his life for decades now.

"Hi, Carolyn," he said casually, getting out of the car and approaching the woman. "Nice morning, isn't it?"

"It surely is," the woman agreed, coming toward him with a smile. "'Specially after that rain last night, Vern. What're you doing up and about so early?"

"Just out for a drive, Caro. Scouting property for a client. You know me, I never stop working."

Vernon's voice and manner were casual, but his

heart was singing, on fire with love for the woman who stood smiling in front of him.

Carolyn Randolph Townsend was almost exactly his own age, just a week younger, in fact, and Vernon Trent couldn't remember a time when he hadn't loved her. Maybe in the years before grade school when he'd only seen her at birthday parties and community picnics... maybe he hadn't loved her then. He couldn't remember. But certainly by the time they were both in first grade he had selected Carolyn Randolph as the woman of his dreams, and in the forty years since he'd never really wavered from that choice.

Carolyn Randolph Townsend, at forty-five, had a figure to put most younger women to shame. Her tall curving body was firm and beautiful and full of promise, even in the old jeans and denim shirt that she wore this morning with her riding boots. Her wide blue-green eyes were vivid, sparkling warmly in her tanned oval face, and her hair, pulled back casually and tied at the nape of her neck with a blue bandanna, was almost the same rich dark gold it had always been. Still, Vernon's keen loving eyes noticed a few scattered streaks of gray that he'd never seen there before, glistening softly in the early-morning light.

Poor girl, he thought, gazing at those silvery

strands, thinking about all this woman had suffered in the past few years. *My poor girl....*

He fought the familiar desire to take her in his arms, to hold her and protect her and shield her from pain.

Get a grip, fella, he ordered himself sternly. *It's not you she wants to comfort her, and it never has been....*

Maybe things would have been different if he'd had more courage when they were young, if he'd ever told her all the things he was feeling. But she and her older sister, Pauline, had been like princesses, growing up out here on this big sprawling ranch that was one the finest places in the area, second only to the McKinneys' Double C. He, on the other hand, was just young Vernon Trent, the druggist's son, living with his parents through most of his boyhood in a little apartment above the drugstore in Crystal Creek.

And in later years, just when all that ceased to matter quite as much and he was ready to open his heart to her, Vernon was drafted. He left Crystal Creek before he was twenty, and came back when he was twenty-three. By that time, everything had changed in the Randolph family. Pauline, Carolyn's sister, and J. T. McKinney had a little girl to go along with their two boys. The Randolph girls' charming dissolute father, Steven, had run off somewhere and dropped out of sight, leaving his wife, Deborah, to run the ranch with the help of Frank Townsend, her young foreman. Pauline Randolph McKinney had a little girl to go with her two young sons. And Carolyn had been married for more than three years to Frank Townsend and was a mother herself.

"Vern? Is something the matter?"

Vernon pulled himself back to reality with a visible effort, banishing all those painful twenty-year-old memories and turning with an easy smile to the woman in front of him, who was now frowning anxiously.

"Not with me, Caro," he said. "I'm on top of the world. But I've got somebody in my car who isn't, I'm afraid."

He opened the passenger door of his car and pointed to the small motionless bundle on the seat.

"I found him out on the road a few minutes ago," he said. "Just past your gates. Looks like he…"

But Carolyn was already leaning into the car, turning back the blanket with gentle hands and gazing in horror at the pitiful little dog curled within the folds.

Vernon watched as her expressive features registered a whole series of impressions—shock, compassion, tenderness, pain and finally outrage. "God, Vern, this makes me so *mad!*" Carolyn said, straightening and turning to her old friend, her eyes glittering in the early light.

"What does, Caro?" he asked gently.

"This," she said, waving her hand at the dog and then reaching down to caress one of its ears. "It's happening more and more these days. Those damn town people, Vern, they just never give a thought to what they do. This little dog is certainly no ranch dog. He belongs to somebody from the city, somebody who's moving away or doesn't want to be bothered with him anymore, so they drive forty miles out into the country and dump him off, figuring he'll just find a happy home at some ranch."

She paused for breath, her chest heaving, her delicate features pink with anger. Vernon was silent, watching her.

"And," Carolyn went on in a lower tone, touching the little dog's head again, "it's just so brutal, Vern. What chance does a little fella like this have out in open country that he doesn't know a thing about? People who treat animals this way should be shot. They really should."

Vernon grinned. "Well, Caro, I can't say I disagree. But it might take a few months to get legislation like that passed, even in Texas."

"Even in Texas," Carolyn agreed, swallowing her outrage and trying to smile back. "Lift him out, Vern, would you? Be real careful," she added. "Just carry him into the barn here, and we'll make him a little nest of straw in one of the mangers."

"Look, Carolyn," Vernon began awkwardly, "I didn't mean for you to have to do all this. I mean, I don't want to make a lot of work and trouble for you. It's just that I thought the little guy needed some help and you were closest...."

"Be quiet, Vern," Carolyn said, laying a gentle hand on his cheek and giving him a smile that made his heart stop, then begin thudding like mad. "Just do as you're told, okay? Bring the little guy in here."

Vernon obeyed silently, carrying the dog into the barn and settling it in the upper portion of one of the mangers, a shallow wooden box designed for oats and other grains into which Carolyn was busily arranging a bedding of soft dried alfalfa.

"This should be nice and cozy for him," she said, leaning in to study the small dog, examining his injuries with competent tanned hands while the animal shivered beneath her touch.

"Do you still have that toy car phone of yours?" she asked over her shoulder without turning around.

"It's *not* a toy," Vernon said with dignity. "It's a completely viable working tool, Caro. An absolute necessity in the modern business world."

"Like hell," his old friend said cheerfully. "It's just a toy, Vern, and you know it. I can never get over the way you men love your toys. But I'll allow that it could be handy at times. Call Manny's office for me, would you, and see if he could drop by and take a look at this little fella?''

''Oh, Caro,'' Vernon protested. ''Truly, I didn't mean for you to...''

She turned to him, her face in the dim interior of the barn softly illuminated by dusty rays of light slanting through the big open doors.

''Vernon Trent,'' she said with amusement, ''if you just don't beat all. You bring me this pitiful little thing, and then you argue with me when I want to help him.''

Vernon laughed with her, then sobered. ''I'm sorry,'' he said. ''It's just that this is getting way more complicated than I'd figured. Do you have any idea what veterinarian fees are these days?''

Carolyn stared at him in disbelief. ''*Do* I?'' she asked him. ''Vern, you know perfectly well I've been running this place on my own ever since Frank died. You think those bills just get paid by magic, somehow, without me signing the checks?''

He paused, stung by her words though she hadn't meant them unkindly. ''I know, Caro,'' he said again, his voice low and strained. ''And God knows, it's been a miracle, the way you've managed things on your own. I just meant...'' Vern hesitated. ''Caro, girl...I'm not sure he's going to be bright and perky again no matter what we do. He looks to be in pretty bad shape.''

Carolyn glanced down at the matted body in her manger, touching the animal's thin heaving side with a gentle hand. As it had with Vernon, the small dog rolled its head feebly and tried to lick her fingers. Carolyn's face softened and twisted.

"He's going to get better," she said, squaring her shoulders and turning to Vernon with sudden decision, her eyes damp and glistening in the misty light. "I don't intend to let him die, Vern. I've seen enough of death these past few years and I'm sick of it, that's all. I just plain won't allow him to die."

Vernon gazed back at her in silent understanding. Within the past ten years, Carolyn had lost both her mother and her beloved sister to breast cancer, and her sturdy vigorous husband to a heart attack. That was a lot of suffering for one woman to endure, even a woman as strong as Carolyn Randolph Townsend.

Perhaps it had been a mistake to bring the dog to her.

But it was too late now. She'd already forgotten about Vernon and was filling a pail with water to wash the dog's livid cut. Vernon watched her a moment longer, then turned quietly and went out to his car to phone the veterinarian's office in Crystal Creek.

CAROLYN DABBED tenderly at the long bloody cut on the dog's shuddering body, trying to be as gentle as she could, wincing as the little animal growled and whimpered with pain.

"Poor little furry guy," she whispered. "Poor little tenderhearted baby. You don't even know what's hit you, do you? You can't figure out why the world should turn so dark and cruel all of a sudden. Poor sweet little thing…"

The dog's bony head lolled wearily and its forelegs twitched. Carolyn rubbed it with another cloth, trying to dry the matted fur without jarring any obvious injuries.

"Carolyn, I called Manny's office," she heard Vernon saying behind her. "He's out on a call, but they'll try to locate him and pass on the message."

"Thanks, Vern," Carolyn said in an abstracted tone, reaching for clean burlap sacks to cover and cushion the little body.

"Well, I'd better be pushing off," he said. "Unless there's something else I can do for you, Caro, before I go."

Carolyn turned around then, smiling at his sturdy form and pleasant anxious face as he hesitated in the doorway of the barn. Vernon Trent was not only one of her oldest friends, but just about the nicest man she'd ever met, she thought suddenly. She was a little surprised at the quick flood of warmth she felt for him as he stood there in the slanting early-morning light.

She smiled and gave him a brisk dismissive wave of her hand. "Vern, for God's sake, quit *fussing,* all right? You just go on into town and sell the hotel or the hospital or something, and I'll look after this little floor mop of ours."

He nodded and turned toward his car, his square features still full of concern. "I'll call you later, Caro, okay? I'm interested in hearing what Manny has to say about him."

"Sure, Vern," Carolyn said, turning back to her small patient. "Not till evening, though, okay? Cynthia and I have a date this afternoon. They roped us into handling one of the tables at the church pie sale."

Vernon grinned, the old teasing sparkle back in his eyes. "Well, now, *that* sounds like fun, Caro. Just your cup of tea."

Her mouth twisted in a wry answering grin. "Go away. Get that ridiculous kiddie car out of my driveway, Vernon Trent," she said calmly, "before I get my rifle and shoot the damn tires."

Vernon laughed and strolled out to climb into his car again.

Carolyn wandered to the doorway, watching him disappear around a bend in the road in a bright flash of silver. She felt strangely wistful as she gazed into the distance, but after a few moments of silence she squared her shoulders and walked briskly into the barn again.

"Mama?" a voice called from the other side of the box stalls. "You in here, Mama?"

"Round the other side, dear," Carolyn replied. "By the tack rooms."

She looked up and smiled as her daughter, Beverly, rounded the bank of stalls. As always, Carolyn was stunned for a moment by the girl's beauty, even though she knew Beverly better than anybody and was often less than impressed by certain aspects of her daughter's personality.

But there was no denying that the girl was lovely. She glimmered like a spring blossom in the dusty interior of the big barn, in her soft pink jumpsuit of crinkled cotton with a wide braided-hemp belt and matching sandals. Her thick golden hair, brushed and shining, held back by a pink shell-shaped clip, cascaded down her slim back.

"What's this?" Beverly asked curiously, bending forward to peer into the manger. "Oh!" she added, and drew back hastily. "Where'd he come from, Mama?"

"Vernon Trent brought him in just now," Carolyn said. "Vern was just driving by, saw this little fella crumpled by the side of the road."

"He was hit by a car?"

"Obviously," Carolyn said dryly. "He's somebody's abandoned house pet, I'd guess, without a lot of back road smarts.''

Beverly was silent a moment, gazing at the quivering bundle of sacking. Then she gathered herself and turned to her mother. ''So he's what that call was about, I guess.''

''What call, Beverly?''

''Manny's secretary called the house just now. She said she raised Manny on his mobile phone and he's somewhere out in this area anyway, so he'll stop by on his way back to town.''

''Oh, good,'' Carolyn said. ''I was sure hoping he could come right away, but I didn't think I'd be quite that lucky.''

''Is Vern still here?'' Beverly asked.

''No, he left a few minutes ago. Why?''

''I thought if he hadn't left yet I could get a ride into town with him. I'm spending the afternoon shopping with Lynn and she can drop me off later, but I still need a way to get in there.''

''What's wrong with your car?'' Carolyn asked, gazing blankly at her daughter.

''It's in the shop, Mama,'' Beverly said patiently. ''I told you yesterday, I'm having that dented fender fixed and painted.''

''Oh, that's right. Sorry, sweetie,'' Carolyn added. ''If I'd known you wanted a ride, I'd have asked Vern to wait.'' She paused, glancing up at her daughter in sudden surprise. "It's awfully early, isn't it, Beverly? What are you planning to do in town anyway, before eight o'clock in the morning?"

Beverly turned away, heading for the door. "Oh, it's just one of the kids on the ward," she said over her shoulder. "He's having his surgery this morning, and I promised him I'd be there when he woke up because his mother has to work. It's okay," she added. "Lori said I could borrow her car if I'm stuck. Bye, Mama. I hope your little guy's going to be all right."

Carolyn nodded and leaned against the manger, watching thoughtfully as her daughter disappeared from her view.

Sometimes she found it so puzzling, this whole business of Beverly and her volunteer work with the children at the hospital. Carolyn wanted very much to believe that Beverly's motives were sincere, that in those sick little kids at the Crystal Creek Community Hospital the restless beautiful girl had finally found something to hold her interest and release her from her intense preoccupation with herself.

Still Carolyn couldn't help being a little skeptical, wondering if the kids were just a new audience Beverly was playing to, a whole new group to dazzle with her gorgeous looks and that beauty-queen smile of hers.

Carolyn's thoughts were interrupted by the sound

of another vehicle in the driveway, then the slamming of a door and brisk footsteps.

Dr. Manuel Hernandez, the local veterinarian, appeared in the doorway, white teeth flashing in his dark handsome face.

"Good mornin', Carolyn," he drawled cheerfully. "What's this big urgent problem of yours?"

Carolyn eyed the young man thoughtfully. "You're awful perky this morning, Manny," she observed. "Seems like every single soul in Crystal Creek got up with the chickens this morning."

"Not me. I was up all night," he said, leaning against one of the box stalls, relaxed and casual in blue jeans and a soft plaid shirt. "Just over at the Double C, in fact. One of J.T.'s mares had trouble foaling, and J.T. and Ken and I worked on her for hours."

"Oh, no. Is she all right?" Carolyn asked with quick concern.

"Mother and baby doing just fine," Manny told her with a smile. "It was that new dark sorrel three-year-old, the one Lynn calls Cherokee. Finally dropped a real nice little bay filly, just a half hour ago."

"Well, that's good," Carolyn said with relief.

"But I'm sure one tired cowboy," Manny said, stretching his lean muscular body and rubbing wearily at his eyes. "I hope y'all don't have a couple of heifers calving, or something. I want to go home and grab a few hours' sleep.''

Carolyn gazed critically at the dark-haired young man, shaking her head. ''Just look at you,'' she commented. ''About three times handsomer than any man has a right to be, and you spend all your nights working. It's time you started thinking about getting married and settling down, Manny.''

''Oh, I think about it, Carolyn,'' he said. ''I think about it a lot, actually. You just find me the right woman and I'll be ready in a minute.''

Carolyn grinned. ''From what I hear, Manuel Hernandez, you've got no problem finding women.''

''That's true,'' he agreed cheerfully. ''It's finding the *right* one that's always the problem.''

Carolyn laughed, leading him across the barn to where the terrier lay.

As soon as he saw the dog, Manny's teasing and laughter vanished and he was all business, examining the little animal with long sensitive fingers.

Finally he straightened and turned to Carolyn, his face grave. ''Most of the injuries are quite superficial, really,'' he said. ''I could put a cast on the leg and stitch up this cut in just a few minutes, but that's not the main problem, Carolyn. I think you'd better let me put him down.''

''Put him down?'' she echoed, staring wide-eyed at the young veterinarian. ''Why would you do that,

Manny, if his injuries are superficial? I'm willing to pay for the treatment, and I'll give him whatever care he needs afterward.''

"I said *most* of the injuries weren't serious,'' Manny said patiently. "The problem, Carolyn, is that his jaw is shattered. Now, this little guy is just a stray from God knows where. I'm sure you don't want to pay for the kind of delicate and extensive surgery that would be necessary to repair his jaw. I doubt that any of my clients would, no matter how crazy they were about their dogs.''

Carolyn hesitated. She was flooded all at once with deep sorrow, an anguish so hot and intense that she was afraid to analyze it. "Isn't there any alternative?'' she asked in a low strained voice. "Anything else we could do?''

Manny shrugged. "The only alternative,'' he said, "is to strap the jaw into position and then feed him liquids by hand until it knits together, if it's ever going to. Otherwise the rest of his injuries will heal, but he'll gradually starve to death. He sure can't chew and swallow, not like this.''

"What kind of liquids?''

"Carolyn,'' Manny said gently, "it's a big job to take on, you know. It would take hours of patience every day to get enough nourishment into him.''

Carolyn knew Manny was probably right. She was

being stubborn and unreasonable over this whole thing, but she couldn't help herself.

"What kind of liquids?" she repeated.

Manny shrugged. "Just about anything that's protein rich and easy to digest," he said. "Bread soaked in milk, soft dog food mixed up in a blender with beef stock or soup, that kind of thing. Whatever you'd normally feed him, only liquefied, trickled down his throat one spoonful at a time."

"Okay," Carolyn said in a barely audible voice, avoiding the younger man's eyes. "Maybe I'll... I'll give it a try for a while. If you'd just patch him up, Manny, I'll take it from here."

The veterinarian nodded, started toward the door and then paused, giving Carolyn a keen thoughtful glance. He seemed about to say something further but apparently thought better of it, turning away and striding out to his van to get his equipment.

CHAPTER TWO

"WHAT KIND OF DOG is he exactly, Manny? Besides being a floor mop, I mean."

Manny Hernandez stretched his body wearily and turned to Carolyn, who was leaning in the doorway of the barn watching as he packed his equipment away.

"Well, Carolyn, what he looks like to me is a very expensive little mistake. I'd say he's a cross between a couple of small terriers, a cross that never should have happened. Probably Yorkshire and Sealyham, by the looks of him."

"I don't know much about lapdogs," Carolyn said. "Those are both furry little mop types, right?"

"More or less. Especially the Yorkie. But I think this fella's got a lot of Sealyham mixed in there, too, and that's where he gets that silky crinkly texture to his coat. Nice little dog," he added. "Probably perky and loyal and intelligent, too, but not worth a hell of a lot."

"You mean because he's a crossbred?"

"Sure," Manny said, pausing by the open door of

his van. "I'd guess that it was an accidental mating, and it produced a litter of hybrids that aren't worth much except as house pets, which is why this little guy ended up where he did, I expect."

"You mean," Carolyn said quietly, "they figured they might as well just dump him if they didn't want him anymore because he isn't worth enough to bother selling him?"

Manny shrugged. "Sometimes their intentions aren't all that bad, Carolyn, the people who do this. They've got a pet they can't look after for some reason, and they genuinely believe that the ranches out here are just spacious limitless places that can give a happy home to any stray animal."

Carolyn nodded. "That was my very first impression when Vern brought him in," she said. "That he was likely an abandoned pet, I mean, who'd been deliberately dumped off out here. But I wonder…"

She paused, moving the toe of her boot with apparent aimlessness in the soft damp dirt of the driveway while Manny waited for her to finish her sentence.

"What if he really is somebody's pet, Manny?" she forced herself to ask, looking up at the young veterinarian. "Some local kid's dog that everybody's out looking for right this minute?"

Manny shook his head decisively. "Not a chance,

Carolyn. A little fella like this wouldn't have traveled far on his own. His pads show that he's hardly covered any ground at all. And I know every dog in the district. He's not from around here—he was brought in by car and dropped off. You can watch the papers for the next few days if you like, but I'd be willing to bet that I'm right.''

Carolyn's slim shoulders relaxed but she waved her hand in a casual gesture, trying to look noncommittal. "I guess so," she said.

"You're not fooling me, Carolyn Townsend," Manny said with amusement, one hand gripping the door handle as he prepared to climb into the driver's seat. "You've completely ignored all my educated warnings, and you're already emotionally involved."

"And a good thing for you, too," Carolyn rejoined tartly, "considering the size of the bill I'm going to be getting for your services this morning, Manuel Hernandez."

"What a life," Manny said dolefully. "Everybody grumbles about the vet fees, and yet they all call me at all hours of the day and night, every day of the year. I just can't win."

"Would you like a cup of coffee?" Carolyn asked, smiling at him, her tartness dissipating in a warm tide of sympathy for the young man. "Or some breakfast? I was just on my way into the house to cook myself up some scrambled eggs and pancakes."

Manny shook his head regretfully. "Sounds wonderful, Carolyn, but I've got calls waiting back at the office and I really need to grab a couple hours' sleep. I'll take a rain check, okay?"

"Okay," Carolyn said.

The veterinarian shot her another keen glance. "Is there something else? Something you wanted me to check on, maybe?"

"No, no…" Carolyn shook her head and then looked up, her clear sea-blue eyes troubled. "I just wanted to ask you what you knew about this damned dude ranch that's opening up next door, Manny."

"The Hole in the Wall?"

"Whatever," Carolyn said grimly. "I thought at first that was such a stupid name, but maybe it fits after all. The place is going to be a real hole, far as I'm concerned."

"Now, Carolyn, it's not that bad," Manny began in a reasonable tone. "From what I hear, Scott Harris has done a real good job of fixing up the ranch, and he's planning to run a first-rate operation out there."

Carolyn shook her head, unconvinced. "Our family neighbored the Kendalls for generations, Manny," she said, "and that ranch was always a real nice little family business. It was called the Lazy J, and it was just about the nicest neighbor ranch you could ever hope for. Now this city lawyer's gone and bought it, and God knows what'll be going on over there at the edge of my property. I just hate it.''

Manny looked at her. ''What is it that you hate about it, Carolyn?''

''Everything!'' she burst out, her face flushed with emotion. ''To begin with, I've hated all the construction, months of bulldozers and heavy machinery rumbling around out there bothering my stock. And now that they're set to open, I hate the thought of a bunch of idiot greenhorns wandering around at the edge of my property leaving gates open and scattering garbage, teasing the bulls and scaring the calves. But most of all, I *hate* this rumor I've heard about the exotic animals.''

Manny looked blank. ''Exotic animals?''

''You know,'' Carolyn told him impatiently. ''Gazelles and wildebeest and all that—exotic African animals brought in and penned up behind fences for city slickers to shoot at. Apparently this man is planning to supplement his income that way. It's happening all over Texas, Manny, and I find it purely disgusting. The thought of it makes me want to go over to the *Hole in the Wall,*'' she concluded, emphasizing the words with bitter sarcasm, ''and shoot something myself. And not some pretty little gazelle, either.''

Manny looked concerned for the first time. ''Well, now,'' he conceded, ''that's a different thing, Carolyn. I hadn't heard that particular rumor, but I'll grant you it does make me uneasy. Not from a moral point of view,'' he added, ''so much as medical.''

''Medical?'' Carolyn echoed.

''Those exotic animals can be a real danger to domestic beef herds. They bring in diseases and parasites that are unknown in North America, and that our native cattle have no resistance to.''

Blood drained from Carolyn's face, leaving it pale as marble beneath the tan. She stared at the younger man.

''Manny,'' she began in a low strained voice, ''we spent twenty years here building one of the finest Santa Gertrudis herds in the state. I can't bear to see everything Frank and I worked for threatened by some…some upstart desk jockey who's decided he wants to play cowboy!''

She fell silent, her chest heaving, her eyes flashing blue fire, and Manny gave her another concerned look.

''I hate to see you getting so upset, Carolyn,'' he said finally. ''You know, I've met Scott Harris and he seems like a nice reasonable type. Maybe there's no real truth to all these rumors, and you're getting worked up over nothing.''

Carolyn collected herself with an effort and forced a smile. ''Sorry to sound off at you, Manny,'' she said. ''It's not your fault. But,'' she added, her voice grim, "I think one of these days I'll just go on over and have a little chat with this Scott Harris myself. And somehow I really doubt that I'm going to share your good opinion of him."

At that moment a sleek little pale blue Nissan rolled out of the triple garage behind the house and started down the driveway just beyond where Manny and Carolyn stood talking.

Lori and Beverly were both in the car, Carolyn noted with amusement. Clearly Lori had decided that she wouldn't lend the younger woman her vehicle, but would give her a ride into town instead. Carolyn grinned privately, forgetting her own concerns for a moment as she thought about the two in the car.

No matter how responsible and mature Beverly was acting these days, she mused, it was going to take a lot to convince Lori that the girl's transformation was genuine. Lori Porter was Carolyn's cousin as well as resident accountant and unofficial assistant, but she earned her living by acting as a professional accountant for most of the other ranchers in the district as well. She had lived with the family at the Circle T long enough to have witnessed much of Beverly's adolescence and young adulthood. Though she usually maintained a discreet silence on the subject, Lori was even more dubious about her young cousin's motives than Carolyn herself. And she was not likely to be impressed by sporadic good works and noble proclamations from Beverly.

Carolyn and Manny both waved at the two women as they rolled down the drive out of sight, and Manny climbed behind the wheel of his van.

"Remember that little dog needs a lot of nourishment on a regular basis if he's going to make it, Carolyn," he said. "Keep him warm, give him liquids every couple of hours, use those drops I left for you and keep the cast dry. And don't move him unless you have to. I'll be back early next week to take the stitches out."

"Thanks, Manny," Carolyn said. She waved farewell and watched as he backed out onto the drive, roaring off just behind the two women in the blue Nissan.

She hadn't even had her breakfast yet, but it seemed she'd already spent hours this morning standing and watching people drive down that same road.

That's all life really is, when you come right down to it, Carolyn thought with a sudden bleak flood of almost unbearable sorrow. *Just standing and watching people drift away from you, watching them disappear around a bend in the road and knowing that you'll never, ever see them again....*

She swallowed a brief anguished sob and then set her jaw firmly, annoyed with herself for this weak and uncharacteristic lapse. With a brisk determined stride, she hurried back into the barn and leaned over the manger to check on the terrier.

The small dog looked up at her approach and thumped his docked tail weakly, setting the silky gray coat quivering with emotion. He was almost dry now and the fluffiness of his coat helped to disguise his pitiful thinness, as well as the gash on his side.

In fact, except for the clean white cast on his hind leg and the clipped area where Manny had inserted a neat row of stitches into the long jagged cut, he looked almost normal. But, studying the little animal closely, Carolyn could see that he was still far from any kind of health and strength. His big dark eyes were glazed with pain, and though he made a gallant attempt he was no longer able to lift his damaged head from the sacking to lick her fingers.

Carolyn swallowed hard and tried to smile at his furry, anxious face.

"Poor little guy," she murmured. "I guess your breakfast is more important than mine, isn't it? I won't try to move you just now. I'll go back up to the house and fix something for you to eat, and bring it right on down here, okay? That'll make you feel better, boy. That'll just be so nice…"

Still murmuring in low soothing tones, she backed away and turned toward the big front doors.

But she'd only gone a few steps when she paused in shock, her hand to her mouth. A shadow flitted past her legs just inches away with a glint of white teeth and eyes in the darkness, a scrabbling of straw and a ragged flash of color swallowed up at once in the dusky stillness of the barn.

"Oh, my *God!*" she exclaimed aloud, badly startled. "What was that? Who's there?" She peered into the dark cavernous shadows of the hay piled next to the door.

"Teresa?" she called. "Is that you? What do you think you're doing, child, spying on me and scaring me half to death?"

There was no response from the shadows.

"Teresa?" she called again. "Are you in there? Is that you?"

The silence was so profound that Carolyn, leaning forward tensely, was almost certain she could hear the child's shallow frightened breathing. She considered crawling into the cavern between the bales and hauling the little girl out bodily, giving her a good talking-to about her behavior. After a moment, though, she changed her mind and started out the door again.

Teresa Martinez had been living at the ranch for almost four months now, since just before Christmas, and Carolyn had never actually talked to the child. As far as she knew, nobody else had, either. Carolyn had hired the little girl's mother, Rosa, to help exercise the horses and also cook the meals for the four men that the Circle T employed on a permanent basis.

Rosa Martinez had just moved up from Fort Stockton, she told Carolyn at her employment interview. She was a dark, slim, quiet woman in her late twenties who would probably be quite attractive if she didn't hold herself under such constant rigid control.

But her personality wasn't any of Carolyn's business. As manager of the ranch, Carolyn was only concerned with the woman's job performance, and that was entirely satisfactory. Rosa Martinez seemed to be as skilled a hand with food as she was with horses. The hired men had never looked so cheerful and well-fed, even though they spent many frustrating hours trying to draw the taciturn Rosa into conversation.

Rosa's daughter was about nine years old, a wild dark wraith of a child with clouds of tangled black hair and glittering black eyes. She didn't seem to attend school at all. In response to Carolyn's worried inquiries, Rosa had said simply, "Teresa, she doesn't do good at school, and they don't want her there. Too wild, they say, so I just teach her at home."

Carolyn frequently wondered if Teresa ever sat still long enough to learn anything. The child seemed to be more wood sprite than little girl, a dark silent flitting presence like a small furtive animal around the ranch. As was the case with Carolyn this morning, people never knew when Teresa might be watching them, or how long she'd been there and what she'd seen. Nobody had ever heard her speak, either, but her unexpected appearances had more than once startled residents of the Circle T.

There were rumors about Rosa and her child, of course. There were rumors about everything and everybody in and around Crystal Creek. They usually originated in the Longhorn Coffee Shop and drifted out across the countryside like an invisible but all-pervasive mist. People talked of some terrible event in Rosa's past, of a drunken abusive stepfather who had threatened little Teresa's life and had finally been knifed or shot by Rosa in a panicked attempt to save her child.

"The kid saw it all," Bubba Gibson reported, wide-eyed and hushed with ghoulish appreciation of the story. "Blood an' everythin'. Never been the same since, they say. Touched in the head, they say."

Carolyn tended to ignore the rumors. She considered it none of her business what had happened in the woman's past. Still, Carolyn Townsend could never quite bring herself to overlook the suffering of small helpless beings, children and animals both, and she often brooded about the strange shadow-child who inhabited the Circle T.

Maybe she'd have another talk with Rosa. After

all, Teresa certainly couldn't go on like this forever, living most of the time out in the open like some wild animal, popping up under people's noses at all hours of the day and scaring them to death. She needed a daily routine, some decent clothes, a few regular toys. She needed to ride the school bus, have the chance to be with other children....

Carolyn slipped in through the side door of the big ranch house, paused in a nearby bathroom to wash her hands, then moved into the gleaming kitchen with a sigh of pleasure.

Carolyn Townsend loved her kitchen.

Of all the rooms and spaces of this house, this one was the most uniquely hers, reflecting her own personality in its shining whiteness and long polished oak table, its pale blue countertops and blue gingham place mats. Muslim curtains, vivid splashes of green hanging plants and rare delft china added to its charm.

About five years earlier, when Beverly was just getting into the beauty pageant scene and her physical setting had been so important to her, she had begun nagging her father and mother about renovating their big comfortable home.

Important people would be coming to visit, she insisted passionately, people who could have a real bearing on her career. What would they think of the scarred leather sofas, the fading wallpaper, the rugged, "lived-in" look of the old stone ranch house?

Carolyn, who had always loved her home, was offended. But Frank Townsend could never deny anything to this only child of his, this beautiful daughter whom he adored, and the two of them had finally prevailed.

All in all, Carolyn thought, looking around with rueful pleasure, Frank and Beverly had probably been right. Though Carolyn had opposed many of the changes at the time, she had to admit that she liked her home the way it looked now.

She crossed the gleaming floor of dark pegged-oak planks, leaning on the counter to gaze out the window at the fields bathed in springtime freshness, and smiled as the curtain fluttered in the breeze and brushed her cheek like a caress.

Then, abruptly, she remembered the animal down in the barn. She pulled out the blender and moved back over to the refrigerator. Resting idly against the open door, she contemplated what she could mix up for little dog.

"Some of that stew from supper last night," she murmured, thinking out loud. "That'd be good, and maybe a little warm milk to go with it…"

As frequently happened these days, Carolyn suddenly had the uncomfortable sensation that she wasn't alone in the kitchen, that somebody was nearby and watching her.

"Teresa?" she called gently, keeping her voice deliberately casual. "Are you peeking in through the window again? Why don't you come inside and have some breakfast with me?"

She waited, listening to the silence. But there was no response, just the soft rustle of the curtains and the morning breeze whispering in the trees beyond the window.

Carolyn felt a brief shiver of alarm, remembering the disturbed young woman who had recently stalked her nephew Tyler McKinney, peering in windows and causing so much trouble at the neighboring ranch. That was different, of course, and much more upsetting. The woman had been unstable. Teresa was just a lonely troubled little girl.

All at once the telephone rang, a harsh sound in the sun-washed morning stillness of the kitchen. Carolyn walked over to the desk.

"Hello?" she said, and then hesitated, puzzled.

"Carolyn?" a voice was saying haltingly at the other end. "Carolyn? Is that you?" The caller was Cynthia McKinney, Carolyn realized, her new sister-in-law. Or, she corrected herself, not exactly her sister-in-law, but the new wife of the man who had been married for more than thirty years to Carolyn's own sister. What did that make Cynthia?

"Hi, Cynthia," she said cheerfully. "I'm just trying to figure out what relation you are to me. You got any idea?"

Normally, Cynthia would have chuckled at this and made some droll reply. Carolyn had been cautious at first about this new woman in J.T.'s life, this sophisticated import from Boston, of all places, but she soon found she couldn't help liking Cynthia. The woman was so smart and strong and humorous, so warm and serious about her responsibilities, so thoroughly dedicated to making J.T.'s life better. Carolyn, always fair, had to love her for that fact alone.

But today for some reason there was no wit or warmth to Cynthia. She sounded distant and strained, not herself at all. Carolyn decided to joke her out of it, whatever the problem was.

"Hey, girl," she said cheerfully, "come on, it's only a pie sale. I know you get real frightened by gatherings of the natives in these parts, but you'll be safely behind a table, and I'll be at your side every minute with my Smith & Wesson in my handbag."

Still no answering chuckle from Cynthia. Carolyn felt a sudden twinge of alarm—an icy finger at the nape of her neck.

"Cynthia?" she said again. "What is it, dear?"

"It's…it's J.T., Carolyn," Cynthia whispered, her voice close to breaking. "He's…oh God, Carolyn, he's…"

"He's what?" Carolyn asked sharply, gripping the receiver so tightly that her fingers hurt. "What's happening, Cynthia?"

"He's…sick, Carolyn," Cynthia murmured in despair. "So sick…"

Panic struck Carolyn like a heavy blow at the pit of the stomach. But with characteristic self-discipline she summoned all her resources and forced her voice to sound calm and soothing.

"What's happening, Cynthia?" she asked gently. "I'll come right over, but just give me some idea for now, okay?"

"He was…he was out in the stables all night with Ken, working over some horse that was foaling." Cynthia paused, struggling to control her voice.

"I know, Cynthia," Carolyn said quietly, though her blue eyes were darkening with worry. "Manny was there, too, and he stopped in here on his way back to town. Doesn't J.T. realize that he's getting past the stage when he should be up all night with foaling mares?"

"Apparently not," Cynthia faltered, still struggling to compose herself. "Anyway, he and Ken came in for breakfast and I thought he looked awfully tired. I wanted him to go up to bed and catch a few hours' sleep but he just scoffed at the whole idea, said no man worth his salt sleeps in the middle of the day. He had to get back out and see to getting the early calves branded. And then all of a sudden..." Her voice broke and she began to sob quietly at the other end.

"All of a sudden what?" Carolyn prompted. There was an increasingly familiar and ghastly feeling to this event. She was beginning to have a panicky sense of déjà vu, as if she'd lived through the same dreadful moment at some time in the past.

"He was putting on his hat, walking out the door and then he just...just kind of sagged, would have fallen if Ken hadn't been right behind him and caught him. We...we helped him upstairs and into bed but he's...oh, Carolyn, he's all gray and sweating, and he seems to be in such pain, he can hardly recognize any of us...."

Gray and sweating...in such pain...

An image flashed unbidden into Carolyn's mind— her tall sturdy husband Frank two years ago just after his massive coronary. Fear stirred and churned at the core of her, choking her, leaving her breathless with terror.

Not J.T.! she screamed soundlessly. *Not him, too! I can't bear to lose any more of the people I love, I just can't bear it, oh God, please don't let it be....*

"Is somebody with you, Cynthia?" she asked.

"Everybody's here. I mean, Tyler and Ruth and Lynn, and Lettie Mae and Virginia, and Ken, and we've called Cal in Wolverton, and Dr. Purdy...."

"Oh, good," Carolyn said. Nate Purdy had been caring for all of them for more than three decades. Now, just the thought of him ministering to J.T. brought her comfort.

"Is there anything else I should do, Carolyn?" Cynthia asked in a low voice, still sounding helplessly childlike, completely out of character. "Anybody else I should call, or anything?"

"Not now, dear," Carolyn said gently. "Sit down, put your feet up and get Lettie Mae to make you a cup of her cinnamon tea. I'll be over right away."

"Oh, thank you," Cynthia whispered, with such relief in her voice that Carolyn knew she had to get over there without delay.

She hung up the phone and grabbed a sweater from a hook by the door, flung it over her shoulders, took her car keys from the countertop and ran out to the garage.

"OKAY, VERN," Martin Avery said cheerfully, riffling briskly through a stack of papers. "I think that finishes it. The transfer of title's in order, the taxes are all paid up to date, and your man owns his property outright, once he signs this last release of funds."

Vernon Trent smiled at his old friend, who paused to answer the telephone and deal with the caller, a solicitor for a local charity.

"When did you start answering your own tele-phone?" Vern asked, chuckling at Martin's glow-ering expression. "Can't you poor underpaid lawyers afford secretarial help these days?"

"Very funny, Vern," Martin grumbled, running a hand through his thick graying hair. "Actually, my secretary called in sick this morning, so I'm doing double duty."

"Billie Jo?" Vernon asked in surprise. "I saw her at Zack's last night, and she looked healthy enough then. Bursting with health, you might say."

Both men were silent for a moment, thinking about the beauteous Billie Jo, with her gorgeous body, her mane of strawberry-blond hair and sexy pouting red lips.

"Yeah," Martin said dryly. "And that's not all she's bursting with, old friend. I'd bet dollars to doughnuts that she's not alone this morning."

"You think Bubba's visiting the sickbed?"

"I'd bet on it," Martin repeated.

"God, he's a fool, isn't he?" Vernon commented absently.

"Maybe we old bachelors just don't understand, Vern. Or maybe we'll be the same if we start to suffer through a midlife crisis. We'll be whining and sniffing around girls thirty years younger than us, buying bad toupees and silver Camaros...."

Vernon threw back his head and laughed at this

skillful thrust. "Maybe you, Martin," he said. "Not me, that's for sure. I'm nowhere near that dumb."

"Speaking of being dumb," Martin said cheerfully, "I was talking to young Ben Waldheim and his wife the other day. They said they made you another offer on your house, and you won't sell."

Vernon shifted awkwardly in the padded chair. "That's true," he admitted.

"How come, Vern? Why're you hanging on to that drafty old barn? Why not let the kids have it? They want to renovate it, got all kinds of plans."

Vernon shrugged. "I don't have time to move and find another place and all that," he said defensively. "Besides," he added with a grin, "that's my ancestral home you're talking about, Martin."

"Bull," Martin said calmly. "Your ancestral home was a little suite above the drugstore. Your daddy didn't even buy that house till you were fifteen."

"That's right," Vernon said with a small faraway smile. "You know, I can still remember the day he took my mama over there and gave her the keys. She looked like he'd given her Buckingham Palace."

"Well, *that* it ain't," Martin said. "Those days were thirty years ago, Vern. The old place is falling down around your ears. You don't have any interest in fixing it up, so why not let it go?"

Vernon frowned stubbornly, thinking about the big

stone house he'd inherited from his parents. Martin was right, it was falling into disrepair, growing rickety, faded and musty, and he was getting to hate it more with every passing year. But still, he panicked at the thought of moving out and getting a little apartment. That would be admitting that this was his whole future and he was never going to have a wife or a family....

"You could move into my building," Martin said, as if reading his thoughts. "It's a real nice little complex, adults only, with a recreation center and a pool and everything. Real sophisticated for Crystal Creek."

"I know, Martin. I've seen it, remember? It's just that apartment living doesn't appeal to me all that much, for some reason. I'd rather just keep living where I am and work real hard so I don't have to go home much, than move into an apartment."

"Then build yourself a new house. Dammit, man, you've got lots of money. Get yourself out of that lonely old place."

"A new house wouldn't be any less lonely, Martin," Vernon said quietly.

Something in Vern's voice made Martin hesitate, then glance down awkwardly at the pile of papers on his desk as if searching for a way to change the subject.

"Well, that's it," he repeated at last with false heartiness. "You can tell Scott the deal's through."

Vernon looked over at the dapper lawyer and mayor of Crystal Creek, then down at the pile of legal documents. He drummed his blunt fingers on the desktop, and his pleasant square features darkened briefly with worry.

"I hear Carolyn's really upset about the Hole in the Wall," he ventured. "Has she said anything to you, Martin?"

Martin shrugged. "Just in passing one night a few weeks ago when we were all over at the Double C for one of Cynthia's fancy dinners. She's not happy about it, that's for sure."

Vernon creased one of the papers thoughtfully, head lowered, eyes concentrated on the careful movements of his tanned hands. "I'm glad we've been able to keep it quiet," he said.

"Now, Vern, you know as well as I do what this town's like," Martin said mildly. "Everybody finds out everything, sooner or later."

"Maybe not," Vernon said. "Nobody knows the details of the sale of the dude ranch but you and me and Scott Harris."

"And J.T." Martin said. "But he's no gossip, that's for sure."

"Right. So if we all stay quiet, maybe we can keep it safely under the rug until Carolyn's had a chance to find out for herself that the Hole in the Wall won't be such a bad neighbor after all.''

Martin chuckled. ''She's not an easy girl to convince of anything, Vern, never has been. What a woman.''

Both men were silent for a moment, but this time their faces were affectionate as they thought about Carolyn Townsend. The phone rang and Martin cursed mildly, then lifted it and barked a greeting.

''Carolyn,'' he said after a brief pause, his voice softening. ''What a coincidence. We were just talking about you. How are y'all this fine spring day?''

Vernon tensed in his chair and sat erect, eyes fixed on Martin's face. But Martin was unaware of his friend. He was listening to the voice at the other end, his debonair face slowly turning ashen.

''God, Carolyn'' he muttered finally. ''That's terrible, girl. What can I do?''

Vern made frantic gestures, but Martin waved him to silence and listened to the caller again.

''Okay,'' he said finally. ''Vern's here with me now and we'll both come right on over.''

He murmured a farewell and hung up slowly, staring at his friend across the desk with a stricken expression.

''That was Carolyn,'' he said unnecessarily. ''J.T.'s had a heart attack. They just brought him in to the hospital by ambulance.''

"Oh, my God," Vernon whispered, gazing un-
seeingly at Martin's face. Despite the shock of the
news his first thought, as always, was for Carolyn.
He recalled the woman he loved and the way she'd
looked earlier in the day, with the spring sun in her
hair and her eyes as blue as the morning, telling him
fiercely that she'd seen enough of suffering and
death....

"I'll go right over there," he muttered, getting
hastily to his feet and stuffing the papers into his
briefcase. "Maybe I can help somehow. Coming,
Martin?"

Without a word, Martin took his suede jacket from
a coat tree by the door and followed Vernon out into
the bright morning sunlight.

CHAPTER THREE

THE SHABBY LITTLE visitors' lounge at the Crystal Creek Community Hospital seemed filled to overflowing with people. Most were crowded into uncomfortable chrome armchairs and long slippery vinyl lounges while a few, like Ruth Holden and Tyler McKinney, stood near the automated hot drink dispenser sipping blankly at foam cups of the vile black liquid that passed for coffee.

Vernon was fairly certain that Tyler McKinney could have been drinking battery acid and he wouldn't have been aware of it. The young man's face was pale and haggard, bleak with fear, making him look twenty years older. In fact, Tyler McKinney, on this bright spring morning, looked more than ever like his father.

Lynn, beside him, had obviously run in from the stables and not taken the time to change her clothes. She was small and shapely in her riding gear. Her beautiful tanned face was wide-eyed and strained, and she kept glancing desperately toward the door as if waiting for someone.

While Vernon and Martin edged toward a vacant couch, Sam Russell followed them into the crowded room and Lynn went to him, moving blindly into his arms like a child, oblivious to everyone else in the room. Sam held her in a close embrace, patting her heaving back and murmuring to her, his blond head close to her auburn one. Vernon swallowed and looked away from them, sinking down onto the couch and glancing around.

Cynthia McKinney sat across the room from him, with Rose Purdy, the doctor's wife, on one side and Carolyn on the other, both of them holding her hands firmly and murmuring to her by turns. Beverly Townsend sat next to her mother, her lovely golden face streaked with tears.

Vernon couldn't help wondering as he looked thoughtfully at Beverly if the tears were real or if they were just there for effect, in case somebody from the media might be around snapping camera footage of the bereaved family.

But as soon as he framed the thought, he chided himself for being uncharitable. He knew Beverly had her good qualities, and that Carolyn, despite her frequent impatience with the girl, loved her daughter deeply. Still, Vernon found himself wondering sometimes how a woman as generous, intelligent and practical as Carolyn Townsend could have produced an offspring so self-absorbed and shallow.

As he was gazing with cool appraisal at Beverly, a couple of children came wandering into the room hand in hand. They were little girls of about seven and three, both wearing institutional gray bathrobes. The older one trundled a mobile IV unit along beside her, strapped to her left arm, and the other one limped badly, trailing a leg in a heavy steel and plastic brace.

While Vernon watched in amazement, Beverly got up, smiling through her tears, and gathered the smaller child tenderly in her arms. She murmured something to the older girl, then took the child's hand and walked from the room still carrying the younger girl. Vernon watched them go, stunned by the little tableau and the obvious warmth and sincerity of Beverly's interaction with the children.

He shook his head and then smiled automatically as Reverend Howard Blake and his wife, Eva, came into the room, followed by Bubba Gibson, who looked hastily assembled and a lot less chipper than usual.

Vern shifted awkwardly on the hard vinyl seat, waiting for his chance to go to Cynthia and offer his own sympathy and support. But she was surrounded, and the crowd seemed to be growing by the minute. There was another stir at the door and Cal McKinney entered, limping slightly from an old rodeo injury.

He was followed by Serena Davis, who looked quiet and pale.

No wonder, Vernon thought, glancing at his watch. Cal was already notorious for how fast he drove that stretch of highway between Wolverton and the home ranch, but he must have set some new records today. His body was tense, his hazel eyes glittering with tears as he was gathered into the arms of his family.

Vernon felt a startling quick stab of pain, wondering what it must be like to be J.T. McKinney and have such a rich legacy, to have all this family loving and fretting for you, these tall handsome sons weeping over you....

He looked up to find Carolyn's blue eyes resting on him with mute appeal. He began to rise, to move toward her. But just at that moment the room fell silent and everyone turned to the door where Nate Purdy stood, weary and somber in his crisp white lab coat.

Immediately all eyes were fastened on the doctor's face and there wasn't a sound in the room except for a few quick ragged intakes of breath. The group waited tensely, watching Nate as he moved into the room and stood by Cynthia and his wife, dropping a hand onto the shoulder of each.

"Well, I think we're through the worst of it, Cynthia," he said. "And we'd better thank the good

Lord that we've got one tough hombre in there, or he wouldn't still be with us.''

Cynthia looked up at him, her brown eyes widening, her cheeks as white as the pale walls all around her.

''Is he...did he..?'' she faltered. Carolyn gripped the younger woman's hand and slipped her free arm around Cynthia's shoulders, holding her close, cuddling her like a child.

''He had a massive coronary,'' Nate said, ''just a few minutes ago. The first attack at home this morning was actually a precursor. As soon as I examined him at the ranch I expected a more serious cardiac event to follow shortly, and we were real lucky that we got him here in time. If we hadn't had the equipment and the medication available, I think we just might have lost him, tough as he is.''

The room stirred and settled. There was a clearing of throats, a restless shuffling of boots, a flurry of hands dashing furtively at tear-filled eyes.

''The worst is over,'' Nate Purdy repeated, turning to address the room in general. ''He's resting comfortably now, but he sure won't be if this gang descends on him. Only two visitors at a time, and nobody but immediate family. The rest of you good people, y'all go on home now, and come back to visit him when he's feeling stronger. And thanks for com-

ing,'' he added with a warm tired smile. ''I'm sure
Cynthia appreciates all the support.''

Cynthia nodded blindly and struggled to her feet,
supported by Carolyn and Rose. She managed to
smile and nod her agreement with the doctor. ''Yes,''
she whispered. ''Thank you all. Thank you so much.
I'm sure that J.T. would…''

With these words Cynthia's poise deserted her and
she choked, then leaned gratefully on Tyler who had
crossed the room to stand beside her.

''You and me first, Cynthia, okay?'' he murmured
huskily, putting his arm around her. ''Let's go see
Daddy.''

Nate Purdy turned to follow them out of the room,
then paused and looked back at Carolyn. ''By the
way, Carolyn,'' he said, ''I certainly consider you
immediate family, if you'd like to wait and see him
for a minute.''

But Carolyn shook her head. ''No, Nate,'' she said
in a low voice. ''That's all right. Too many of us
right now will just tire him. Cal and Lynn can go in
next, and I'll come back tomorrow when he's
stronger.''

People began to file out, still murmuring to one
another in hushed tones. Vernon took advantage of
the general exodus to cross the room and sink down
beside Carolyn.

"Hi, Vern," she said, giving him a small bleak smile. "It's nice of you to come."

"Oh, Caro," he murmured, deeply moved by her evident pain and weariness. "How could I stay away, girl? Is there anything I can do for you?"

She shook her head automatically, then paused. "Actually, there is, come to think of it," she said. "I drove over to the Double C this morning as soon as I heard, and left my car there. I came in with Tyler and Lynn. Now Lynn's giving Beverly a ride home later this evening and she'll be bringing my car back then, so I guess I'm on foot. Could you… could you give me a ride home?"

"Nothing would please me more," Vernon told her with warm sincerity. "That is," he added solemnly, trying to make her smile, "if you don't have any moral objections to riding in a Camaro."

"It'll probably wreck my reputation completely," Carolyn said, responding gallantly to his effort at humor, "but what the hell. A good reputation's a dull kind of thing, isn't it, Vern?"

"I NEVER THOUGHT it would be J.T.," Carolyn murmured, gazing blindly out the window as Vernon's car skimmed along the curving country roads. "Of all the people in my life, I've always looked on him as the strongest, the most indestructible, somehow."

"I guess we all have," Vernon said. "I remember

looking up to J.T. as a boy, way back when he was a football and basketball star at school and a rodeo star in the summertime, everything a kid could ever dream about.''

''I know,'' Carolyn said with a distant smile. ''He was ten years older than you and me, Vern, but I had such a crush on him when I was little. I envied Pauline so much when she started going out with him, I could hardly talk to her for a year or so.''

She stared out silently at the trees shimmering in the afternoon sun, recalling the vivid agonies and delights of that long-ago childhood time.

Vernon grinned. ''You got over it, though, I hope. Just look at the bluebonnets in that field, Caro. I've never seen them so spectacular so early.''

''I know,'' Carolyn said absently. ''I was thinking the same thing, just this morning. Seems like a century ago. Yes, I got over it,'' she added, returning to their earlier topic. ''But after I recovered from my crush, J.T. turned into one of my best friends. I've always depended on him, and more than ever since Frank's been gone. I just can't bear the thought of…''

She choked and fell silent. Vernon gave her a quick glance. ''He's going to be all right, you know, Caro,'' he said. ''Nate sounded optimistic, and you'll notice that he mentioned several times how tough the man is. Nate's a square shooter. He doesn't say things like that just to hear himself talk.''

''You know what I keep thinking?'' Carolyn said as if Vernon hadn't spoken. ''I keep thinking it's my fault, that I should have seen it coming. I noticed lately how gray and tired he'd been looking, and how he's been rubbing his left arm a lot. I actually teased him once about old cowboys and arthritis, but I never thought about heart attacks. You'd think that of all people, I would have been alert to warning signs like that.''

''You were just like the rest of us,'' Vernon told her calmly. ''J.T.'s always seemed indestructible, so we all just chalked it up to stress. After all, there's been a lot of that in J.T.'s life lately, even though most of it's happy stress. He's got a brand-new wife, and a new business venture starting up at the ranch, and a whole crew of prospective new family members, considering the way his kids are all getting paired up these days.''

''That's not all,'' Carolyn said, her voice bleak as she stared out the window.

''Not all what?''

''Not all the new family members,'' Carolyn said miserably. ''Vernon, don't tell a soul because nobody knows yet, okay? Cynthia's pregnant.''

Vernon gripped the wheel and stared at Carolyn,

his square cheerful face reflecting his stunned amazement.

"Oh, my God," he muttered aloud.

"You bet," Carolyn said grimly. "I thought this morning that Cynthia wasn't looking well, and wasn't dealing with this whole thing as well as I would have expected her to, either. I managed to corner her at the ranch before the ambulance came and asked her if anything else was wrong, and that's when she told me. Nobody knows yet but Nate Purdy."

"And J.T., of course," Vernon said automatically.

Carolyn shook her head. "Not even him. She's just about a month pregnant, Vern. In fact, she only found out for sure yesterday, and she was going to tell him tonight. They were planning to go out to a romantic candlelight dinner at the country club, just the two of them, and she was going to tell him then."

"The poor kid," Vernon murmured, gazing straight ahead through the smoky curved windshield, his face deeply troubled.

"I know," Carolyn said. She brushed absently at the slow tears that trickled down her cheeks. "And now, on what should be the happiest day of her life, she's got this to deal with. And I know she's blaming herself, Vern, thinking that she's the cause of all this because she's brought so much upheaval into J.T.'s life, first with her opposition to Tyler's vineyard, and

then the wedding and the renovations to the house...
she feels just awful.''

"That's ridiculous," Vernon said. "She's been
damned good for J.T. He may have an ailing heart,
but he's looked happier these past few months than
I've seen him in years.''

"Tell her that, Vern, if you get a chance," Carolyn
said, wiping her eyes and trying to smile at him.
"She really needs to hear it.''

"You bet I will," Vernon said. "You know," he
added haltingly, "it sounds ridiculous, but I almost
envied J.T. this morning, while I was sitting there in
that hospital waiting room.''

Carolyn stared at him. "You *envied* him? Why on
earth, Vern?''

"I don't know," he said awkwardly. "I just
thought what a lucky man he is to have so many
people who love him, all those pretty women crying
over him, and those two big tall sons....''

"You would have liked a family, wouldn't you,
Vern?" Carolyn said softly, looking with affection
at the man beside her. "Why didn't you? Ever get
married, I mean? Lots of girls were after you when
we were in high school. You were considered quite
a catch.''

His mouth lifted in an engaging lopsided grin, and
he swerved skillfully to avoid a little cottontail rabbit

scuttling across the highway. "You're kidding. Me, a catch?"

"Well, sure," Carolyn said. "Remember Sally Thompson? She was crazy about you. She wrote your name all over the walls in the girls' washroom."

Vernon gave a theatrical sigh. "*Now* she tells me," he commented sadly. "Thirty years too late. Actually," he added in a more serious tone, "I guess that the years when I might have been interested, Carolyn, I was running around in the jungle carrying ammunition clips. And then when I came home, everybody was kind of settled already and I was odd man out, and I just decided to stay that way. Less complicated," he added.

Carolyn gave him a thoughtful glance. There was something strange and guarded in his tone and she was on the point of questioning him further, probing a little more deeply. But just then something came into her line of vision and she stiffened in annoyance, turning sharply to gaze out the window.

"Look at that!" she burst out, peering at a set of intricate wrought-iron gates adorning a low curving stone wall. "He's even got it on the *front gates* now, for God's sake."

"What?" Vernon asked.

"The Hole in the Wall. He's had those gates

mounted since the last time I was by here. Look at them. Isn't that awful?"

"Well, Caro," Vern said reasonably, "it *is* the name of the ranch, you know. He's entitled to put it on the gates if he wants to. I've heard that it's easier for customers to find the place, you know, when you have the right name on the gate."

Carolyn ignored this attempt at humor. "I hate it," she said darkly. "I just hate it, Vern."

"Why, Caro? What's so bad about it?"

Carolyn repeated her grievances, telling Vernon all the same things she'd told Manny earlier in the day, while he drove through her own gates and parked by the house, listening in silence.

"Well, I agree with Manny," Vernon said finally, turning to her and resting his arm along the top of the seat. "A lot of this could just be gossip and conjecture, Caro. You've never been one to pay much attention to gossip, far as I can recall. Why don't you wait till the place opens and then judge for yourself?"

Carolyn tensed, irrationally annoyed by the calm reasonableness of his words and his tone. "Well, I sure don't have much choice, do I?"

"I think it'll be great for the community," Vernon went on. "Bring in all kinds of new business."

"Yeah, sure," Carolyn said gloomily. "Thousands more dudes and rock hounds, littering and trespassing and bothering the cattle. Tyler says Cal and Serena are thinking of opening a boot shop out at the dude ranch. They're expecting so much business that they feel it would actually be viable.''

"Well, don't you think that's good news?'' Vernon asked. "Aren't you glad to see the kids prospering?''

"Not at the expense of my ranch and my herds.''

"They won't bother your herds,'' Vernon said comfortably. "Besides,'' he added with his wry grin, "just think how much business those greenhorns are gonna bring in to the hospital, what with all the rope burns and cactus spines and saddle sores and broken bones. Maybe the nursery will finally be able to afford those new baby incubators they've been lobbying for.''

Carolyn chuckled in spite of herself, then looked gloomy again. "I just wish I knew where he came from, Vern.''

Vernon glanced at her in surprise. "Everybody knows the man's biography by now, Carolyn. He comes from Austin, grew up there and got his law degree from—''

"From Baylor,'' Carolyn interrupted impatiently. "I know all that, Vern. And he's a highly successful divorce lawyer who's decided he wants a new challenge, some wholesome country life, etc. etc. I could recite the man's pedigree in my sleep, I think. What

I want to know is how he got to be *my* neighbor. Who told him the place was for sale? It was never advertised in the city. Who sold it to him? Where did he come from?''

Vernon was silent, gripping the wheel of his parked car and looking with apparent deep interest at the quiet deserted veranda of Carolyn's sprawling stone ranch house.

''I know, I know,'' Carolyn said, gazing at his quiet profile. ''You're not going to tell me, are you? Realtors stick together and protect one another just like any other profession. But believe me, if I ever get my hands on whoever sold that man the ranch next door without even so much as coming over to mention to me that it was for sale…''

She paused and her beautiful face tightened briefly with emotion. Then she collapsed against the seat, washed under by a sudden flood of dark misery.

Vernon turned to her, his face full of concern. ''Caro? What's the matter, girl?''

''Oh, I don't know, Vern,'' she said helplessly. ''Somehow it all just seems too much to bear, you know? The place next door bringing disease and problems to my herd, and poor Cynthia and J.T., and everything…seems like this day's been getting more and more awful ever since you came through the gates this morning with that pitiful little mop dog.''

As she spoke the words, her face twisted suddenly

and she stared at Vernon, her blue eyes wide with
wretched appeal.

"Vern," she whispered. "The *mop dog!* Oh, God,
when Cynthia phoned I forgot all about him till this
moment! Oh, no..."

Still murmuring distractedly, she flung herself
from the car and ran across the driveway to the barn.
Vernon watched her for a startled moment and then
hurried after her, his face drawn with anxiety.

"I was in the kitchen," Carolyn said hastily over
her shoulder, running through the wide double doors
of the barn. "I was just getting something ready to
feed him, and then Cynthia called and I forgot all
about him. Oh, Vern..."

She paused beside the manger and looked up at
Vernon who stopped beside her, a little out of breath
from this unexpected exertion.

"Manny said he needed to be fed by hand, with
liquids dribbled from a spoon because his jaw was
broken. And he had to be fed all the time, regularly,
because he was half-starved already and he was so
weak and sick that he'd die otherwise. Oh, God, he's
dead, Vern, I just know it...."

Her eyes were wide and terrified, very blue in the
dusky interior of the barn and glittering with unshed
tears as she reached down with a shaking hand to
touch the motionless bundle of sacking.

Vernon slipped a gentle arm around her. "Caro,

please don't let it matter so much, okay? He was just
a stray, and he was so badly hurt that it's probably
going to be better this way.''

"You don't understand,'' she burst out, swallowing a sob of misery. "You just don't understand,'' she repeated in lower voice. "As soon as I
saw this little dog, Vern, I told you I wasn't going
to let him die. I said I'd seen too much of death
already. And now he's dead, and J.T.'s...''

She choked and fell silent while Vernon gazed
down at her, obviously bewildered by this train of
feminine logic.

"Let me get this straight, Caro,'' he began. "Are
you telling me that little dog was a symbol, or something? Is that it? That if he didn't make it, then in
your mind J.T.'s doomed too, somehow?''

She hesitated, gazing up at him in miserable appeal. "I know it sounds crazy, Vern,'' she whispered.
"But I'm beginning to feel that death is all around
me and I have no control over it, that it can just take
anybody from me anytime. I feel so... so goddamn
helpless!''

He took her in his arms, holding her close to him
for the first time in his life, patting her slender back
and murmuring in her ear, whispering words of comfort.

But her body remained tense and unyielding in his
embrace. After a moment she pulled away, turning

to reach for the silent folds of sacking where a few tufts of the terrier's silky gray coat were visible.

Vernon tried to stop her, grasping her hand and holding it firmly. "Caro, don't," he said huskily. "Go on up to the house and let me look after it, girl."

But she ignored him, her face pale and expressionless as she gently pulled aside the rumpled folds of burlap, then gasped in astonishment.

The little dog's dark eyes looked up at them, brighter and softer than Carolyn remembered. His pink tongue lolled and a small undulating disturbance in the thick springy gray coat indicated that he was making a feeble attempt to wag his stump of a tail.

Carolyn stared at him, openmouthed, her face alight with wonder.

"But he's… Vern, he actually looks *stronger*. He looks better than he did this morning. How can he possibly be…?"

Vernon was examining the small dog in a quiet businesslike manner, touching the clean white plaster cast, running his hand gently across the silky coat with its neat shaved channel crisscrossed with dark stitches, patting the bony tufted head.

"Look, Carolyn," he said quietly.

She leaned in beside him, so close that their cheeks were almost touching, and then caught her breath. The sacks beneath the little dog's head were lightly stained with a thin brownish liquid, and a few spots were scattered here and there across the remainder of the clean sacking. The dog's muzzle was similarly stained, and his pink tongue licked occasionally at the matted fur with evident enjoyment despite his slack useless jaw.

"Someone's fed him," Carolyn murmured in wonder. "But who? Nobody else even knew he was here except Beverly, and she hasn't been home since this morning. Besides, she'd hardly want to—"

"Look at this," Vernon said suddenly, pulling a small multicolored object from the folds of burlap. "Looks like a kid's toy."

Carolyn stared at the object. It was indeed a child's toy, a tiny cloth doll about six or seven inches long, wearing plaid rompers, with wide button eyes and a smiling mouth stitched onto its soft fabric face. When the furry gray dog caught sight of the doll his tail thumped weakly once more and he rolled his head toward the small bright object. Vernon tucked it tenderly back down near the dog's muzzle, while Carolyn stared in amazement.

"Now, who on earth would think to give him that little toy?" she said.

"He seems to like it," Vernon commented, watching as the little dog rested his head against the soft stuffed toy and whined quietly.

Carolyn was silent. The child's toy reminded her

of something, and suddenly she captured the elusive memory…that furtive scramble of feet in the straw in front of her, the flash of eyes and teeth and her own heart-stopping terror. And then, more slowly, she recalled standing by the refrigerator as she wondered aloud what to feed the injured dog, and the prickly nervous sensation that she was being watched.

She leaned closer, sniffing at the stains on the burlap, then straightened. "Stew," she announced. "And milk."

She felt a sudden flood of warmth and gratitude, an emotion so intense that it left her feeling a little dizzy and unsteady on her feet.

"Teresa," she called into the musky silent depths of the barn, her voice shaking. "Teresa, you were such a good girl to do this for me. You were just a wonderful little girl. Why don't you come out and let me give you a big hug?"

Vernon stared at her in alarm. Carolyn ignored him, leaning forward intently and listening to the silence.

"You hear me, Teresa?" she said. "I know you're out there somewhere. Thank you for looking after him, dear. I surely appreciate it."

"Carolyn," Vernon began hesitantly, "I wonder if you should…"

"I'll tell you later," Carolyn whispered, turning

to him with a weary but radiant smile. "As a matter of fact, why don't you come in for supper and spend the evening with me, okay, Vern? Lori has a meeting and Beverly won't be home till later, and I really don't feel like being alone right now."

Vernon hesitated, looking at her thoughtfully.

"I'd like to stay Caro, but I don't want to intrude. Won't you be going over to the Double C right away? Maybe you all just want family there now."

"Oh, go on, Vern, who's family if not you? Come on," she urged, suddenly full of energy, as she took his arm and pulled him from the barn. "I just have to check with Karl about a few things and see how Rosa made out with the colts, and then you and I can make a sandwich or something and go right on over there. Please, Vern," she added when he continued to hesitate. "I'd like for you to come along. Truly I would."

"Sure, Caro," he said instantly. "In that case, I'd love to come. Just let me grab my phone and tell the office where I am."

Beside the car he paused, casting an inquiring glance at Carolyn, who was already heading across the ranch yard toward the corrals.

"Carolyn," Vernon called.

"Yes, Vern?" she said, taking a few steps back toward him.

"Carolyn, don't you think maybe we should move

the dog up into the house where it'll be easier for you to take care of him?''

She hesitated, then shook her head. ''No, I think we'd better leave him where he is, Vern. I think that little dog has a guardian angel, and he's going to need all the help he can get. And,'' she added, her eyes darkening as she recalled all the events of the day and the problems ahead, ''God knows, so do I.''

He continued to look at her in silence, and she gave him a wan smile. ''I'll explain later,'' she promised again. ''I'll tell you all about the ghosts and guardian angels that haunt my ranch these days, Vern. You call your office and get squared away, and then come on up to the house with me. We can put all these problems out of our minds for a while. We'll eat potluck and talk some more about how much I hate dude ranches in general and the Hole in the Wall in particular.''

CHAPTER FOUR

THERE WAS NOTHING in the world that could compare with an April afternoon in the Texas Hill Country, Carolyn thought, gazing around her with pleasure. In the week since J. T. McKinney's heart attack, the whole world seemed to have exploded with color and brightness. The rolling countryside was fresh and lovely, rich with bursts of green and rainbow splashes of wildflowers.

Carolyn smiled, pausing for a moment by her parked car and looking over the lush quiet grounds and rolling acres of the McKinney ranch. Then she started up the circular drive toward the front veranda, her step light and springing. The afternoon was mild and Carolyn wore a white cotton shirt with the sleeves rolled up, a khaki skirt belted snugly at her waist and woven leather sandals. Her golden hair was tied back with a soft scarf of white and tan silk. She looked as fresh and beautiful as the spring day all around her, though her blue eyes still showed traces of strain and weariness.

"Hi, Grandpa," she said cheerfully, climbing the

veranda steps and smiling at the old man, who sat in a circle of deep shade behind one of the pillars. "How's it going?"

Hank Travis glanced up at her, grunted something noncommittal and turned away. Chuckling, Carolyn moved across the veranda to stand close to him. She gazed down at him fondly.

Hank looked the same as always, thin and neat and self-contained, his shoulders straight and his hawk-like profile as belligerent as ever. He wore crisp jeans, a pale straw cowboy hat, handmade leather riding boots and a clean white snap-buttoned shirt with the round yellow tab on his tobacco pouch hanging from the corner of one pocket.

For as long as Carolyn could remember, Hank Travis had dressed exactly the same way. The old man had only been in permanent residence at the Double C since J.T. had moved him over from Pearsall, house and all, about fourteen years earlier. But before that he had visited the Double C often, and Carolyn had always seen right through the crusty exterior to the man beneath and paid scant attention to Hank's gruff offhand ways.

It was strange, Carolyn mused, gazing down at his seamed leathery cheek beneath the brim of the cowboy hat, just how little age had affected this remarkable man. When he was sixty he'd looked incredibly ancient to her five-year-old eyes. Now that he was ninety-nine, almost a century old, he seemed hardly changed from those long-ago days.

She felt a sudden flood of love for the cantankerous old man, an emotion compounded with nostalgia for her lost childhood and sorrow for all those dearly beloved people who were already gone. Hot tears rose behind her eyes, almost blinding her, and she blinked them back impatiently. "Hank Travis," she said sharply. "If you aren't just the rudest old man in Claro County. Don't even have the decency to give a person a proper hello."

Hank glanced up at her, rearing back to raise his head, his brown eyes bright and unrepentant.

"When I'm fixin' to draw into a straight flush," he said, "I sure don't wanna be bothered by no women wantin' to chat."

Carolyn chuckled again and sank into a chair nearby, smiling at him.

A couple of winters earlier when Hank was fretting in the cold, unhappy because he couldn't get out and time was hanging heavy on his hands, Tyler had startled the family by buying the old man a sleek little laptop computer and patiently teaching him the rudiments of its operation. Everyone was puzzled, trying to figure out what Tyler hoped to accomplish by introducing Grandpa to the computer age. Even more, they were stunned by Hank's uncharacteristic patience, his diligent efforts to master the operation of this newfangled contraption.

But after a while it became very clear what the two were up to. Once Tyler was sure Hank understood the basic operation of his expensive little machine, he installed a Las Vegas casino program on it and his great-grandfather spent many contented hours playing blackjack and draw poker, watching the colorful cards flash up on the screen, planning strategies, cursing at his losses and happily drawing up long secret lists of unintelligible symbols and statistics that he updated with painstaking care after each game.

"A straight flush," Carolyn said, impressed, gazing at the row of cards on the computer screen. "That must pay a lot. Did you make it?"

"Missed it by one card," Hank said in disgust. "I was countin' cards an' I figured the three of clubs was fixin' to come up right then but it fooled me. Come up the next hand instead."

He waved a sheet of paper at her, rows of figures in his shaky hand, arranged in a complex series of columns and lines.

Carolyn gazed at it blankly. "What's all that, Grandpa?"

"My strategy," the old man said. "My draw poker system. When I get this perfected, I'll sell it for a million dollars."

Carolyn grinned. "No kidding. What will you do with a million dollars?"

"Just watch," he said mysteriously. "Just watch me, young lady. You might be surprised."

All at once his leathery face darkened briefly and he glanced up at Carolyn, his faded brown eyes troubled. "I guess the boy's feelin' a little better," he said.

Carolyn nodded, understanding that in Hank's eyes J. T. McKinney would always be "the boy," even if he was fifty-five years old with a couple of sons in their thirties.

"That's what I hear," she said. "Nate thinks he might even be able to come home soon, if he keeps improving like this."

"Imagine a young man like that havin' a heart attack," Hank commented with a bleak expression, punching his keyboard in perfunctory fashion and frowning as a row of cards turned up.

"Nines!" he said in disgust. "Goddamn nines ain't worth a plugged nickel. You can't never fill with nines."

"Why not?" Carolyn asked, genuinely interested, but the old man's thoughts had already veered away to another topic.

"She's pregnant, you know," he commented.

Carolyn stared at him.

"The new wife," he said impatiently. "With the fancy big-city name."

Carolyn grinned again. Hank didn't feel that Cynthia was a proper Texas name, and avoided saying it if at all possible. The family got quite a few chuckles out of his elaborate efforts to address or refer to Cynthia without actually saying her name.

"Did she tell you that?" Carolyn asked, looking at him curiously. "About being pregnant, I mean?"

Hank shrugged. "Didn't have to tell me," he said.

Carolyn was silent, still gazing at him thoughtfully. Hank Travis occasionally exhibited this kind of uncanny prescience, an apparent ability to see and know things unknown to others that almost amounted to second sight. This facility was a little unnerving to family members but Hank himself was completely offhand about it and scoffed loudly if anyone ever suggested that his insights might be unusual.

"Anybody with half a brain an' a glass eye can see somethin' right in front of their noses," he would protest. "Or y'all should be able to, if you just wasn't so damn *dumb*." Now he looked directly at Carolyn, his eyes shadowed beneath the brim of the cowboy hat. "Does the boy know?" he asked.

Carolyn shook her head. "Nobody knows but the doctor. And you, of course," she added with a smile. "I think she's waiting to tell J.T., maybe till he's a little stronger. She thinks it might be a shock for him in his weakened condition.''

"She should tell him," Hank said firmly, surprising Carolyn again.

"Why, Grandpa? Why should she tell him?''

"Well, because he's a man," Hank said impatiently. "Because he's prob'ly feelin' his age these days, worryin' about how old he is, now that he's had this damn heart attack. If she tells him about the baby, he'll feel just like a young rooster again. Set him right back on his pins.''

Carolyn nodded thoughtfully, getting to her feet and watching as Hank's fingers punched a couple of keys and another series of cards sprang up on the screen.

"Tens!" he exclaimed in delight. "Now, that's more like it. With tens I can go for a full house on the sevens. Now let me think....''

Carolyn patted his shoulder, dropped a kiss on his cheek and walked away toward the door, followed by the old man's smug exclamations and the beeping musical whir of the computer as it counted his payoff.

She opened the heavy front door and stepped inside, taken aback a little as she always was these days when she first entered the McKinney house now presided over by Cynthia. Carolyn had liked Cynthia from the beginning, and was growing to care more deeply for the younger woman all the time, to feel an affection so strong that it could even be termed love. She knew that, as Vernon had pointed out, this marriage had been good for J.T., and that Cynthia's addition to the family had been a positive step for everybody.

Still, it felt vaguely disturbing to walk into this familiar place, this house that J.T. had built expressly for his first wife, Pauline, Carolyn's beloved older sister, and see it changed and transformed under the hands of another woman.

"Hello?" she called. "Anybody home?"

But the big house was clean and silent in the afternoon stillness. Carolyn strolled through the tiled foyer and down the hall, past the open doors leading into the living room and dining room. Briefly she paused at the entry to J.T.'s empty study and gazed at the broad scarred desk still littered with papers and brand slips from his last shipment of cattle. Then she moved on toward the kitchen.

She felt as if the walls were talking to her, sending back whispered echoes of all the things that had happened in this house. She heard J.T.'s affectionate teasing and Pauline's answering laughter, her husband Frank's deep masculine voice singing while somebody played the piano, the ribald merriment of big groups of friends and neighbors at a springtime barbecue, the crying of babies and the happy shouts of a generation of children long since grown.

Carolyn paused in the hallway by the kitchen and swallowed hard, gripping the doorframe while she struggled to compose herself. They had been such good years, such rich sun-filled happy times, and she'd never dreamed they would end. But everything was so different now.

For one thing, people were gone who would never be back. Frank, Pauline, their mother Deborah, their father... And now J.T. was gone, and the intense silence seemed to highlight his absence. Even the house itself saddened her. It was beautifully re-decorated in Cynthia's spare and elegant fashion with appealing light colors and gracious appointments, but today it seemed to Carolyn like another little death, an absence of something familiar and deeply loved.

Carolyn shook herself and squared her shoulders, determined not to give way to this kind of emotion. She glanced into the kitchen, prepared to say something cheerful and teasing, but it, too, was deserted. Through the window above the table, she could just glimpse Lettie Mae, J.T.'s cook, in her vegetable garden behind the house. She was hoeing among the neat rows of young plants, jabbing at the ground with quick choppy strokes.

Carolyn walked through the kitchen and opened the doors into the sunny yard, waving at Lettie Mae, who called out a brisk cheerful greeting and continued with her work.

"Hi there, Lettie Mae," Carolyn called. "Where's Cynthia, do you know?"

"Here I am," a voice said nearby.

Carolyn glanced around, startled, and then smiled. Cynthia McKinney knelt beside the path a few yards away, half-obscured by spreading rosebushes, wielding a trowel busily among the new growth. She wore a plain white T shirt, baggy faded denim bib overalls, sneakers and a wide-brimmed straw coolie hat on her head.

"Hi, Cynthia," Carolyn said, sinking onto a wicker chair nearby, just at the edge of the flagstone patio. "You look like Huckleberry Finn. I trust those are designer overalls?"

Cynthia grinned back at her and rubbed a gloved hand over her face, leaving an appealing smudge of dirt on one cheek.

"Now don't *you* start teasing me, like everyone else," she said to Carolyn. "You should hear old Hank's opinion of these overalls."

Carolyn chuckled. "I can imagine," she said, choking a little. "I can certainly imagine."

Then she sobered, watching with thoughtful affection as the younger woman stood, massaging the small of her back in a weary gesture, then lowered herself into the opposite chair.

"How are you, Cynthia?" she asked. "Really, I mean. How are you coping?"

Cynthia made a face, peeled off her gardening gloves and gazed down at her hands in rueful silence. Beneath the brim of the hat her shining golden hair fell forward, partly concealing her face as Carolyn looked at her.

"Oh, not too well," she said with an attempt at lightness. "I find that it's kind of hard to be brave and serene, you know, when you're chucking your cookies every ten minutes."

Carolyn laughed. "I declare, girl," she said, "you're fitting in better all the time. A few months ago, I couldn't possibly imagine you 'chucking your cookies,' let alone talking about it that way."

Cynthia gave her a wan smile. "I know," she said. "Spending time with Grandpa has totally corrupted me, I'm afraid. At least, my vocabulary is getting a lot more colorful."

"So you're having morning sickness already, Cynthia?"

Cynthia nodded. "Nate says it's pretty early, but it could be because of all the stress. I don't know what's causing it," she added, trying to smile, "but I sure know I'm not imagining it."

"Oh, I know," Carolyn said with sympathy. "There's not many things as awful as morning sickness. Twenty-five years later, and I still recall it vividly.''

Cynthia nodded, her pale face flushing delicately as she leaned back in the chair and gazed across the rolling green fields dotted with grazing cattle.

''You know,'' she said, ''last year at this time, I was fully involved in passionate discussions on the Savings and Loans problem and my own efforts to track interest rates for corporate clients, things like that. If somebody had told me then that twelve months later I'd be living among hundreds of cows and concentrating mostly on how to get through the day without throwing up on my shoes, I'd have told them they were crazy.''

Her words were meant to be humorous but her voice trembled as she finished. Carolyn reached over and gripped her hand, and Cynthia returned the pressure gratefully.

''God knows, it's hard enough under the best of circumstances,'' Carolyn said. ''Dealing with pregnancy, I mean, and all the doubts and questions and changes your body's going through. I can't even imagine how hard it must be when your husband is seriously ill and you're forced to cope with it all on your own.''

Cynthia turned aside and began to toy with the gloves again, her face strained and silent. Carolyn understood that she was reluctant to risk her voice for fear of breaking down.

"Hank thinks you should tell him," she said casually, watching Lettie Mae's spare figure as she plied her hoe energetically in the vegetable patch. "Tell J.T. about the baby, I mean."

Cynthia turned abruptly in the chair to gaze at her friend, brown eyes wide and startled.

"Hank *knows?*" she asked. "About the baby? How does he know? Did you tell him, Carolyn? I haven't told anybody. Not a soul but you."

"I didn't tell him," Carolyn said. "He just knows. There's times," she added, "he just knows things, and nobody can explain how."

Cynthia nodded. "Of course. I'd forgotten about his sixth sense." She was silent for a moment, then she looked over at Carolyn again. "He thinks I should tell J.T.? Why?"

"He thinks J.T. will be worrying about his age, having just had a heart attack. In Hank's opinion, when he hears about the baby it's going to make him feel like a new man. A "young rooster," were Hank's words, I believe."

Cynthia grinned unexpectedly. "Men," she said. "They're all so predictable, aren't they? You know what?" she murmured to Carolyn, leaning forward confidingly. "There's something about this baby that even old Hank hasn't found out yet."

"Really? What's that?"

"Well, it sounds incredible, and I'm almost reluctant even to say it out loud, but you know what, Carolyn? The baby's actual due date is Hank's birthday. His hundredth birthday. Can you imagine such a coincidence?"

Carolyn stared at her, openmouthed. "Cynthia!" she exclaimed. "Really?"

Cynthia nodded solemnly. "Really. Nate worked it out twice, just to be sure. I don't know what to do," she went on after a moment. "I don't know whether to tell Hank or not. If he knows it might make him like me a little better, or at least win me a few points. But if I…"

"If you mess up and don't deliver on the right day after all, he might never forgive you," Carolyn finished cheerfully.

"Exactly," Cynthia agreed, turning to smile at her again. "If I happen to go a couple of days over, or deliver two weeks early, he'll be disgusted. He'll chalk it up to me being a lightweight or an incompetent city slicker and never speak to me again." Cynthia got to her feet and headed toward the kitchen door, still carrying her trowel and gloves. "Come on in and have some coffee, Carolyn," she said. "I don't think I can stomach coffee myself, but I can nibble some soda crackers and keep you company. You know, maybe Hank's right," she added, as Carolyn followed her into the kitchen and sat down at the table.

"About what?"

"Maybe I should tell J.T. about the baby. I keep thinking it'll be too big a shock for him right now, but maybe I'm underestimating him."

"How is he, Cynthia?" Carolyn asked quietly. "Really, I mean. How is he?"

Cynthia's face shadowed again. She pulled the coolie hat off and hung it on a peg by the door, then paused to wash her hands before moving over to get a mug and glass down from the cupboard. "He's doing pretty well, but not as well as *he* thinks he is," she said briefly over her shoulder.

"Can I help with something?" Carolyn offered, and then protested, "Oh, Cynthia, no cake or anything. I just had lunch."

"Good," Cynthia said with relief, putting a covered cake tin back into the refrigerator. "Just looking at that rich gooey icing makes me start to heave."

"What do you mean, he's not doing as well as he thinks he is?"

"Oh, you know what he's like," Cynthia said wearily, bringing a steaming coffee mug over to Carolyn and sitting down opposite her with a glass of milk and a couple of soda crackers on a plate. "He was a little stunned by the fact that he, the original Iron Man, had actually suffered a heart attack. But now he's put that all behind him as if it never happened and he's pushing himself already, doing way more than he should, ignoring all of Nate's warnings...."

Cynthia fell abruptly silent, gazing into her glass of milk with a brooding expression while Carolyn watched her quietly.

"You know what he did yesterday?" Cynthia asked, looking up miserably. "He's supposed to go for a walk every afternoon, two trips down the hall to the nursing station and back. Well, yesterday when it was time for his walk, he just hopped into his jeans and boots and went on over to the Longhorn for coffee."

"Cynthia!" Carolyn said, aghast.

Cynthia nodded grimly. "Did you ever hear of anything so insane? When Nate told me I was so damned mad I could hardly talk to J.T., and he genuinely couldn't understand why I was upset. He said it's just a few blocks over to the Longhorn and the fresh air was good for him after being cooped up in the hospital for a week."

"What did Nate say?"

"Nate was just as mad as I was, but with a lot more self-control. He's worried that J.T. just hasn't grasped how much damage was done to his heart, and that if he overdoes it now he'll be running the risk of congestive heart failure, whatever that is."

Carolyn shuddered, plunged all at once into the blackness of memory. "That's what Frank died of," she murmured, and then instantly regretted her words when she saw how the color drained from Cynthia's face. "But with him it was almost instantaneous, Cynthia," she said hastily. "It all happened at once."

"What do you mean?"

"I mean, Frank had the heart attack and then a couple of days later, before he ever had a chance to rally, he suffered congestive heart failure. His heart stopped, his lungs filled up with fluid and that was it."

Cynthia nodded. "That's what Nate said. Apparently it's the real danger after a heart attack. He says that if J.T. would just take it really easy and give the damaged heart tissue a chance to mend, than he'd be a prime candidate for angioplasty in a few months."

She cast Carolyn a quick inquiring glance, took a reluctant sip of her milk and continued. "Angioplasty is the procedure with the little balloon, you know, that they inject into the artery and then inflate to remove the blockage?"

Carolyn nodded. "I know. But they'd have to do that in a bigger hospital, wouldn't they?"

"In Austin. Nate says it's a relatively simple operation, and J.T. would probably be able to live a normal life after that, a long healthy life, Nate says, with just a little more attention to diet and reducing the stress in his life. But, Carolyn, I'm just so scared...."

Her voice broke and she fell silent, staring blindly down at the table. Carolyn reached over to cover Cynthia's hand with her own.

"I'm so scared," Cynthia whispered, choking a little, "that he'll push himself too hard too soon, and not ever have the chance to have the corrective procedure done. Oh, Carolyn..."

Carolyn watched, aching with sympathy, as Cynthia raised her face and gazed at her friend with tragic dark eyes.

"I love him so much, Carolyn. I never dreamed I could love a man the way I love J. T. McKinney. I can't bear to lose him now, after such a little time together. I just can't bear it!"

Carolyn swallowed hard and forced herself to smile. "You're not going to lose him," she said firmly. "You're not. Here's what we're going to do, Cynthia. You're going to tell him about the baby, and make him aware that he has some new responsibilities. You know, I think Hank's right," she went on. "I think that hearing about this new baby is going to be a better therapy for the man than anything else in the world."

Cynthia still looked miserable, but there was a little color creeping back into her cheeks and her dark eyes showed the faintest glimmer of hope.

"And then," Carolyn said, heartened by Cynthia's expression, "I'll go talk to him. I've been real gentle with him up till now out of respect for his invalid status, but not anymore. Just as soon as you've told him about the baby, I'll go and put the fear of God into that cowboy. Believe me, Cynthia," she concluded grimly, "when I get finished with J. T. McKinney, it'll be a while before he crawls out of his hospital bed and takes a stroll down to the Longhorn for coffee again."

Cynthia smiled wanly. "Thanks, Carolyn," she said. "It's wonderful to hear you say that. Sometimes I feel so lonely, trying to deal with all this on my own, not knowing what I should do."

"You're doing just fine," Carolyn said gently.

She smiled back at the younger woman, trying hard to battle her own feelings of fear and anxiety. But part of her mind still held the image of J.T.'s erect figure on the street in Crystal Creek, heading cheerfully down the block for a visit with his friends. She saw his handsome graying head and quick smile and lithe springing step, and the dangerous dark shadow that hung over him, threatening him, clouding his life and stealing away his future....

"When will you go?" Cynthia was asking. "When do you want to talk to him?"

"Well, as soon as we can, right?" Carolyn said, forcing herself back to reality, pushing the troubling images away. "After all, hearing the way he's started to carry on, there's no time to waste. When are you seeing him next?"

"In an hour or so," Cynthia said, glancing at her watch. "He's having X rays right now, and I promised I'd come in later in the afternoon and stay with him for supper."

"All right," Carolyn said. "You make sure you tell him he's going to be a daddy again. And then after supper when we go to see him, I'll let him know exactly what kind of responsibilities a daddy has, in case he's forgotten."

Cynthia nodded gratefully and took another long sip of milk, grimacing a little. "I hate this stuff," she said with a small apologetic smile, "but it's doctor's orders."

Carolyn grinned. "And God knows, *somebody* in this family's got to obey the doctor's orders," she said dryly.

Cynthia smiled, her cheeks pink, looking more like her old self all the time. "This makes me feel so good, Carolyn," she said, looking fondly at the woman across the table. "I think you and Hank are both right. I think this little bundle—" she patted her still-flat abdomen beneath the baggy overalls "—might be just the shock therapy that my stubborn husband needs. Who's 'we,' by the way?'' she added casually, watching as Carolyn strolled across the kitchen to pour herself another cup of coffee.

"What do you mean?" Carolyn asked.

"You said tonight 'when we go to see him,' and I just wondered who was going with you. Isn't Beverly still in Dallas at the spring fashion show?"

"Oh, I meant Vern," Carolyn said, distressed by the sudden flush that warmed her cheeks. "Vernon Trent. He was planning to drop out to the ranch for supper tonight, and we'll probably drive in together to visit J.T. afterward."

She turned aside, busying herself with the sugar bowl while Cynthia gazed at her with cheerful speculation.

"Hasn't Vernon Trent been around quite a bit lately? Or am I just imagining it?"

Carolyn continued to ignore those bright dark eyes, stirring sugar into her coffee with great concentration. "I guess maybe he has been around a bit more than usual," she said cautiously. "I've been really upset about J.T. and Vern's such an old friend to both of us, and then we have this dog to worry about...."

"Dog?" Cynthia asked. "What dog?"

"Oh, a little guy that was hit by a car outside my gates last week, the same day that J.T. got sick. Vern found him in the ditch early that morning and brought him in, and I called Manny to patch him up and started looking after him, so Vern and I have both taken kind of an interest in him. Vern comes out a lot to check on him, that's all.''

Cynthia nodded, her eyes amused and skeptical. ''I see,'' she said. ''It's just the *dog* Vern's interested in, is it? And how's he doing? The dog, I mean,'' she added with a grin.

''He's doing all right,'' Carolyn said with dignity, ignoring Cynthia's teasing glance. ''But he's still got a lot of problems, the poor little fellow,'' she added, sobering as she thought about the furry gray terrier in her barn.

''What's wrong with him?''

''Well, a broken hind leg, for starters, and a big gash in his side that Manny stitched up and a shattered jaw, plus unspecified internal injuries.''

''Oh, my goodness,'' Cynthia murmured. ''That doesn't sound good, does it? Where did he come from?''

''We're assuming that somebody dumped him off,'' Carolyn said. ''You know how they do it, figuring this nice big ranch will be the perfect home for their poor unwanted pet?''

Cynthia nodded and braced herself to drain the last of her milk.

''I've been watching the papers for the past week, but there's been no 'lost dog' ad in any of them,''

Carolyn said, "and Manny's not expecting one. He can tell by the dog's pads that he's not a stray. He was dumped off nearby."

"Poor little guy," Cynthia murmured.

"He sure is," Carolyn agreed. "And he's so weak, and he can't eat, you know, because of his jaw. He needs to be fed liquids by the hour, and he seems to have something else wrong with him now. He's not really getting any stronger, and he runs a temperature a lot of the time like he's battling infection. I don't really know what to do for him, but I don't like to bother Manny about him too much, either, because I know Manny thinks I'm crazy."

"He does? Why?"

Carolyn shrugged, leaning against the counter and sipping her coffee. "Well, to be trying to keep the little fella alive in the first place when he's so badly hurt. Manny thinks it's impractical, I believe."

"Don't you think Manny might be right?" Cynthia asked cautiously, glancing up at her friend. "I mean, if the dog's that badly hurt and he's not a beloved pet of the family or anything, shouldn't you just…let nature take its course? For his sake, too?"

"You're right," Carolyn agreed. "I should. I know that. It's just that I feel…"

She fell abruptly silent, gazing out the window at Lettie Mae, who was now on her knees weeding by hand around the rows of tiny new lettuce plants.

"I feel like I owe it to him somehow," she finished lamely. "Having taken on the job, I can hardly quit now. And besides, there's Teresa."

"Teresa?" Cynthia asked in surprise. "What's Teresa got to do with it?"

Cynthia knew all about the troubled waif who haunted Carolyn's ranch. In the early days, she'd expressed sympathetic horror when she heard the child's history, and a couple of times when she visited Carolyn she'd even made futile attempts to draw the child out, to corner her in the barn and engage her in conversation.

"Teresa's helping me look after the dog," Carolyn said. "She's doing most of the tedious part, actually."

"You're kidding," Cynthia said, amazed. "I didn't think you'd ever managed to talk to her."

"Oh, I don't *talk* to her," Carolyn said. "She watches me all the time, I can feel her there watching, but I never see her. I leave supplies and food nearby and she creeps out after I've gone and spends hours dribbling liquid food into his mouth, coaxing him to drink water and take his medicine, that sort of thing."

"Well, that's a different story," Cynthia said. "If she's showing that much interest in something, even if it's just a stray dog, it'd be a real shame to take it away from her. This might be just what she needs to bring her out of her shell.''

''I think it might take more than a dog,'' Carolyn said thinking of the child's furtive ways. ''But I guess you're right, it's a good sign.''

''And what about Vern?'' Cynthia asked, returning to the main topic of interest. ''Is he helping to feed this dog, too? Is that why he's around all the time?''

Carolyn faced her friend squarely. ''Why are you looking at me like that, Cynthia? Why do you keep asking me about Vern?''

''Oh, come on, Carolyn,'' Cynthia said, smiling. ''Anybody can tell what's going on. I think it's great.''

''What?'' Carolyn asked, genuinely bewildered. ''What's going on?''

''Oh, Carolyn,'' the younger woman said in exasperation, munching on one of her dry saltines. ''How can you be so dense? The man's crazy in love with you. Everybody knows it but you.''

''Vernon Trent?'' Carolyn asked, astounded. ''In love with *me?*''

''You really don't know it, do you?'' Cynthia said in wonder. ''You've really, truly, never noticed.''

''Noticed what?'' Carolyn asked impatiently, beginning to feel uncomfortably warm in the sun. She walked back to the table and sat down with her coffee mug.

"The first time I ever saw you two together," Cynthia said, "way back before J.T. and I were married, I could see how Vernon Trent felt about you. Every time his eyes rest on you, Carolyn, his face is just transformed. The man adores you. J.T. says he's adored you all his life, and that's why he never married anybody else even though he's such a darling and lots of women wanted him."

"Well, I don't want him," Carolyn said sharply, growing more and more distressed by the warmth that crept over her cheeks, and the strange erratic fluttering of her heart. "I think this is ridiculous. Vern and I are friends, that's all. We've been friends since forever, since we were born, practically. I don't know why all these gossips around here have to insist on making things more than they are!"

"Okay," Cynthia murmured. "Okay, dear. That's fine, if that's how you feel. But just as a matter of interest," she added, "why would you be so violently opposed to the idea? I mean, he's a terrific guy, and he's crazy about you...."

"I'm not sure I believe that," Carolyn said with dignity, "just because you and J.T. are busy matchmaking. Besides," she added after a moment's hesitation, "he's not my type."

"Not your type? What do you mean? Don't you two get along well together?"

"Oh, sure," Carolyn said a little desperately. "We get along real well together. We always have. But for me to fall in *love* with him, well, that's a different thing altogether."

"Why?" Cynthia persisted gently. "Why is it so different? I remember reading once that love is just friendship set to music. If you two already have the friendship," she concluded with a smile, "maybe you just need to start making the music."

Carolyn returned her smile wanly, and then shook her head. "You're right, Vern's terrific and we have all kinds of fun together, and I don't know what I would have done without him lately. But I couldn't ever fall in love with him, Cynthia."

"Why not?"

"He's too out of shape," Carolyn said, surprising both herself and the woman across the table.

"Too *out of shape?*" Cynthia echoed blankly. "That's a major consideration?'

"Damn rights it is," Carolyn said grimly.

"In what way? How come? Carolyn, I didn't know you were a jock."

"I'm not," Carolyn said. "But I'm concerned about healthy-life styles, Cynthia, and you of all people should understand why. I lost a mother and a sister to breast cancer, and a husband to heart disease, and now another man that I care deeply about is threatened by the same thing. Then I look at Vernon Trent, and I just feel scared to death,'' she concluded bleakly, running her finger in little random circles around the handle of her coffee mug.

"Scared?" Cynthia said. "Why?"

"Look at him," Carolyn said in despair. "Just look at the man. He's about twenty pounds overweight, he works all the time in a high-pressure sales job, he never exercises, he lives on fries and doughnuts and chicken-fried steak.... What woman in her right mind is going to let herself fall in love with a man like that?"

Cynthia nodded thoughtfully. "I see what you mean. You're afraid you might have to go through what I'm suffering right now. A few wonderful months with somebody and then he—" Her voice broke.

"Exactly," Carolyn agreed. "But with J.T. you couldn't really have known that a heart attack was in his future because he looks so lean and fit. A man like Vern just looks to me like a walking time bomb. I'd be too scared to get close to him, Cynthia. I can't stand to lose anybody else I love. I really can't."

"Okay, Carolyn," Cynthia said, getting to her feet and trying to smile. "Then for now, let's just concentrate on keeping this stubborn cowboy of mine around for a lot more years, shall we? We'll give him the one-two punch tonight and put 'the fear of God' into him, as you express it.''

''You bet we will,'' Carolyn said, forcing herself to smile as Cynthia moved toward the door, elegant and graceful even in her baggy overalls.

Cynthia paused to smile over her shoulder. ''I have to shower and get changed,'' she said. ''If you're gone before I come back down, I'll see you at the hospital tonight, okay?''

''Okay,'' Carolyn promised again.

She watched as Cynthia vanished, her sunlit hair bright as spun gold in the dimness of the hallway. Then she sank back in her chair and gripped her coffee mug in both hands, her face bleak and troubled as she gazed out the window at the cloudless Texas sky.

CHAPTER FIVE

TERESA LAY FLAT on her stomach on the floor of the loft, oblivious to the prickling of dry straw under her chest and arms and the hardness of the wooden planks against her bare skinny knees. All of her small being was concentrated fiercely on what was happening in the barn some fifteen or twenty feet below, a scene that she was watching through a ragged knothole in one of the loft floorboards.

She had discovered this particular knothole just a week earlier. Now it was one of the most important things in her life, because the vantage point was situated directly above the manger where the little gray terrier lay, still sick and listless with fever. The hole in the floor gave Teresa a full view of everything that happened to him. A further advantage was that the loft stairs were nearby, so close that she could scamper up soundlessly at the first sign of somebody's approach and then watch what was going on below from a cautious distance.

Most of Teresa's life was organized around escape routes like this, places where she could safely vanish whenever she needed to, elude pursuit and melt away into nothingness. The child's intimate knowledge of this big sprawling ranch would probably have amazed everyone, even Carolyn who had lived there all her life.

Teresa had only been in residence a few months but she already knew dozens of secret hiding places, tunnels through haystacks and behind buildings, hidden caverns in the tall weeds and along the riverbank. Any time danger threatened she could fly like a bird across the rooftops of the ranch buildings or slither quiet as a snake beneath the raised floor of the stables, or disappear instantly in the prickly tangle of mesquite and cactus behind the windmill.

"Oh, Vern," Carolyn was now saying hesitantly, far below Teresa's watchful eye. "The poor little guy. He's so sick, isn't he? Poor little guy."

Teresa stiffened, knowing exactly what Carolyn was thinking. She was thinking that the dog was too badly hurt to get better, and they should get the handsome smiling man with the black bag to "put him to sleep."

The child scowled, clenching her dirty little chapped hands.

Put him to sleep, she thought bitterly. What a dumb thing to say. Everybody knew what it meant. It meant make him dead, that was what it meant. Why didn't they just say so, and be done with it?

She glared down at Carolyn, who stood near the manger box, gazing unhappily at the suffering animal.

From Teresa's lofty position the woman below looked strangely small, like some dainty little doll. Teresa could see the glow of fading spring sunlight on her golden hair with its pretty silk scarf.

In spite of herself, Teresa's face softened. Besides her mother, Rosa, who was always there and didn't really count, there were only two beings in Teresa's whole world that she loved, and they were Carolyn Townsend and the little gray terrier.

Teresa had adored Carolyn from the very first time she saw her. The child loved Carolyn's tall regal look, her gentle smiling tanned face and thoughtful sea blue eyes and her quick graceful way of moving. In her private thoughts Teresa referred to her mother's employer as Gloriana, a name that, in her opinion, suited the woman far better than her real name, Carolyn, which was far too plain and ordinary.

Teresa had been to school for only one year and part of a second term before the terrible thing happened, the thing she never thought about. But she had learned a lot while she was there, and she'd known a lot before she even started school. In fact, Teresa Martinez had taught herself to read before she was five. Years ago, at the last place they'd lived, she used to spend most of her afternoons lying in the haystack with an ABC book, struggling to master the words and sounds while her mother exercised horses out on the track.

Now she secretly devoured all the books Rosa brought home from the library, even books intended for adults. Her mother's tastes tended toward historical romance, and Teresa thrilled to the lush descriptions of knights and ladies, of castles and moats and shining armor.

The woman below her in the barn would have fit well into that kind of setting, in Teresa's opinion. She'd look just lovely as Gloriana, sweeping through the halls of a beautiful stone castle in a rustling gown of palest blue silk, with a net of woven gold on her shining hair....

Teresa sighed and shifted noiselessly on the straw, brushing at a sleek little gray mouse that scampered across her bare arm and then sat up a few feet away to stare at her with comical astonishment, his whiskers twitching.

"Go away," Teresa whispered. "Can't you see I'm busy?"

The mouse nodded, his furry pointed face wise and bright like that of a cheerful little old man, then vanished into the piled straw. Teresa shifted and gazed downward again, watching as the man moved into view and stood close to Gloriana.

The man was called Vernon. All in all, Teresa ap-

proved of the name. Normally she preferred to give
her own names to the people and animals in her
world, but Vernon suited this man pretty well. The
sound of it was strong and rich and golden brown,
like him, with the soft velvety whisper of fire licking
at dry wood, warming the darkness of the night.

Teresa didn't love the man the way she adored
Carolyn. But she still approved of him, liked his
square smiling face and big stocky body, the warmth
of his sudden happy laughter and the gentle way that
he spoke to Gloriana. He wasn't a knight, or even a
duke or an earl, but he was a nice man. Besides, he
was the one who'd brought Bluebonnet to them, and
that was enough for Teresa.

Carolyn, not Teresa, had been the one to name the
injured gray terrier Bluebonnet, but again it was a
name that Teresa had warmly approved from the very
first time she heard Carolyn use it. Now she gazed
down at the little dog with passionate melting adoration, watching as Vernon moved closer and
touched Bluebonnet's soft silky gray fur with a gentle hand.

Bluebonnet was the perfect name for him, Teresa
thought. He was so pretty, with a delicate rare beauty
that almost made you cry. His gray coat even had a
bluish sheen sometimes in the dim light of the barn
and his fluffy topknot was almost white, just like the
flowers blooming in the fields beyond. And he'd

come to them like a wondrous magical gift from the sky, at exactly the same time the bluebonnets were getting sprinkled all over the pastures and hillsides.

Teresa watched, her heart beating faster as Bluebonnet lifted his injured head weakly the way he always did, trying to lick the man's hand.

"I don't know, Caro," Vernon was saying. "He really does looks awfully weak, doesn't he? Is he improving at all?"

Yes! Teresa shouted silently, her stomach knotted in an agony of fear. *Yes, he is! He's getting better every day. You should see how he eats. And he smiles at me every time I come in, and tries to wag his tail. And yesterday he…*

But nobody heard her, of course. She wouldn't make any sound, wouldn't talk to them. She was locked in a soundless bubble that nobody could penetrate, trapped inside the world she'd built to protect herself. This world of hers made big strong walls between Teresa and all other people except her mother. It was lonely sometimes but it was worth it. The walls kept out everything bad, the shouts and cruel grasping hands, the harsh voices and scary things and noise and splattering blood and dreadful numbing pain.…

"We'll give it a while longer," Carolyn was saying below her, as she pulled the sacking tenderly over the dog's thin shivering body. "I don't…I just don't want to give up quite yet, Vern. Not after we've done all this.''

Teresa's heart swelled and throbbed with adoration. She longed to tumble down the loft stairs and embrace Gloriana's knees, kiss her slim brown hands, pour out her gratitude for this reprieve.

But of course she never would. Teresa had seen how the beautiful lady flinched when she caught sight of her, how she pulled away and looked startled and cool. They couldn't ever be friends because it wasn't possible for Teresa to be friends with other people, not ever again. Still, she was so thankful that they were going to let Bluebonnet stay alive.

If they didn't, Teresa decided, her small dirty face suddenly fierce with determination, then she'd just steal him and run away. She'd take Bluebonnet and they'd vanish somewhere far away where they'd be safe together and nobody would ever find them again. Not ever, not in a million years.

The man below moved over beside the woman and slipped a casual arm around her shoulders. Teresa saw how Gloriana leaned gratefully against him, how she smiled up at him and drew briefly closer to him. His handsome pleasant face softened and glowed with tenderness when he looked down at Gloriana's golden head, but she'd already pulled away and started briskly toward the house. He hesitated, looking a little sad and troubled, then followed her.

Teresa sat up, hugging her knees and peering out through a narrow ventilation slit in the wall of the loft, waiting patiently until Gloriana and the man were safely out of sight before she climbed down to visit with Bluebonnet. Teresa Martinez was a thin delicate child, just past her ninth birthday, with a slender fine-boned body that was small for her age. On this warm spring evening she wore ragged cut-offs, a stained shapeless T-shirt and torn gray sneakers that had once been white. A thorough scrubbing and a vigorous brushing of that dark cloud of hair would have revealed a little girl of startling pretti-ness, with huge liquid dark eyes, a shy oval face and a gentle sensitive mouth. But not even Rosa ever got very close to Teresa Martinez, so her prettiness went unnoticed.

The mouse crept out and looked at her again, his eyes bright in the fading twilight.

"Hi, Edgar," Teresa said in the low husky voice only her mother, her favorite toys and a few animals ever heard. "It's okay now. They're gone, and I'm going down to see Bluebonnet for a little while. I won't bother you anymore tonight."

The mouse, who was a good friend of hers, nodded cheerfully and watched as she moved over to the stairs and climbed down, her slim dark form as quick and graceful as a little fish as she slipped through the dusky recesses of the big barn.

VERNON STOOD by the counter in the soft lamplight, a blue-and-white gingham apron tied around his stocky body, whistling tunelessly between his teeth and tossing a green salad with exaggerated flair.

Carolyn passed behind him carrying a plate of warm garlic toast and gave him a cheerful nudge with her elbow. "For goodness' sake, quit showing off," she said. "Always remember that I knew you when you were still trying to figure out how to use the pencil sharpener. You're never going to fool *me* into thinking you're some kind of hotshot French chef."

"That's the whole problem here, you know," he said amiably. "It's hell, trying to impress someone who grew up with you."

"So, why bother?" Carolyn asked. "Why should you want to impress me anyhow, Vern, when we've been friends all our lives?"

Vernon turned to look at her. She was standing by the counter filling an omelet with sauteed sliced mushrooms and green peppers, and she seemed unaware of his scrutiny. She bit her lip, frowning in concentration as she slid the folded omelette cautiously onto a serving plate.

"There!" she said in triumph and cast him a bright glance. "I always feel so incredibly competent when I manage to do that."

Her cheeks were pink and little tendrils of golden

hair had escaped her scarf and curled around her face. To Vernon's loving eyes she looked altogether adorable, a woman expressly designed and richly fashioned to bring pleasure to a man. He struggled again with the urgent longing that was growing stronger all the time, the need to gather her into his arms and press her close to him, feel her heart beating next to his own, whisper in her ears and drown her in kisses.

"Why *bother?*" he echoed, watching her.

"Hmm?" she asked, and rummaged in the drawer for a serving fork.

"You're so smug about getting that damned omelet out of the pan intact, you've already lost the thread of the conversation," he complained. "I was talking about how hard it is to impress you, and you asked me why I should bother. Well, I think maybe it's time I told you why I should bother, Carolyn."

Carolyn avoided his gaze, fidgeting by the counter and looking down at the omelet on its graceful fluted tray, clearly distressed by the sudden tension that charged the atmosphere of her kitchen.

"Vern…" she began abruptly, her voice low and strained.

"Yes, Caro?" he said, watching her quietly. "What is it?"

"You see this meal?" she said, surprising him.

"The meal?" he asked blankly.

"Yes. Salad with low-cal dressing, a light two-egg omelet, garlic wheat toast. You see it?"

"Of course I see it, Caro," he said, growing steadily more puzzled. "I helped to make it."

"But would you have made it on your own?" Carolyn asked, looking up at him, her eyes very blue and strangely challenging. "Is this the way you eat at home, Vern? What would you be making for yourself tonight if you weren't eating with me?"

He shrugged, still gazing at her in astonishment. "I don't know, Caro. I don't usually cook for myself, actually. If it's supper time and I'm at home, I usually just walk on over to the Longhorn and get Dottie to fix something for me."

"What kind of thing?" she asked tensely. "What does Dottie fix for you, Vern?"

"*I* don't know," he repeated with a helpless wave of his hand. "Just the usual stuff. I guess I'd order a burger or chicken fried-steak, home fries, a piece of pie...just the same stuff everybody else eats, more or less."

"And gravy and ice cream," Carolyn finished tonelessly. "And white Texas toast with gobs of butter, and six glasses of Coke."

"Caro," he said in disbelief, "I'm not really sure where we're heading with all this. You're saying you disapprove of my *eating habits?* Is that it, or am I going completely crazy?"

She hesitated, looking up at him with that same baffling expression, a sort of angry defiance mixed with serious concern.

"Vern," she began, "I just—"

The phone rang and she walked quickly over to answer it, while Vernon continued to watch her in openmouthed astonishment. But when she hung up and moved briskly back to the counter, she had clearly decided to put the whole issue behind them.

"Come on, let's eat," she said with forced cheerfulness. "Get that salad over here, *monsieur*. My omelet needs to be savored at its peak of perfection."

"Carolyn," he began, "I want to—"

"That was Cynthia on the phone," she interrupted firmly. "She says she told J.T. about the baby and he's just thrilled out of his mind. She's hoping he'll be very humble and receptive to any lectures I might want to deliver. And let me tell you, I intend to deliver a lecture!"

"Caro, what did you mean by—"

"So," she interrupted again, taking off her apron and seating herself at the table, "you don't think little Bluebonnet's looking very good, do you, Vern? What should we do about him?"

Vernon gave up, accepting the fact that she obviously didn't intend to resume that strange conversation no matter how hard he tried to introduce the subject again. "I don't know," he said finally. "What does Manny say?"

"Oh, you know." Carolyn reached for the garlic toast, smiling automatically as she passed it across the table. "He feels it's a waste of time and money, and that the dog should be put to sleep. I think it's his opinion that otherwise, this low-grade fever will persist until poor Bluebonnet's so weak that he'll finally just fade away."

"I see," he said evenly, serving himself a helping of the omelet. "And what do you think, Carolyn?"

"I don't know," she said. "For one thing, I don't feel that it's entirely my decision to make. Teresa's kind of a partner in this endeavor, after all. She's actually doing most of the work."

"You could call her a silent partner, right?" Vernon said, his good humor beginning to reassert itself. He was rewarded by Carolyn's warm bubble of laughter.

"Yeah," she drawled in agreement. "*Really* silent. But she must love the little dog, Vern, or she wouldn't spend all that time with him, giving him his medicine and trying to trickle food into him. And I hate to have Manny put him down without the chance to explain to her why it's necessary."

"Do you ever see her? Have you ever actually talked to her?"

"Oh, Lord, no. Nobody ever *talks* to her, Vern. I

can hardly imagine a conversation with Teresa, to tell you the truth. It'd be like talking to a…hummingbird, or something.''

Vernon took a thick slice of brown toast, thoughtfully spread it with a generous dollop of garlic butter and then bit into it, closing his eyes in rapture. ''Mmmm,'' he said. ''Just delicious, Caro. You know, this wheat bread doesn't taste so bad if you have lots of butter on it.''

''Have some salad, Vern,'' she said dryly, passing the heaping bowl of greenery across to him. Something in her voice caught his attention again, but when Vernon looked at Carolyn, her eyes were lowered and she was picking at her omelet in careful silence.

''Bubba has all kinds of stories about Teresa and her mother,'' he volunteered after a moment's silence. ''I never pay much attention to the gossip down at the Longhorn, but after you told me what was happening here with the dog, I've been trying to recall some of it.''

Carolyn glanced up quickly. ''Yes? What's Bubba been saying?''

Vernon shrugged. ''Something about a child molester and the mother attacking him with a butcher knife, the kid being scared out of her wits and not normal anymore… I can't recall the details.''

Carolyn's face clouded. ''I wish,'' she said slowly,

"that Bubba Gibson would pay more attention to his own business, and leave other people's alone." She glanced up at the man opposite her, trying to smile. "I don't like him much, you know," she confessed. "Never have, even though Frank and J.T. always looked on him as a real good ol' boy. But Mary's a darling," she added, taking another bite of omelet.

"She sure is," Vern agreed.

They were both silent for a moment, eating their meal and thinking about the strained marriage of Bubba and Mary Gibson.

"So," Vernon said finally, returning to their earlier topic, "does Bubba have the straight goods? What really happened to the kid, Carolyn?"

"Pretty much what Bubba says, actually. More wine, Vern?"

He nodded, watching as Carolyn refilled his crystal wineglass. "Pretty soon we'll be drinking a Double C vintage, if Tyler and Ruth can get their project off the ground," he said with a grin, raising his glass. Carolyn laughed with him, then sobered.

"Rosa Martinez told me the basics of their story when I first hired her," she said, toying with the stem of her wineglass. "Her boyfriend at the last place she worked was a real jerk, I guess, though she didn't realize it at first. Teresa complained about him a few times, but Rosa didn't really take her seriously. The kid was about six or seven at the time, and Rosa thought she was just jealous of her mother's new relationship. Then one night Rosa caught him beating the little girl, drunk and out of control. She tried to get him to leave her alone but he wouldn't. Finally she picked up his gun and shot him.''

''Right in front of the kid?'' Vernon asked in horror.

Carolyn nodded grimly. ''He died in the hospital a few hours later. Teresa was traumatized, couldn't talk, couldn't go to school, nothing. Rosa left her job, went on welfare, was charged and acquitted and finally wound up here. She seems fairly contented now—Rosa, I mean—but Teresa hasn't recovered at all.''

Vernon gazed at the woman across the table, his sunny pleasant features wretched with sympathy. ''Isn't there something that can be done, Caro? Couldn't she be helped by...I don't know...a child psychologist, or something?''

''I offered, Vern. I told Rosa I'd pay for the sessions if counseling would help. But Rosa believes it isn't possible. She thinks the kid would have to be manhandled badly, I mean literally trapped and hogtied, to get her into treatment, and that would likely do more harm than good.''

''So what's the solution?''

''I don't know,'' Carolyn said. ''Time, I guess. And the chance to see that the world is essentially good and loving and nonthreatening. And something to love, too. That's why it's such a good thing the way she's taking an interest in this little dog.''

''Maybe we could…buy another dog for her,'' Vernon suggested, still looking troubled. ''I mean, if this one doesn't make it, you know?''

Carolyn glanced up quickly, her face clouding. Vernon looked at her keenly but she bit her lip and stared down at her plate, avoiding his eyes.

''That's not the whole story, is it, Caro?'' he asked gently. ''I mean, about this sick dog. You want to keep him alive for the child, but you've got a stake in it, too, don't you?''

''Don't be silly, Vern,'' she said, trying to keep her voice light, though she still couldn't look at him. ''What kind of stake would I possibly have in a poor little stray mop dog?''

''You've got an idea in your mind,'' Vernon said. ''It's because of when we found him and all. You think that if he doesn't get better, then J.T. won't, either. They're all connected in your mind somehow.''

She glanced up then, her blue eyes swimming with tears. ''Look,'' she murmured, ''just quit being so damned perceptive, would you? I don't like having anybody know that much about my silly private thoughts.''

''Oh, Caro…''

One tear slipped down her cheek, glistening in the muted lamplight, and the sight of it was too much for Vernon. Propelled by an urge that he couldn't have resisted no matter how hard he tried, he got out of his chair, rounded the table and drew Carolyn to her feet, folding her in his arms and patting her heaving back, whispering to her, kissing her cheeks and neck and forehead, her ears and eyelids and the soft warm hollow where a rapid pulse beat in her tanned throat.

"Caro," he whispered huskily. "Oh, Carolyn, my sweet darling…"

His mouth roamed across her face, tasting the warm fragrance of her skin and the salty tears. At last he found her lips and kissed her more deeply, thrilling to her response. He could feel her slender body softening and curving into his, feel the rising warmth of her and the passion in her mouth as she returned his kiss.

Vernon's hands moved slowly over her body, the elegant beautiful body that he'd always adored, touching her full shapely breasts and her narrow waist and the soft firm swell of her hips, caressing her with a rough sweet passion that was almost reverent in its intensity.

"God, you're so beautiful," he whispered, still lost in their kiss, his mouth moving against hers.

"You're just so beautiful, Caro. There's never been a woman as beautiful as you."

She sighed and moved closer to him, clinging to him, her body supple and warm against his, her lips softly parted to receive his kiss.

But then as suddenly as it had begun, the moment ended. He could feel when it happened, feel how she stiffened and drew away, gathered herself back in hand and forced her emotions under control and retreated hastily to some remote guarded place where he couldn't follow. Even though she was still in his arms, still pressed close to him with her face hidden in the hollow of his neck, she was gone, and Vernon was chilled with sorrow.

"Caro?" he whispered against her bright hair. "Caro, what's the matter? Is it me? Have I upset you somehow?"

"No, Vern," she murmured, pulling away abruptly and turning aside.

She sank into her chair again and moved the cutlery around aimlessly, still not able to look at him.

"I'm sorry," she said at last, her voice low and trembling. "I'm really sorry, Vern. I don't know what got into me. Must've lost my head for a minute. Let's just forget it and finish our meal, shall we? We have to be at the hospital soon."

He stared at her bent head, his whole body throbbing with frustrated longing. But he loved her enough to see the painful tension in her shoulders, the unhappy droop of her neck, and he knew it would be unkind to push her any further.

"Okay, Carolyn," he said, forcing his voice to sound normal and cheerful. "I guess you're right. We both just lost our heads for a minute. No harm done, though. As a matter of fact," he couldn't resist adding, "I personally found it most enjoyable."

She glanced up quickly, gave him a weak embarrassed smile and returned at once to her plate, eating with great determination. Vernon watched her for a moment, then nodded.

"You're right," he said heartily. "Hurry up, girl. Visiting time starts in an hour, and we still have all these dishes to do." They continued to eat in silence, sitting at opposite sides of the kitchen table, while the blue and mauve springtime dusk deepened beyond the windows and a solitary owl sounded his mournful evening call across the meadows.

"WELL, WELL. Look who's here," J. T. Mckinney drawled from his hospital bed. "A pair of bright-eyed kids, come to visit the poor ol' codger on his sickbed."

"Lord, J.T.," Carolyn protested with a grin, sinking into one of the vinyl armchairs next to the bed. "You'd better watch out, cowboy. You're getting to sound more like old Hank every day."

J.T. grinned back at her, white teeth flashing in a face that was still tanned and handsome though the strain of the past days showed clearly around his eyes and mouth, and in the weary tilt of his head against the bank of hospital pillows.

"How you feelin', J.T.?" Vernon drawled, seating himself next to Carolyn and extending his legs casually as he smiled at his old friend. "Say, those sure are sexy pajamas you got on there, boy. They treatin' you good enough in here?"

"Vern, these nurses are so damned nice you can't believe it. Matter of fact, all this terrific feminine attention is purely wasted on an old married man like me. You should have a heart attack, Vern, just to get to spend a few days in here."

"Don't say that!" Carolyn said sharply, then flushed in embarrassment as both men turned to look at her in surprise.

"Just kidding, Carolyn," J.T. said amiably.

Carolyn tried to smile. "I know. I just don't like people to kid about heart attacks," she said.

The men were silent, watching her.

Carolyn shifted uneasily in her chair, wondering crazily if what had happened earlier was somehow visible on her face. She felt as if Vernon's passionate kiss must be branded there for all the world to see, along with her own embarrassing reaction, her flood of intense sexual desire, the warm sweet thrill that still coursed through her whole body whenever she thought about his lips and hands....

Again she smiled brightly, looking around at the flowers that covered every available surface and even spilled out into the hallway. "I declare, J.T., you must be the most popular man in the county. I never saw so many flowers in all my life."

"Well, I'll tell you, I could do without the damn flowers," J.T. grunted, shifting on the hard mattress. "I'd trade 'em all for the chance to be at my ranch getting my calves branded. The work's piling up out there, and I'm lying here. It just doesn't make sense."

"It makes all kinds of sense, you blockhead," Carolyn said briskly. "Ken Slattery's the most capable foreman you've ever had. I'm sure he can look after getting the calves branded, and if he needs any help I'll send Karl and a couple of my men over for a few days. *You,*" she concluded, giving the handsome man in the bed a cold level gaze, "can just damn well lie here and get better. And that means doing everything Nate says."

"And," Vernon added cheerfully, "we're pretty sure Nate never said anything about taking a daily constitutional down to the Longhorn and back, J.T."

"Oh, God," J.T. groaned in mock despair. "The woman's been talking, hasn't she?"

"The woman's been begging for help, that's what

she's been doing,'' Carolyn told him, leaning forward, her face intent and pleading. "She's scared to death, J. T. McKinney, that's all. Cynthia loves you, and she doesn't want to lose you. Especially *now,*" Carolyn added in a tone of warm significance.

"Especially now," J.T. echoed, his rugged face softening with emotion. "I guess you've known for a while, Carolyn?"

Carolyn nodded. "Since the day of your coronary. She had to tell somebody, poor girl."

"I could hardly believe it," J.T. told them, his voice rough with feeling, his dark eyes full of wonder. "You know, it was one of the things we fought about before we got married. Cynthia wanted a baby and I was opposed to it. Now," he concluded simply, "I just feel like the luckiest man on earth."

"Well, so you should," Carolyn said, trying to sound brusque. But the softness in her eyes gave her away, and she had to swallow hard before she could go on. Vernon reached over and took her hand, squeezing it gently. She returned the gesture in grateful silence, then looked up again at the big man in the hospital bed.

"You have to pay attention, J.T.," she told him earnestly. "You have to quit pushing things and do as Nate says. You owe it to Cynthia, and to this new baby. She has a right to have her husband with her, and the little fella has a right to grow up with his daddy.''

J.T. shifted impatiently in the bed, his face suddenly bleak. ''Yeah, sure,'' he said bitterly. ''But what kind of daddy, Carolyn? Some broken-down old guy sitting in a wheelchair with a rug over his knees? Is that how I'm supposed to live from now on? Will my new baby have to be real careful not to play rough with his daddy?''

''Oh, J.T., you know that's ridiculous,'' Carolyn said impatiently. ''Nate told Cynthia there's every chance you can lead a normal active life, if you'll just take some care right now and give your heart a chance to heal.''

J.T. regarded them both quietly, his brown eyes level and calm. But beneath the quiet exterior Carolyn could see the emotions that raged in him, his helpless anger and frustration and his dreadful visceral fear of an invalid life and a loss of manhood.

''It'll be okay, J.T.,'' she whispered, aching with love and sympathy. ''It really will. Just do what the doctor tells you and give it a little time. Everything will be just fine.''

J.T. watched her a moment longer in thoughtful silence. Finally he shifted on the bed and turned his attention to Vern with the air of a man determined to change the subject.

"I hear things are moving right along out at the Hole in the Wall, Vern. You been out there yet?"

Vernon cast a cautious sidelong glance at Carolyn and cleared his throat. "No, J.T., I haven't seen it since....since all the renovations started. Apparently most of us are getting invited to the opening-day barbecue, which should be in a month or so."

"I wonder if I'm going to be invited," Carolyn said dryly. "Or maybe your Mr. Harris has heard how I feel about having him as a neighbor, and he'd just as soon avoid me."

"Now, Carolyn," J.T. said mildly, "are you still holding on to all that? Relax, girl. This dude ranch won't be any problem to you."

"Oh, sure," Carolyn said bitterly. "Hardly any at all. The latest gossip, J.T., is that he's going to allow hunting of exotic animals out there, and Manny says those imported animals are a real threat to our domestic beef stock."

J.T.'s dark eyes narrowed thoughtfully and he exchanged another glance with Vernon, but said nothing.

"Believe me," Carolyn went on, warming to the subject, "if my Santa Gertrudis cattle start getting sick and dying from some fancy imported parasites, I'll be over there with a gun myself. But *first*," she said grimly, "I'm going to find out who brought this man into the county, and tell him what I think of what he's done. And it won't be pretty, let me tell you.''

Again the two men's eyes met in a quick significant glance and then they both looked away, elaborately casual.

''What's going on here?'' Carolyn asked with sudden suspicion. ''Why do you two keep looking at each other like that?''

''Like what, Caro?'' Vern asked in wide-eyed appeal. ''Were we looking at each other, J.T.?''

''Come on, Vern,'' J.T. said easily. ''Would I waste time looking at an ugly mug like yours when there's somebody as pretty as Carolyn in the room?''

''Okay,'' she said, suddenly furious with both of them. ''Okay. I get it. I know you men. You both know who sold Scott Harris that ranch, and you're not going to tell me, are you? Men always stick together on things like that. But I'm going to find out just the same,'' she went on, her eyes flashing with anger. ''Just as soon as I can stomach the prospect I'm going on over there to have a little talk with Mr. Scott Harris, and we're going to get a whole lot of things out in the open.''

There was a brief strained silence, interrupted by the arrival of a cheerful nurse with a tray full of medication. She was a local woman, the daughter of one neighboring rancher and wife of another, and both Vernon and J.T. turned to her with relief, joking and exchanging gossip and quips.

Carolyn sat quietly looking on, her angry flush slowly fading, thinking ruefully about how infuriating these two men were, and just how deeply she cared for both of them.

CHAPTER SIX

TERESA SAT in her magic place with the sun covering her in a blanket of gold. She sighed and stretched like a cat on the sun-warmed grass. Then she crept stealthily across the clearing and parted the bushes to peer out.

She was on a tiny island in the Claro, the river that flowed past most of the major ranches in the district and provided a lifeline for stock and ranchers all through this high valley. Most of the time the Claro was shallow and slow-moving, more like a creek than a genuine river, but longtime residents still told fearful stories of the Claro in flood, of gigantic walls of water crashing along the riverbed, wiping out buildings and drowning stock. Those flash floods were growing less frequent all the time as the rural population and demands on the river increased.

This particular spring the Claro was still low enough in early April that Teresa was able to wade across to her island. She accomplished the journey by means of a deliciously scary row of stepping-stones, big tumbled half-submerged boulders that were slippery with lichen and the wet foamy spray from the current.

She watched with bright interest through her screen of brush as three riders passed by, trotting single file along the path that edged the river. They were her mother, Rosa, whom Teresa referred to in her private thoughts as Rosalind, along with the ranch foreman and another rider not yet fully visible. Rosalind was in the lead, her dark hair shining like a raven's wing in the sunlight, her quiet face pink with happiness and looking unusually pretty.

Behind Rosalind was Sir Galahad, the rugged soft-spoken foreman at the Circle T, known to everyone else as Karl Walters. In fact, Teresa Martinez was probably the only person in the world able to see romance and dashing gallantry in this solid dependable young man with his sturdy muscular body and the wholesome blond look of his German forebears.

But then, only Teresa noticed the growing warmth between her mother and Karl, or the way her mother's stern self-contained features softened and brightened when Karl came by to visit in the evening, to sit on the veranda of their little cottage and talk with Rosa about horses and ranch business and whatever other conversation he could coax from her.

Teresa knew that Rosalind was growing closer to Sir Galahad. She didn't mind. Knights and ladies

should be together, and Galahad was a brave handsome knight. All Teresa asked was to be left alone,
not to have to talk to Sir Galahad or even be in the
same room with him. She knew that these feelings
of hers upset her mother, that Rosa would have liked
Teresa to be more friendly. And Teresa loved Rosalind, wanted desperately to please her mother and
make her happy, but it just wasn't possible.

The little girl's eyes darkened briefly, then brightened again as the third rider came into view. It was
Gloriana, beautiful in faded denims that looked like
soft blue velvet.

The three of them passed in slow procession along
the riverbank, their colorful shirts and saddle blan-
kets glistening like gems, their silver-mounted bri-
dles flashing in the light. Teresa sighed in bliss,
watching them.

She knew where they were going, Rosalind and
Sir Galahad and Gloriana. She'd heard her mother
talking about it over breakfast. They were riding out
to gather the cows in the hill pasture so the new
calves could be vaccinated, and soon there would be
all kinds of noise and dust and activity down at the
corrals.

But Teresa preferred to think that they were riding
off to the Crusades, and that they'd be coming home
with a priceless treasure trove of gold and jewels,
riches that they'd spread all over the lawn at the big

house. There'd be a shining mountain of treasures, so huge that everybody could have everything they'd ever wanted. And they'd bring back a special magic stone from a witch's cave, a stone that Bluebonnet would lick and he'd get better in a flash and be able to run and play like other dogs....

At the thought of Bluebonnet, Teresa's rapt expression faded and her little face took on a determined look. She dropped back behind her screen of brush, waiting until the three riders vanished into the trees, then hurried over to a big wooden crate half obscured by trailing willow branches.

Teresa had stolen this crate from the barn and wrestled it across to the island a couple of months earlier, a task that had taken one whole moonless night and a staggering amount of physical effort. Her storage chest was now fitted with a makeshift lid of thick plywood, weighted down with a couple of rocks so heavy that the child puffed and grunted when she lifted them off.

She reached into the box and took out an armful of burlap sacks, shaking them and folding them into a soft little nest in the sunlight. Frowning, she examined a few other objects in the box: a book of illustrated fairy tales, a can of cookies, a couple of water bottles, a special piece of smooth wood and a magic feather, a ragged sweater, an old hairbrush, a jar of liquefied dog food and a spoon. She put everything carefully back inside, then replaced the lid, weighted it again and darted out of the clearing and into the shadows along the island's edge.

With noiseless agility the child skipped across the damp uneven boulders and vanished into the shrubbery along the shoreline. She took a shortcut through the hay meadow, thudded past the feed stacks and wound up in the barn. Panting a little, she glanced around cautiously before she crept over to the manger where the little gray dog lay.

"Hi, Bluebonnet," Teresa whispered, gazing at those big shining eyes in his furry quizzical face. She loved Bluebonnet so much that she could feel her heart breaking as she looked at him, feel how it swelled inside her chest and beat harder and harder till it nearly burst. She wondered what would happen if her heart actually broke someday, exploded right inside her so she collapsed like Gloriana's friend, the man on the next ranch, and had to go live in a hospital.

But Teresa didn't like to think of sickness and bodily harm. She pushed the thoughts aside and smiled down at the little dog. Bluebonnet rolled his head gamely and whimpered, trying to smile back.

"Oh, Bluebonnet," Teresa whispered. "We're going to have such a good day today. I'm taking you to my secretest place, and you can see all the animals and the birds and I'll tell you their names, and then

I'll read to you and you can have a nap in the sunshine. Won't that feel good? And I already got stuff over there for your dinner...come on, Bluebonnet...."

Murmuring and whispering, the child worked with infinite care as she folded the little dog within the bundle of sacks and lifted him gently from the manger box.

He was so thin and tiny that he didn't weigh more than a bird, Teresa thought. It was as if he wasn't even there, as if she was just holding a puff of air, or a dream. She glanced around furtively a few more times, checking her surroundings like some shy woodland animal. Then she faded back through the barn and across the meadow, heading for her sunlit island with the bundle of sacking cradled protectively in her arms.

CAROLYN STROLLED up the curving flagstone path from the stables, pleasantly weary from her long ride and the day's activities down at the corrals.

She smiled, thinking how little it really took to make a person happy. A warm sunny day, the new purebred calf crop looking so good, the knowledge that J.T. was getting stronger every day, the prospect of a deep hot sudsy bath and a good meal...

Carolyn sighed with contentment and turned up the walk toward her kitchen door. But just as she was about to let herself inside she paused, startled, as a burst of merriment drifted around the corner of the big stone ranch house. There were people on the patio, it appeared. And whoever they were, they were certainly having a good time. Another gale of laughter drifted past the tall forsythia bushes that were, just now, laden with blossoms like showers of gold. And she could hear voices in disconnected and cheerful snatches of conversation, carried lightly on the late-afternoon breeze.

Smiling, Carolyn slipped around the side of the house and through the picket gate, feeling the welcome coolness of the deep shade at the back. The ranch house was U-shaped, with two long wings that extended to the rear and provided spacious private living quarters for Beverly Townsend as well as for Lori Porter, Carolyn's cousin.

Outside, the same two wings sheltered a huge patio furnished with brightly cushioned wicker, a swimming pool and a small tennis court, all with a sweeping view of the river winding below. This pleasant area was a favorite retreat for everyone, and from April to November it was seldom deserted if there were people at home.

Just now it was anything but deserted. Carolyn paused behind a tall rose trellis, enjoying the sight of the boisterous group assembled in the shade, none of whom had yet noticed her. Beverly was there, with her friend Amanda Walker, as well as Lori, Lynn McKinney and Vernon Trent.

Beverly and Amanda wore brief white tennis dresses, and their rackets and equipment bags were piled casually nearby. Carolyn grinned, observing that Amanda looked a little winded. Her delicate beautiful face was flushed, her blue eyes misted with fatigue as she sipped at a tall iced drink. Beverly, on the other hand, was as cool and lovely as if she had just slipped on her tennis dress to pose for a couple of photographs.

And yet, Carolyn mused, she'd probably beaten Amanda three straight sets. Beverly Townsend was a formidable competitor despite her air of sophistication and graceful lassitude. Her own personality combined with years of competition with her neighboring older cousins, Tyler and Cal McKinney, had made her tough and boyishly aggressive at sports. In fact, this fierce fighting spirit was one of the things Carolyn liked best about her daughter.

Lynn McKinney, though, obviously hadn't been involved in the tennis match. The small auburn-haired girl wore the comfortably shabby riding clothes she always did, and looked as if she'd just run in from the stables.

About the same as I look, Carolyn thought ruefully, glancing down at her own dusty jeans and shirt.

Lori Porter was delicately pretty, as always, in a

bright Mexican sundress, a silver belt and sandals. While Carolyn watched, Lori poured a glass of iced tea from a tall frosted pitcher and handed it to Vernon, and he looked up at her with a smile. Carolyn felt a sudden stab of wholly irrational jealousy, an emotion that distressed her as soon as she recognized it for what it was.

My God, she thought in alarm. *What in hell is happening to me? After all, it's hardly as if he...*

But just then Vernon caught sight of her, and there was no mistaking the warm glow of pleasure that lit his face.

"Here she is," he announced to the rest of the group. "Home from the range. Come have a glass of iced tea, Carolyn."

She hesitated as the four young women joined Vernon in a chorus of greeting. "I really should go in and have a bath first, and change my clothes," Carolyn said, looking longingly at the pitcher of iced tea, realizing suddenly how thirsty she was. "I've been riding all day, and working with the calves...."

"Oh, forget it," Vern said cheerfully. "Come sit by me. I love earthy women."

Carolyn chuckled and crossed the patio to a soft padded chair next to his, smiling her gratitude to Lori for the tall glass of icy liquid that appeared like magic in her hand.

"Well, Vern," Carolyn said, taking a long appreciative sip and extending her booted feet in blissful relaxation, "you're certainly doing all right for yourself out here, aren't you? Like a sultan with his harem."

"More like a thorn surrounded by roses," Vernon said placidly, waving his glass at the four younger women.

"Vern was just telling us about these clients of his," Beverly said, grinning. "Wait'll you hear it, Mama."

"Telling about his clients?" Carolyn echoed in mock horror. "Isn't that a breach of professional confidence, Vern?"

"Absolutely," he said solemnly. "I'll lose my license and be defrocked and everything if you tell on me."

"We won't tell," Amanda Walker said, leaning forward, her beautiful face sparkling with laughter. "Go on, Vern. The old man said…"

"He said they wanted a house with a self-contained suite in the basement," Vernon said obediently. "And I asked if it was for a family member, an in-law or somebody?"

"And he said…" Lynn prompted.

"He said, 'You might say so. It's for the wife.' So I looked a little blank, you know, and I said, 'For the *wife?*' And he said, 'Fer Gawd's sake, man, it's bad enough I gotta share a *house* with that woman.

Y'all truly don't expect us to live on the same goddamn *floor,* do you?''"

The group erupted with laughter, and Carolyn took
advantage of their mirth to give Vernon a private
smile. ''You're terrible, you know that?'' she murmured.

''How could I help knowing it?'' he said, his
warm brown eyes brimming with laughter. ''You
keep telling me, Caro.''

She grinned back at him, warmed by his glance,
thrilling in spite of herself to the memory of his lips
on hers, their bodies melting together in sweet yearning passion....

''So, Amanda,'' she said hastily, turning to the
pert dark-haired young woman who had been Beverly's friend since their college days. ''When did you
arrive? I haven't seen you for ages.''

''I know, Carolyn. I've really missed you all, you
know that? New York's great, but the people there
just aren't like Texas people.''

''So I've heard,'' Carolyn said dryly. ''Beverly
tells me you're back in Austin to stay.''

''Only if I can make a go of my new business,''
Amanda said.

''That's why she's here,'' Beverly said cheerfully.
''She's not here because she likes us, Mama, not a
bit. She's just drumming up business.''

''Well, she's sure got mine,'' Lynn McKinney

said, speaking up for the first time. "I think it's a great idea."

Carolyn smiled at this niece she'd always loved. Lynn was not only one of her favorite people, she was the image of her mother. Looking at Lynn, Carolyn sometimes had the wistful notion that she and her sister were girls again, full of laughter and dreams, that none of the rest of it had ever happened and Pauline had never died and left them....

"What's a great idea?" Carolyn said, pulling herself firmly back to reality again. "What *is* this business of yours, Amanda?"

"I'm thinking of opening a personal shopping service, based in Austin," Amanda said.

Carolyn looked at her, puzzled. "What's that, Amanda? You mean you pick up people's groceries for them, or what?"

The others dissolved in gales of laughter. Carolyn looked calmly from one face to the other, sipping her tea in silence.

"Okay," she said at last. "Now that you've all had so much fun ridiculing me, why doesn't somebody explain what a personal shopping service really does?"

"Oh, *Mama*," Beverly said in exasperation. "If you spent less time working with cows and more time paying attention to the real world, you'd *know* what a personal shopping service is."

Carolyn gazed thoughtfully at her beautiful daughter, but refrained from any comments about Beverly's perception of the real world. Instead she turned to Lynn, who leaned forward with a confiding grin.

"I didn't know either, Aunt Carolyn," she whispered. "Not till they told me."

"It's sort of an image consultant service," Amanda said. "I dress people, you know."

"A light begins to dawn," Carolyn observed. "You mean, you help them to learn what their best colors are and how to achieve a total coordinated look, that sort of thing?"

Amanda nodded. "And I shop for my clients as well. I search the stores and mail order houses and national suppliers for the best items at the best price. It's a service, actually, for people who want a certain style but don't have the time to manage it for themselves."

Carolyn nodded thoughtfully.

"We were over at the Double C earlier today," Beverly said. "Cynthia's really excited about it, and so is Lynn."

"I can understand Cynthia loving the idea," Carolyn said. "I know she's been really frustrated by how hard it is to shop around here, and now she's going to need a whole new wardrobe, too. But *Lynn?*" she added, turning to look at her niece. "It doesn't seem like your thing, somehow, Lynn."

"Sam keeps saying I need to do something about my wardrobe, and I know he's right," Lynn said, her face softening as she mentioned the name of the man she loved. "It's just that it's so hard to find the time, and I hardly know where to begin. I'd love to have somebody take me in hand and do it for me."

Carolyn nodded again, turning to smile at Vernon. "Well, what do you think, Vern? Is the Hill Country ready for this New York image maker?"

"Oh, absolutely," he said solemnly, though his brown eyes were still sparkling with humor. "Now, take this big fancy opening day barbecue at the Hole in the Wall next month. I'd love to see Amanda dress you all. Wouldn't that be something, Amanda? They'd all be swishing around in feathers and sequins and designer pajamas, scaring the horses...."

Amanda punched him cheerfully on the arm and returned to an earnest conversation she was having with Lori and Beverly about colour draping.

Lynn listened for a moment, then turned to Carolyn with a wry grimace and a private grin. "How are the calves looking this year, Aunt Carolyn?"

"Just great," Carolyn said with enthusiasm. "That new bull was worth every penny we paid for him. And believe me," she added grimly, "it was a pretty penny."

"Your little Santa Gertrudis calves are always so

beautiful,'' Lynn said with a smile. ''Their hide is so rich and silky.''

''I know,'' Carolyn said, giving her niece an answering smile. ''I just hope...'' she began, and fell abruptly silent.

''Hope what?'' Vernon asked.

Carolyn swirled the dregs of her iced tea and gazed moodily into the glass. ''I hope this damned Hole in the Wall isn't going to hurt my calves,'' she said. ''I hate to think about it, Vern.''

He looked at her bent head for a moment, then cleared his throat and turned to Lynn. ''I hear there's a big event at your house on the weekend, Lynn.''

''Yes, Vern, Daddy's coming home, and Cynthia's so excited, she's just like a little kid. Oh, I almost forgot,'' Lynn added, looking around at the group on the patio. ''Lettie Mae and Virginia are planning to barbecue briskets, and the family wants you all to come on over on Sunday. You too, Vern.''

Carolyn hesitated. ''Won't that be too much excitement for J.T. on his first day out of the hospital?''

Lynn shook her head. ''Dr. Purdy says it's okay. He says company won't hurt him, he just has to avoid any kind of strenuous physical activity for a while. Daddy and Cynthia wanted a party just for friends and family, you know, partly for Daddy getting out of the hospital and partly to celebrate the new baby.''

"How do you like the idea of a little brother or sister, Lynn?" Vernon asked, reaching for the pitcher to fill Carolyn's glass.

Lynn's face brightened and her eyes glowed. "I love it," she said softly. "I think it's wonderful. It's certainly done wonders for Daddy, just knowing about it."

Carolyn nodded, smiling at her niece, and was about to say something when Beverly interrupted. "Mama, what happened to that poor little gray dog?" she was asking. "Did he die?"

Carolyn looked blankly at her daughter. "Of course not, Beverly. What made you think that?"

Beverly and Amanda exchanged puzzled glances.

"Beverly?" Carolyn repeated, feeling suddenly tense.

"Where is he, then?" Beverly asked. "Did you move him?"

"She won't move him," Lori said impatiently. "I keep telling her it'd be so much easier to have that dog up at the house, but she insists on leaving him down in the barn and then having to go out there at all hours to tend to him. It's crazy, if you ask me."

Carolyn was silent. Vernon, who was the only one with any knowledge of Teresa's involvement with the injured dog, and Carolyn's feelings about the mystical tie between the animal and J.T.'s well-being, reached over to lay a hand on her shoulder.

"Well, he's not in the barn anymore," Beverly announced. "He's disappeared."

"*What?*" Carolyn said, turning to her daughter in alarm. "What did you say, Beverly?"

"When Lynn and Amanda and I got here, Lynn wanted to look at one of the horses so we went down with her and I took Amanda in to see the little dog. But that manger place where you keep him was empty, Mama. Just a couple of sacks there, no dog."

Carolyn's face turned pale beneath her tan and her blue eyes widened in fear.

Lori gave her cousin a concerned look and crossed the flagstone patio to sit next to her. "Don't worry, Carolyn," she murmured. "Maybe he…he's started feeling a lot better, and he just jumped down by himself and hid somewhere. He'll be fine."

Carolyn shook her head. "He's not ready to be doing any jumping, Lori. He still has his cast on, and Manny just took the stitches out last week. Besides, he's almost too weak to move, let alone jump. I'm going down there," she added, setting her glass aside and getting to her feet.

Vernon followed suit at once, standing up beside her and putting a casual arm around her shoulders while the four younger women watched them in silence.

"Mama," Beverly began hesitantly, "why do you care so much about that little stray dog, anyhow?

You should see your face. You look like you've just
a seen a ghost.''

Carolyn turned, trying to smile. ''Sorry, girls,'' she
murmured. ''I know it's silly, but I guess I've just
gotten…kind of attached to him, that's all. I just really want him to get better.''

She was already moving away toward the edge of
the house, her slim shoulders tense. Vernon cast a
brief glance at the others, then followed her.

By the time they reached the barn Carolyn was
almost running, her heart pounding with terror. Everything was jumbled together in her mind. She saw
the empty manger—its pitiful little occupant dead
and gone. And shadowed over that picture was the
fearful image of J.T. coming home from the hospital,
fragile and vulnerable once he was beyond all those
protective surroundings….

''He can't be dead, Vern,'' she muttered. ''He just
can't.''

''Caro…'' Vernon began, his face taut with love
and concern.

But Carolyn was already around by the tack rooms
with their neat rows of saddles. She leaned leaning
over the manger, turning back the top layer of sacking.

Bluebonnet lay within the soft nest of burlap, his
big feverish eyes bright with welcome.

Vernon came up beside Carolyn and they both gazed down at the little dog.

Vernon bent to sniff at the terrier's sun-warmed gray fur, and picked a couple of blades of dried grass from his flowing coat.

"I think," he announced, "that Bluebonnet's just been on a picnic."

Carolyn nodded agreement. "I think you're right," she murmured.

She leaned in anxiously to check the dog's eyes, look into his ears and throat, feel the temperature of his soft silky belly while Vernon stood nearby, watching her.

At last she straightened, trying to smile. "Well, he looks all right, Vern. In fact, maybe he looks a little better than he did this morning, even."

She raised her head and glanced around the silent empty barn, frowning.

"Is she listening?" Vernon whispered. "Is she watching us somewhere?"

Carolyn nodded. "Oh, I think so," she whispered back. "But I can't imagine where she might be. I've had Karl take away all the piled straw she used to hide in, and we've even started locking the tack rooms and closing the shutters on the windows. I was hoping that if all the hiding places were gone, she'd be anxious enough about the dog that she'd come out in the open and I could talk to her. But she's found some way to watch me anyhow."

"Does it bother you?" Vernon asked.

"Not really. I'm getting to care more for her all the time, even though I never see her. I'd just like to have the chance to break through and communicate with her, the poor little girl. But I..."

Carolyn paused abruptly, her face troubled, and reached down absently to caress one of the dog's trailing silky ears.

"Look, Vern, she's brushed him again," Carolyn said, trying to smile. "She brushes him all the time. I'll bet our Bluebonnet is the best-groomed little fella in Texas."

It was hard to hide the desolate sorrow that flooded her, and the terrible fear. Especially from Vernon Trent, who always seemed to know exactly what she was feeling no matter how she tried to disguise her emotions.

He bent toward her. Carolyn knew that he was going to take her in his arms, kiss her again the way he had the other night. And suddenly she wanted him more than anything else in the world. She wanted his mouth on hers, his hands on her body, his strong masculine love and comfort washing over her like a warm sweet tide.

But Carolyn was still deeply conscious of the child watching them from some unseen place, a child who might be troubled or confused by the sight of passionate contact between two adults.

Smiling a rueful apology, Carolyn turned aside to lead the way out of the barn. Vernon smiled back at her automatically but she was unhappily aware of the shadow of pain and disappointment on his face and of her own deep aching need, a need that seemed to be growing stronger and harder to control with every passing day.

CHAPTER SEVEN

"DAMN FOOL GAME," Hank Travis said, snorting, his eyes scornful beneath the brim of his cowboy hat. "Grown men, actin' just like a buncha idiots."

Carolyn smiled at him. "Oh, Grandpa, you're so harsh," she said cheerfully. "It's a very ancient, very civilized game that dates all the way back to the thirteenth century. In fact, it's even older than Texas."

Hank reared around in his chair to scowl at her, outraged by this heresy. "Is that so? Well now, missy, I'll have you know that *Texas* dates all the way back to the Garden of Eden. Look at them ol' dinosaur fossils they keep findin'."

"Oh, Grandpa, that's not what I—"

"If I'm gonna keep havin' to argue with women," he interrupted bitterly, "then I guess I'll just get up an' go set on the front porch again. I like my big ol' rocker better than this damn fool little city-slicker chair, anyhow."

Suiting actions to words, Hank struggled to rise, pressing his hands on the arms of his chair, one of a set of elegant washed-oak kitchen chairs that had been carried out onto the patio to accommodate the crowd.

"Don't go, Grandpa," Carolyn said hastily, grasping his hand. "Stay and keep me company. I promise I won't fight. Look at Cal," she added. "In a minute, he's going to get mad and whack Tyler over the head, just like he used to when they were kids." Always attracted by the prospect of imminent violence, Hank lowered his creaking body back into his chair and turned his eyes in the direction Carolyn indicated.

They were sitting together on the shaded patio at the rear of the big McKinney ranch house, looking down over the cropped green lawn on which a lively group was engaged in a fiercely competitive game of croquet.

Carolyn grinned privately, thinking that old Hank was right. There was something really strange about the sight of tall Texas men like Cal and Tyler McKinney playing croquet. But they both loved the game, which had been introduced to the ranch years before by Lynn after weekends spent with wealthy college friends from Austin.

Lynn refused to play with her brothers anymore, however, and it was no wonder. Their game of croquet bore little resemblance to the genteel pastime that Lynn had first brought home. Tyler and Cal played croquet like a contact sport, a ruthless brutal contest where no quarter was given and none was expected, and striped wooden balls whistled through the air with the dangerous velocity of small missiles.

"*Damn* you, Tyler," Cal howled in anguish, wincing as his ball was struck with punishing force and lofted in a dizzy trajectory toward the stables, landing in a dusty clump of mesquite just beyond the windmill.

Tyler chortled, then looked a little abashed as Ruth gave him a quiet reproachful glance.

"It was a perfectly legal maneuver," he told her defensively. "His ball was touching mine, Ruth. I'm entitled to hit it."

"But not into the next *county,*" Ruth protested, watching as Cal's long lean form was swallowed up in the distance while he trudged off to search for his ball.

Serena, Cal's partner in the game, grinned and patted Ruth's bottom gently with her mallet. "Oh, it's good for him, Ruth," she said cheerfully. "Any man as arrogant as Cal McKinney can benefit from a little humiliation every now and then."

The game was briefly halted while the combatants waited for Cal, now just a speck in the distance, to find his ball and lob it back toward the house.

While they waited, they stood casually chatting on the vivid green lawn. Ruth leaned against Tyler, apparently forgiving him for his aggressiveness, and smiled at Serena who was practising her wrist shot with earnest concentration. Beverly Townsend and Sam Russell watched and offered pointers while the final couple, Vernon Trent and Amanda Walker, took advantage of the hiatus to stroll back to the edge of the patio for a cold drink.

Carolyn watched them approach and smiled, delighted by everything...the warmth of the afternoon, the knowledge that J.T. was safely home from the hospital, the fun of the company and the prettiness of the young women in their brief colorful outfits. Vernon noticed her smile and his face lighted.

"Well, what mischief are you two plotting?" he said to Carolyn and Hank, pausing by the rose trellis to sip from his frosted glass and munch on a handful of Lettie Mae's delicious pralines. "Why are both of you just a-sittin' and a-grinnin' like that?"

"We're taking on the winners," Carolyn announced, her face solemn. "Aren't we, Hank?"

"Damn right," Hank agreed placidly. "We'll blow 'em away."

This phrase coming from the crusty old man was more than Carolyn and Vernon could bear. They dissolved in laughter, while Hank looked on, his leathery face impassive.

"Vern! Get on back here!" Cal shouted. "It's my turn, and I'm fixin' to send Tyler right into the river. Hope you got your swimmin' trunks on, brother."

Vernon gulped manfully and turned away, pausing to drop a hand on Carolyn's shoulder with gentle warmth before he left.

"That's a good boy, that Vernon Trent," Hank said unexpectedly, watching the stocky figure head back across the lawn. "I always liked that boy."

Carolyn was silent, startled both by hearing Hank praise somebody and by the sudden alarming tumult of her own emotions. She squinted into the sunlight as Vernon retrieved his mallet, exchanged some cheerful banter with Beverly and resumed his position on the lawn.

A bewildering tide of feelings battered at Carolyn with relentless force. She frowned and reached up unconsciously to caress the place on her shoulder that was still warm from Vernon's hand. Part of her emotion was purely physical, a warm fluttery sexual throbbing that was sweet and unsettling. But on a deeper level she sensed other feelings, shadows of tension and unease and a dark nameless dread.

Carolyn watched Vernon assume his position amid much affectionate teasing and knock his ball expertly through a hoop. He stood erect, waving his wooden mallet triumphantly in the air, and Carolyn saw how his body strained soft and flabby against the waistline of his casual corduroy slacks.

All of her emotion crystallized suddenly into a violent and inexplicable surge of anger. She was coldly furious with Vernon Trent all at once, furious over the twenty extra pounds that he carried and didn't seem to care about, over the lack of conditioning in his square heavy body, over the quantities of sugary soft drinks and chips and sweets he'd been casually consuming all afternoon. "Carolyn?" Cynthia was saying. "What do you think? Should we set another table out here or just let some of them eat in the kitchen?"

Carolyn pulled herself back to reality with an effort and turned to the younger woman, trying to smile.

Cynthia was carrying an armful of blue linen place mats. She wore a loose bronze silk shirt and white slacks, and her delicate face was still quite pale. She appeared to have lost some weight during J.T.'s illness but her smile was genuine, her brown eyes shining with happiness.

Carolyn's emotional balance, always a little shaky these days, tipped once again so that she found herself fighting back tears.

"It's great to have J.T. back home again, isn't it, Cynthia?" she murmured. "It's so wonderful to know that he's down at his corrals right now looking at the calves, instead of lying in that hospital bed."

"Oh, Carolyn," Cynthia began, sinking into a chair nearby. "Nobody can ever know how I feel today. I feel just like…"

Now it was Cynthia's turn to fight for composure. She paused, her smooth golden hair falling forward to hide her face as she gazed down at the pile of place mats in her lap. She toyed with the fringe on one of the mats, struggling for words, then looked up at Carolyn and bit her lip. Her eyes were brimming with tears that she brushed aside impatiently, then smiled.

Carolyn looked deep into Cynthia's wide brown eyes, and was jolted to see the same emotion reflected there that she was battling in herself. The expression hidden in the depths of Cynthia's eyes was one of fear, of cold naked terror.

God, Carolyn thought desperately, *it's hell being a woman!*

Hank rescued the moment by addressing himself to Cynthia's original question. "Well, I don't know about y'all," he announced, "but *I'm* gonna eat in the kitchen like a civilized human bein'."

Both women turned to him with relief, grateful for once for the outspoken old man's presence. "Oh, come on, Grandpa," Cynthia teased. "Don't you like picnics?"

"*Picnics!*" he echoed, his voice full of disgust.

"They're all the rage up north," Cynthia said innocently, giving Carolyn a tiny wink. "In the city, people just love picnics."

"Oh, sure," Hank said bitterly. "That's 'cause

them dumb city slickers don't know their head from a hole in the ground. What man in his right mind is gonna eat outside with the flies an' the bugs when he can sit inside at a table like a decent human bein'?''

The two women chuckled and Cynthia rose gracefully, patting the old man's bony shoulder.

''Okay, Grandpa,'' she said cheerfully. ''You've solved my problem. I'll seat you inside at the table, and put a few others there to keep you company, and then we won't have to move another table out here after all.''

She smiled at him and moved away toward the door, pausing as a small disturbance drifted around the corner of the house.

The croquet players stopped in the middle of an argument, staring at something that was not yet discernible from the patio. Then Tyler and Cal dropped their mallets and sprinted out of sight, followed by the others.

Carolyn glanced at Cynthia, who stood very still, clutching the place mats in her hands.

After what seemed like hours, though it could only have been a couple of seconds, the group appeared once more around the corner of the house, all of them bunched together, obscuring something from view. Carolyn got up and moved over next to Cynthia, automatically dropping her arms around the other woman's slim shoulders.

She could make out a shape now in the midst of the hushed silent group. It was a long piece of plywood, carried by Ken Slattery and one of the ranch hands, and on it was stretched a man's body. Straining forward, she could see J.T.'s crisp jeans, his fine leather boots and white shirt, the brown Stetson placed tenderly on his chest.

"Oh, no," Cynthia was whispering beside her. "Oh, God, no…"

Nate Purdy came rushing out of the kitchen where he and Rose, his wife, had been happily assisting while Lettie Mae and Virginia prepared the killer chili that was a specialty of the Double C kitchen. With a speed surprising in a man of his years, Nate rushed to meet the group, as he shouted to Rose to fetch his bag from the car. He bent over J.T.'s still form as Ken and his helper settled the slab of plywood carefully onto one of the tables.

Cynthia stood frozen on the patio. Carolyn hugged the younger woman close, her heart breaking in sorrow and sympathy. She could actually feel the anguish in Cynthia's slim body, feel the deep chill that was creeping over the woman beside her and turning her slowly to ice. Nate finished his examination, exchanged a few quiet words with Ken Slattery and then looked up, meeting Cynthia's eyes.

"There was a big ol' wooden gate down next to the barn that was stuck, Cynthia," Nate said. "J.T. pushed on it, trying to get it open, wouldn't wait for one of the men to come and help him."

Cynthia shuddered and Carolyn hugged her fiercely.

"Is he...oh, God, Nate..." Cynthia whispered brokenly.

"Oh, he's all right," Nate said. "In a lot of pain, I expect, but that serves him right, the stubborn fool. We'll take him up and put him to bed now, maybe in a straitjacket if y'all got one, to keep him from moving till I say it's all right."

Cynthia sagged with relief and would have fallen if Carolyn hadn't been supporting her. They watched in silence as the two ranch hands lifted the plywood slab again and followed Nate Purdy into the house, bearing J.T.'s long body through the kitchen and up the stairs.

Cynthia pulled away, murmuring something incoherent, dropped the place mats in a heap on the flagstones and rushed after the men.

When she was gone Carolyn stood alone, gazing into the shadowed yard. She hugged her arms and shivered, not even conscious of the others around her. She was locked in the cold prison of her own thoughts.

VERNON PULLED UP the curving driveway and parked in front of Carolyn's garage, glancing over cautiously at the silent woman beside him.

"Caro?" he ventured. "You want to talk about it, girl?"

Carolyn shook her head, a small tight gesture that made his heart ache. He turned to look at her.

Outwardly she seemed composed, but Vernon Trent had loved this woman far too long to be fooled by outward appearances. He could see the tiny tense lines next to her mouth, the strain around her eyes, the way her hands were gripped so tightly together that the knuckles whitened.

"Oh, Caro," he whispered, reaching over to take both her hands in his. "Damn, I wish I could…"

"It sure spoils a barbecue, something like that, doesn't it, Vern?" she said in the small brittle voice that told him she was dangerously close to tears. "Just plumb takes all the fun out of it."

"He's going to be all right, Caro," Vernon said urgently, leaning toward her. "You know what Nate said. This little episode was just like a warning, sort of. J.T.'s going to be just fine."

"Oh, sure," Carolyn said bitterly, turning to gaze at the man beside her, her eyes wide and glittering with unshed tears. "He's going to be just fine, until the next time this same thing happens. Then what?"

"It won't happen again," Vernon said. "Not if he's more careful."

"*Careful!*" Carolyn echoed in that same grim toneless voice. She sat for a moment, brooding over her thoughts, then gathered herself together with a visible effort and turned to Vernon again.

"Would you mind coming in for a while, Vern, please?" she asked. "I don't think I can stand to be alone just yet."

"Of course," he said, getting out and rounding the car to hold the door for her, a courtesy that came naturally to him though it often made Carolyn smile and offer some small teasing remark.

But tonight there was no teasing or humor in her face as she got out of the car, stood wearily on the crushed rock drive for a moment, then started walking rapidly toward the barn.

"I just wanted to have a quick peek at Bluebonnet," she said in response to Vernon's questioning glance. "I can't ever seem to go to sleep if I haven't looked at him."

Vernon wanted to protest, but he couldn't think of the words to say. Instead he fell into step beside her, worrying about the little gray terrier.

The problem, in Vernon's mind, was that the stray terrier was looking weaker all the time. One of these times, like tonight when she was desperate with concern over J.T., she was going to go down to the barn

and find the dog dead in his manger and Vernon
didn't know how she was going to cope with it.

He watched, his face troubled, as Carolyn bent
over the manger to study the small furry body. She
touched Bluebonnet's black nose and soft thin belly
and ran a gentle hand over his long silky coat. Then
she turned with a wan smile and motioned for Vernon to move over closer.

"He's sleeping," she whispered in relief, her eyes
dark with emotion in the shadowed recesses of the
big barn. "I think he's still pretty feverish, but at
least he doesn't seem any worse. Look, Vern."

Vernon stood beside her, his arm draped casually
around her shoulders, and gazed down at the little
dog. Bluebonnet was curled in a small furry ball, the
stiff cast on his hind leg protruding at an awkward
angle, his nose tucked under his front paws. His
breathing seemed rapid and shallow and he whimpered occasionally, but Vernon wasn't sure if the little animal was in pain or if he was just having pleasant doggy dreams about rabbits and cats.

He stood beside Carolyn, both of them grinning
fondly like young parents gazing into a baby's crib.

"What's that on his head?" Vernon whispered.

"A ribbon," Carolyn whispered back. "Teresa's
started tying his topknot back like that. She must
have found a book somewhere on dog care because
I looked it up the other day and sure enough, they

say this breed should have the topknot tied back to keep their eyes from getting irritated.''

Vernon gazed thoughtfully at the jaunty blue bow on top of the dog's head. ''You know, I find it really hard to picture Teresa reading books on pet care,'' he said.

Carolyn nodded. ''I know. But Rosa says she reads all the time. The poor kid,'' she added, her face softening. ''I wish I could—''

She broke off abruptly and leaned forward to pull the little dog's burlap blanket up over his body again, then turned toward the door.

Vernon followed her out into the velvet twilight. They stood for a moment watching the nighthawks wheel and swoop above the trees, the white markings on their wings standing out in sharp relief against the soft purple and gold of the sunset sky.

Carolyn shivered. ''Their cry is always so melancholy,'' she said, and then added, ''I wish the girls had stayed until tomorrow. The house is going to feel so empty tonight.''

''Where's Lori? Won't she be home later?''

Carolyn shook her head. ''She's going into Austin with Beverly and Amanda. We've bought a new truck for the ranch and she's driving it back on Tuesday after she gets some business done in the city. And Beverly will be staying in town with Amanda most of the week.''

"So you're all alone here for a few days?" Vernon asked, glancing down at her in concern.

"Well, not really," Carolyn said. "Rosa is here, and the men, of course. It's just that my own house is going to seem awfully big and empty."

Her face was still pale, though the sight of the little dog seemed to have relaxed her somewhat. The dusky evening light caressed her, highlighting her golden hair with rich shadows and softening the elegant contours of her face.

She turned to Vernon with a small awkward smile and he gazed at her, enchanted by her loveliness. "Oh, Caro," he whispered huskily. "You should see yourself, girl. You look about eighteen."

"Well, I feel about a hundred," she said with a brief grimace. But her face softened and her smile was tender and tremulous as she linked her arm through his and drew him toward the house.

Vernon followed her, his heart beating fast, his mouth suddenly dry.

He looked down at the woman beside him, his whole body tense with yearning, so deeply in love with her that he could think of nothing else. And when they entered the house and closed the door behind them, he took her into his arms with wondering joy like a man who has dreamed for a lifetime about finding a treasure, and suddenly has that treasure placed in his outstretched arms.

VERNON LAY PROPPED on the soft pillows in Carolyn's wide bed, his hands behind his head, waiting for her to come out of the bathroom.

Her bedroom had surprised him. The rest of the house with its gracious Southwestern decor was like a rich cool showplace, the embodiment of the perfect ranch house. But this room was intensely personal, reflecting Carolyn's own taste in its soft creamy tones and delicate appointments, the touches of pale yellow, green and apricot, the drapes and sheets trimmed with wide bands of embroidered eyelet.

Vernon smoothed the edge of a pillowcase. He would not have guessed that Carolyn's private place would be this feminine. She always seemed so brisk and practical, so confident and businesslike in her jeans and denim shirts. There was a rich sensual pleasure in picturing her here at night, dainty and womanly in the lamplight, wearing a lacy nightdress....

His throat tightened and his loins ached with anticipation. He stared at the closed door of the bathroom, willing her to appear.

Just then the door opened and Carolyn came out, pausing beside a white Jacuzzi that was recessed in the floor near the windows and partially screened by tall leafy greenery.

Vernon's heart began to pound like a schoolboy's and he stared at her, speechless. She wore a delicate peach silk nightgown with tiny gold straps. Her shoulders and arms were slim and firm, her figure ripe and curving beneath the clinging fabric. The muted indirect light gleamed on her soft golden hair, her high cheekbones, the long elegant lines of her body.

"Oh, God, Caro," Vernon whispered, sitting upright in the bed and pulling the covers across his broad hairy chest. For an unhappy moment he was painfully conscious of his own body, of the thickness of his waistline and the soft look of his shoulders. He wished desperately that he could be different for her tonight.

But it was too late for thoughts like that. She was already moving toward him, pausing to switch off the lamp so the room was cast into velvety darkness. The only illumination was a band of bright moonlight falling though the wide mullioned window, flinging silvery rectangles across the carpet and walls.

Vernon watched, holding his breath while she paused next to the bed, slipped the straps of her nightdress from her shoulders and let it fall into a silky pool at her feet.

Carolyn stood naked beside him. Vernon reached out with trembling hands and touched her waist, ran the palm of his hand up over one breast and then the other, and slowly down across her stomach. Carolyn watched him silently, her face shadowed and unreadable in the dusky stillness.

"Caro," he whispered huskily, cupping his hands around her hips and drawing her down onto the bed next to him. "Oh, darling, I've thought about this all my life. You don't know how many dreams I've had about you...."

"Don't talk, Vern," she whispered against his ear. "Just love me."

He was intoxicated by her, by the spicy flowery scent that she wore, the soft fragrance of her hair, the silky texture of her skin against his fingertips. Her slim naked body was like a vessel of warm molten gold, spilling all over him, anointing him with fiery sweetness.

He caressed her in slow wondering delight, marveling at the beauty of her, loving the way her nipples hardened at his touch and her body moistened and opened to him. She lay still, curving toward him while he ran his hands over her shoulders, around her breasts and across her rounded hips, into the soft downy thatch between her thighs, overwhelmed by her womanly sweetness. She was so wondrously, richly feminine, so entirely satisfying in every way that she took his breath away.

Under his hands she was the embodiment of all women, the essence of every woman he'd ever known or touched. But in a mysterious transcendent way she was also unique, the one irreplaceable woman he'd yearned for all his life, so that caressing her in this intimate way seemed like a sacrament, a fundamental affirmation of his own existence. When her hands sought him, cupped and fondled him, the fingers moving with delicate mesmerizing purpose, he quivered like a boy just learning the art of love. But he continued to stroke her with a delicate touch, his hands gentle and slow, and she moaned and shivered, her mouth open against his throat, her body straining against his.

Vernon sensed her need and her hunger, but even in the midst of his own consuming emotion he understood that her passion wasn't just for him. Carolyn's response on this night had more to do with her fear of the future, her anxiety and pain and her deep need to search out some kind of life and hope in the midst of despair.

Loving her as he did, Vernon wasn't hurt by this knowledge. Instead he was humbly grateful that she'd turned to him in her time of need, trusted him with this inmost expression of her own anguish and yearning.

But by now he was burning up with love for her, huge and thrusting with need, and he moved over her and into her, murmuring softly, desperate not to hurt her with the intensity of his passion. Her body opened and received him, silky and soft and caressing, taking him into a world of velvet and perfume and throbbing rich sweetness that filled his soul, drove all thoughts from his mind, carried him on a wave of mounting pounding driving pleasure, past the moon and stars and on toward the blazing depths of the sun.

He climbed and soared for a long time, an eternity of happiness, and he could feel her climbing with him, journeying beside him toward that fiery brilliance. Then, at last, he crashed into exploding brightness and lay still, emptied and shivering, drained of breath and substance, limp with ecstasy while the stars wheeled slowly around him and the moonlight bathed him in radiance.

Slowly he came back to himself and felt Carolyn's slender body resting pliantly in his arms. He lifted himself onto one elbow and gazed down at her. Her face was gentle and soft, her lips parted, her eyes wide and glazed in the shadows.

"Oh, my," she breathed. "Oh, my goodness, Vern."

"I'm sorry, Caro," he began, feeling a little awkward. "I kind of lost track of things there for a minute. Was that...was it all right for you?"

"All *right?*" she echoed in disbelief. "The man takes me on a one-way trip to heaven, and then asks if it's all *right?*"

He grinned at her, ridiculously gratified by her response. "You're just trying to make me feel good," he said.

"No, actually that's what I was trying to do earlier," she said with a little crooked smile. "Did it work?"

"Oh, Caro... Oh, God, girl..." he began helplessly.

She burrowed against his chest, giggling. Vernon was delighted by the sound of her laughter, so relaxed and girlish and full of happiness. It was a long time, he realized suddenly, since he'd heard Carolyn laugh like that.

"Who'd have thought," she murmured into the curly graying mat of hair on his chest, "that we could do that, Vern?"

"I always knew we could do that," he said with dignity. "Most people can do it, after all, Caro. It's not exactly a unique talent."

"That's not what I mean." She drew away and looked up at him, suddenly serious. "I mean, we've been friends for so long, Vern. It just never occurred to me that we could be lovers, too. I'm amazed by how good we are together. I never imagined it."

"Well, I did," Vernon said mildly. "After all, a man can't love a woman the way I've loved you all these years and not indulge himself in the occasional fantasy."

For some reason that seemed to make her uncomfortable. She turned away and sat up, swinging her legs over the edge of the bed, stepped into her night-gown and padded across the room to switch on a small lamp.

Vernon watched her, blinking a little though the light was very subdued, astonished to see her lean over behind a screen of tall plants and switch on the gold faucets above her sunken tub.

"What's happening, Caro? What are you doing?"

"I'm having a bubble bath," she announced, turning to smile at him over her shoulder. "And you're going to join me."

He chuckled. Despite the years of fantasies he'd told her about, this was something he hadn't really expected from Carolyn, this playfulness and sponta-neity as a lover. "If you don't watch out," he said solemnly, climbing out of bed and crossing the room to stand beside her, "I'm going to get really fond of you."

He took a huge pale green towel from a rack by the tub and wrapped it around his stocky middle, watching as Carolyn bent to pour a froth of scented bubbles into the steaming tub.

She stood erect, dropped her nightgown on the floor again and faced him. With a quiet purposeful movement she reached out and removed his towel, gave his body a slow deliberate appraisal while he stood nervously waiting, then grasped the excess flesh at his waist and squeezed it hard in her two hands, staring into his eyes.

"If you don't watch out," she echoed, "I'm going to get really fond of you, too, Vern. And then, God help us both."

Without another word she released him, swept her hair onto the top of her head and secured it with a silver clip that was lying on the washstand nearby. Then she stepped into the swirling frothy depths of the tub, motioning him to join her.

Vern lowered himself with a blissful sigh onto the seat opposite her, feeling the warmth of the water rising all the way to his chin as the steamy fragrance swirled and mounted.

"Now, this is living," he murmured. "A gorgeous woman, a warm beautiful room, a tub full of bubbles..."

"A nice roll in the hay..." Carolyn supplied, grinning at him.

"Don't be coarse, woman," Vernon said with dignity. "That was not a roll in the hay. That was a transcendental experience."

She laughed and soaped him with a soft green washcloth, rubbing lather all over his chest and then tenderly rinsing it away, chatting while she worked as if they had a bath together every night of their lives.

Vernon was so enchanted by her, so lost in the

wondrous pleasure of the whole experience that he was hardly paying attention until something she said caught him off guard.

"What, Caro?" he said abruptly, turning to look at her over his shoulder while she scrubbed his broad back. "What were you saying just then?"

"Pay attention," she threatened him, "or I'll get soap in your eyes on purpose, Vernon Trent. I was telling you what I'm going to do tomorrow," she continued, rubbing more lather onto the cloth. "I was saying that you've made me feel so good I'm even ready to face up to my problems. First thing in the morning, I'm going over to the Hole in the Wall to have a chat with our Mr. Scott Harris."

Vernon's body felt suddenly tense in the steaming water, and his mind whirled. "Why, Caro?" he asked. "Why would you do that?"

"Oh, Vern," she said impatiently. "You know why I want to do that. Here, it's your turn," she added with a grin, handing him the washcloth and turning her slim body away from him.

He soaped her back automatically, his hands still tingling at the feel of her skin, his fingers slipping around of their own accord to cup her breasts, even while his mind was groping for some kind of response to what she was saying.

Carolyn chuckled and moved away from his questing hands. "I want to find out if there's any truth to this horrible rumor about the exotic animals for hunting,'' she said over her shoulder. ''And I want to find out who sold him that property.''

''Why?'' Vernon repeated, his voice sounding jerky and awkward in his own ears. ''There's nothing you can do about it now, after all.''

''I know,'' she said. ''But I still like to know who my enemies are. Maybe,'' she added with another sparkling glance at him, ''I can get into a good rip roarin' fight with somebody, and take my mind off all my troubles.''

He smiled back automatically, amused at the bitter irony of life in general. Just when he finally won the greatest prize of his life, just when he held the woman of his dreams and found her to be even more wonderful than he ever could have imagined...just at that very moment in his life, it seemed that he was destined to lose her.

The cruelty of it was staggering. He soaped and rinsed her back, trying to joke and respond to her cheerful comments while his happiness was evaporating like the mounds of dying bubbles in the water all around him.

Unaware of his discomfort, Carolyn turned around in the tub with another frothy swirl of bubbles. She seated herself opposite him and gazed at him, her face solemn, her eyes sparkling wickedly as she reached beneath the water.

"Hey!" Vernon said, jumping a little. "What are you doing, girl?"

"I'm looking for the soap," she said innocently.

Vernon chuckled in spite of himself. His spirits began to rise and his natural optimism reasserted itself. Maybe everything would be all right after all, he told himself. He'd just make sure to get hold of Scott Harris early in the morning and caution him not to reveal anything about the sale of the dude ranch. Then later, when he felt that Carolyn was ready to hear it, he'd...

He shuddered with pleasure and leaned back, closing his eyes briefly.

"You keep that up much longer, girl," he muttered huskily, "and you're going to find more than the soap down there."

"Oh, good," she said shamelessly. "I was hoping that might happen. Do you think it's possible to do it in a bathtub, Vern?"

"I believe it is," he said after some consideration, "but in the interests of research, maybe you should just come over here a little closer."

Laughing, she slid into his arms and settled down onto him, sheathing him in a warmth even more silky and caressing than the steaming scented bathwater. And by that time, there were no thoughts or worries at all in Vernon Trent's mind. There was nothing but ecstasy.

CHAPTER EIGHT

CAROLYN STOOD on the driveway that circled in front of her house, smiling and waving as Vernon's Camaro rounded the bend and disappeared into the trees.

Even after his car was gone, she stood watching the empty road, her eyes narrowed against the early-morning light, her face tender.

At last she turned and started slowly toward the big front doors of the barn. As she walked her smile gradually faded and her face took on a look of intense preoccupation.

Carolyn had known Vernon Trent all her life, liked and trusted him as long as she could remember. But she had been sincere the previous night when she'd told him how astonished she was to find that they could be lovers as well as friends.

And it wasn't that he was merely acceptable in bed, she mused, pausing by the entry to the barn and gazing dreamily off into the grove of young trees below the well pasture.

The amazing, incredible fact was that Carolyn

Townsend had never had a sexual experience like the one she'd enjoyed the night before. She and Frank had been good partners, both in business and in life, and they'd had a solid faithful marriage. In fact, Frank Townsend was the only man Carolyn had ever slept with. But Vernon was a completely different man than her husband had been, more tender and imaginative, more playful, more able to give himself over to the needs and wishes of his partner. And he made it so evident that he adored her....

Carolyn shivered, remembering the warmth of their lovemaking, the passionate whispers, the hours of warm embraces in the deep caressing darkness. Her body moistened and softened of its own accord, yearning for him again.

Probably, she reminded herself with a small grim smile, he was heading off to the Longhorn for a big greasy breakfast right this second.

They'd had a light breakfast together in Carolyn's kitchen, feasting cheerfully on fruit cup and cottage cheese and wheat toast, and Vernon had claimed to enjoy the meal. But Carolyn didn't trust the man. She knew how much he loved sausages and fries, greasy eggs and hotcakes and big thick breakfast steaks. She could just see him now at a table in the Longhorn, laughing with Dottie Jones and Bubba Gibson as he stuffed himself with calories and fat, while the cholesterol swirled through his bloodstream and settled relentlessly and lethally in his arteries....

This is ridiculous, she told herself sternly. *I've got to quit tormenting myself.*

She approached the manger box with its warm pile of burlap and drew back the top covering, looking down at Bluebonnet, who blinked sleepily and then roused himself and tried to lick her hand.

At first glance, the dog looked much better. His stitches had been removed and the wound was healing nicely. His gray coat was already growing in to hide the long scar. His leg cast was still in place but would be coming off in a couple of weeks if he continued to progress.

Even his shattered jaw appeared to be knitting well. The young veterinarian was encouraged by the way the little dog appeared to have more control over his jaw movements, and seemed to be in less pain when he opened his mouth to swallow or lick the hands of his attendants.

But, as Manny was always careful to point out to Carolyn, those superficial injuries, serious though they were, weren't the major problem.

Bluebonnet was still in danger, but what threatened him now was the recurrent low-grade fever that never seemed to go away completely. The fever was sapping his strength, making him weaker and more feeble all the time even as his bones knit together and his body healed. He didn't even have the strength to hold himself erect on his three good legs or take a few wavering steps when lifted down from the manger.

But when Carolyn questioned Manny in frustration, pleaded for some kind of medication to help the animal, the vet could only shrug.

"There's just nothing that will help him, Carolyn. Only time, and a roll of the dice."

"A roll of the dice?"

"I call his chances at fifty-fifty. One day, he might just shake this, stabilize his body temperature and start to make a dramatic improvement within days, even hours. Or he might just roll over and die. It could go either way."

"When will that be? When will he reach the crisis point?" Carolyn would ask.

Again Manny would shake his head. "Could be anytime. Maybe today or next week, could be a month or more. I'll maybe know when he's getting close, and be able to give you some warning."

Carolyn frowned now, remembering, as she toyed with one of Bluebonnet's ears, then touched his nose, dry and hot with fever, and gazed into his huge dark eyes. Abruptly she squared her shoulders and looked around the barn. The far recesses remained in deep shadow but the broad dusty floors were washed with slanting rays of early sunshine. The whole building smelled richly of hay and horses and summer.

"Teresa?" she called. "How are you this morning, dear? It's a lovely day. The radio said it's going to be really hot."

Carolyn was developing a kind of sixth sense so acute that she could always tell when Teresa was nearby. It was a mystery where she must be hiding because, as Carolyn had told Vernon, all the obvious places of concealment had been carefully eliminated. But still Carolyn knew that there were eyes upon her, ears straining to hear what she said.

Strangely enough, it was no longer such an unpleasant sensation. Even though Carolyn never saw Teresa, except as a running flash of brown legs and arms or a dark tangled cloud of hair, she was growing to love the little girl.

Carolyn's own tender instincts were stirred by the child's loving care of the sick dog and her touching clumsy attempts to make Bluebonnet comfortable, to brighten his captive existence. In fact, Carolyn would have given a good deal to be able to gather the shy wild child into her arms, hug her and comfort her and convince her that the world was really full of good and loving people.

But it seemed impossible to make any progress with Teresa. Coaxing, pleading, long earnest talks with Rosa Martinez, the child's mother—everything was futile. Carolyn had to be content with this strange one-sided kind of relationship where she talked to the air and knew that the air was listening.

She stood silent for a moment longer, conscious only of the gentle hum of insects and the cheerful early-morning clatter from the ranch yard. At last she gave up, moving off toward the door. In the entryway she paused, turning back toward the shadowed depths. "Maybe you should just play with Bluebonnet inside today, Teresa," she suggested, making sure that her voice carried well. "It might be too hot to take him outside when he's still feverish."

Again she waited, glancing hopefully into the big hushed building. She thought she heard something...a rustle of straw, a furtive step, maybe a soft muffled cough....

But there was no further response. Finally Carolyn shook her head and walked out into the sunlight.

CAROLYN PULLED through the wide stone gates that marked the beginning of the dude ranch property, grimacing as she always did when she saw the Hole in the Wall logo emblazoned on a heavy wooden sign above the gates.

But even though her body was rigid with distaste, she felt her curiosity mount as she drove slowly up the tree-lined approach road and onto the property of the new development.

There had certainly been dramatic changes since her last visit to the old ranch, known for years as the Lazy J, that bordered her own property. The modest frame house and battered corrals that had served the Kendall family for generations had vanished. They had been replaced by a big lodge nestled in the trees, a new set of pens and outbuildings and an imposing spread of recreational facilities, including swimming pools, tennis courts, hot tubs, one huge barbecue pit and several smaller ones, shady picnic areas and groomed hiking trails.

Most impressive of all though, was the huge central building. This rustic structure housed the guest rooms as well as a number of small shops, a bar, a dining room, a games room, and a big lounge for dancing and informal socializing.

The vast central complex was also where Cal and Serena's new boot shop would be located, Carolyn assumed.

She braked her small car at the entrance to the ranch yard and stared out at the Hole in the Wall, a little nonplussed. The place was undeniably intimidating in its aggressive newness and efficiency, a mute testimony to the power, wealth and business acumen of the man behind the project.

You could just tell, Carolyn thought gloomily, that the man who owned this place was going to make a success of it. He clearly didn't choose to do things by halves. And like it or not, she had to admit that he'd designed a glossy and well-packaged operation.

She glanced around, wondering what she was looking for, half-expecting to see a gazelle come bounding over the hill pursued by camouflage-clad gunmen, or a herd of wildebeest languishing in a pen, sick with some dreadful tropical illness.

But the morning was silent and pleasant, and there was little sign of activity around the sprawling grounds. Of course, the ranch wasn't yet open for business, and Scott Harris wouldn't officially be receiving paying guests until after his dude ranch's much-vaunted opening-day barbecue.

With another small shudder of distaste, Carolyn parked in front of the lodge, got out of the car and went slowly up the walk to the front door. She was admitted instantly by a gray-haired Mexican woman in a flowered apron. Carolyn greeted her and was ushered into a study opening on the wide cedar deck that fronted the house.

"Mr. Scott, he's been out ridin', and now he's just down at the big place checkin' on some supplies," the woman said in her soft musical voice. "I'll buzz him on the intercom, and he'll be right up, okay?"

"No rush," Carolyn said cheerfully, smiling at the woman, as she sat on a heavy couch covered in a tweed fabric. "This is comfortable, and I'm not in any hurry."

While she waited she looked around, unashamedly curious. The room was pleasant and unpretentious, paneled in light oak, and decorated in subdued desert tones of tan, pale blue and soft rust.

Carolyn found herself approving the comfortable ambience, and glanced thoughtfully at the broad desk to find some clues to the personality of the man who used this room. But the desk was bare and polished, empty except for a small dark brown telephone, with a neat leather blotter and small matching notebook arranged with mathematical precision on the gleaming golden oak surface.

"Not much character to that desk, I'm afraid," a cheerful voice said behind her, making her jump. "I'm just a pretty dull, harmless kind of guy."

Carolyn turned with a start and gazed at the man who stood in the doorway. He was tall and handsome, perhaps ten years younger than she, with dark blond hair, gray eyes and high patrician cheekbones. He wore casual jeans and boots and an open-necked golf shirt, and moved with the easy powerful air of a man comfortable with his own masculinity.

"I wonder," Carolyn said dryly, returning his handshake with a firm challenging grip.

"Wonder what?" he asked, moving over to sit behind his desk, his eyebrows raised in polite inquiry.

"How dull and harmless you are," Carolyn said abruptly, troubled by the uncomfortable suspicion that she was being teased. "I'm Carolyn Townsend," she added. "Your next-door neighbor."

His face brightened and his gray eyes softened with a genuine smile of welcome. "Beverly's mother?" he said. "Well, this *is* a pleasure. I've heard such a lot of things about you, Mrs. Townsend. All incredibly flattering."

"Well, I'm not real fond of flattery," Carolyn said, knowing that she was being brusque and graceless but unable to help herself.

She studied the man opposite her, realizing that of course a man as attractive as Scott Harris would have come to Beverly's attention. She was irritated that Beverly hadn't mentioned that she'd met the dude ranch owner and let her mother know a little about the man.

He sat across the desk watching Carolyn calmly, his eyes sparkling as if he could read all her thoughts and found them quietly amusing. Carolyn tensed, not sure how to begin, growing angrier as her awkwardness mounted.

"I understand," he said finally, his voice gentle, "that you're somewhat less than thrilled about my new business venture, Mrs. Townsend."

Carolyn nodded. "I guess that's common knowledge, Mr. Harris. And," she added, "I wish you'd call me Carolyn. I can't remember anyone ever calling me Mrs. Townsend when I was this close to home.''

He grinned easily. ''Gladly, Carolyn. And I'm Scott. All right?''

Carolyn nodded a little stiffly.

''Now,'' he continued, ''about my dude ranch. You were saying?''

''I guess you've learned already that this place runs on gossip, Mr....Scott,'' Carolyn amended, feeling her cheeks turn pink. ''This whole town and all the ranches around it are hotbeds of gossip. And I haven't been real happy with some of the things I've heard about your place.''

''Really? Like what, Carolyn?''

''Like...'' Carolyn began, her voice trembling a little. She took a deep breath, steadied herself and continued. ''Like the fact that hundreds of people with little or no knowledge of ranch life or respect for fences and property are going to be all over this area, no doubt trespassing on my land, bothering my cattle—''

''You really care about those cattle of yours, don't you?'' Scott interrupted, his eyes fixed gravely on her face. ''I've heard that's a pretty special herd.''

''It certainly is,'' Carolyn said. ''It's one of the finest Santa Gertrudis herds in the state. Do you know anything about Santa Gertrudis cattle, Scott?''

He shook his head, still watching her intently.

"The breed was developed right here in Texas," Carolyn said, "over the course of the past century. The first herd was produced down on the King Ranch. They achieved it by crossing Brahma and Shorthorn."

"An interesting combination," Scott Harris said.

Carolyn gave him a quick glance but decided that he wasn't being flippant. He really did appear to be interested. Encouraged, she continued. "It really was. The idea, of course, was to produce a breed with the beef characteristics of the Shorthorn and the hardiness and heat resistance of the Brahma."

"And it worked?"

"Better than anybody could have expected. The Santa Gertrudis is a wonderful beef animal. And nowadays, bulls sell for six figures, Scott. I've got a lot of dollars on the hoof out there on the property adjoining yours, and it's a real concern to me."

"Why?" he asked, leaning back in his chair and keeping his eyes fixed on her intently. "Why should my commercial operation be any threat to yours, Carolyn?"

"The Santa Gertrudis is a sensitive, intelligent animal," she said. "They're quite high-strung, especially the bulls. They certainly wouldn't respond well to a bunch of city types wandering into their pasture and playing cowboy, chasing them around the field for the fun of it, something like that."

"Don't worry," Scott said dryly. "Nothing like that will ever happen, I can assure you. I intend to supervise this whole operation very closely. I have an excellent staff, and their instructions are clear. I will never, at any time, allow activities here to encroach on the rights or property of my neighbors. *Never.*"

Carolyn looked into the younger man's face and realized that he was dead serious. And there was something in the set of his jaw, in the cool light behind those gray eyes, that told her rules laid down by Scott Harris weren't likely to be broken.

Still, there was…

"You don't look convinced," he commented. "What else is bothering you?"

"It's…" Carolyn hesitated, feeling a reluctance even to frame the words. "It's these damned exotic animals!" she burst out finally. "I purely can't stand the thought of it, Scott. It's driving me crazy."

"What about them?" he asked blankly. "What are you talking about?"

Carolyn made an abrupt little gesture of impatience and told him the whole story, the rumors about the African prey animals and the hunting safaris, and her own fears for the health of her herd.

Scott listened, his eyes widening in disbelief, and then threw back his head and shouted with laughter.

Carolyn's anger slowly mounted as she watched

him. She was about to make an indignant protest when he sobered and leaned forward.

"You're absolutely right, Carolyn" he said quietly. "The gossip in this place is terrible, especially when it's far from the truth. It's true," he added thoughtfully, "that we do plan to have a game park with exotic animals. But the only hunting our guests will do will be with a camera."

Carolyn stared at him. "A camera? So there'll be no shooting zebras or wildebeest?"

Scott Harris's handsome face darkened. "Look, Carolyn," he said slowly, "I don't want to belabor the point, but I really find that whole suggestion incredibly offensive. I'm a member of Greenpeace, Wildlife International and the Sierra Club. Anybody who shot a zebra within a hundred miles of me would be very sorry if I had any say in the matter, let me assure you."

Carolyn looked into those steely-gray eyes and found that she had no trouble believing him. She felt a flood of relief, and for the first time in the interview she gave her new neighbor a warm smile. "Well, Scott, that's real good to hear," she began. "I'm sorry I—"

But her apology was interrupted by the arrival of Scott's cook, bearing a tray with two lemon-garnished glasses of iced tea, a tall silver pitcher for refills and a plateful of freshly baked oatmeal cookies, which she offered immediately to her employer and his guest.

"Thanks, Carla," Scott said, giving the woman a cheerful boyish grin. "Those cookies smell wonderful, don't they, Carolyn?"

"Mmm," Carolyn agreed, her mouth already full.

"By the way, any messages, Carla?" Scott asked, as the cook beamed on him with maternal fondness and turned to leave.

"Let's see," Carla said, frowning, her plump body rigid with concentration. "The hardware store called about the trampoline, and the travel agent wants more information about your holiday package offer. Oh, and Vernon Trent wants to talk to you. He's been calling all morning, says it's really important. Matter of fact, he sounded kind of frantic."

"Vernon Trent?" Scott said. "I thought our business was all tied up. Maybe he's just interested in having lunch sometime."

"Didn't sound like it," Carla said. "Sounded like he was having a fit, actually."

Carolyn felt a cold chill. She stared at the handsome young man across the desk. "Vernon Trent?" she said.

"The local realtor," Scott told her. "You must know him, Carolyn. Vernon's a native of Crystal Creek, isn't he?"

Carolyn nodded stiffly. "I've known him all my

life," she said, her cheeks warming a little as she remembered those dark secret hours of passion, the sweet hot feeling of their bodies joined so intimately. "We went to school together. I just didn't realize that the two of you were acquainted."

"Oh, very much so. Vernon Trent sold me this property," Scott said cheerfully. "And he did a terrific job of it, worked for months putting the deal together. He..."

But Carolyn was no longer listening. She stared at her new neighbor, her face white, her mind whirling.

"*Vernon Trent?*" she whispered. "*Vern* sold you this property? He's the one who made the deal? He worked on it for...for months, you say?"

"That's right," Scott said, looking a little startled by her reaction. "I met Vern a couple of years ago in Austin, told him then what I was considering and asked him to keep his eyes open for a likely property for a dude ranch. When he heard this place might be available, he contacted me and we started working right away on the terms and conditions. I was really impressed with him as a businessman."

Carolyn was silent in her comfortable tweed chair. All she could feel was shock and disbelief, and a dreadful overpowering sense of betrayal.

"Carolyn?" Scott Harris was asking in concern. "Carolyn? Is something the matter?"

With a valiant effort Carolyn pulled her scattered

thoughts together and forced herself to smile at the young man opposite her. "Of course not," she said brightly. "I'm happy to have met you, Scott," she added, setting aside her glass and gathering up her handbag. "But I'm afraid I have to run. I wish you all success. I'm glad I came over to talk with you today. *Real* glad." Her voice sounded grim in her ears, though her host didn't appear to notice.

"I'm glad, too," Scott said, rising courteously as she prepared to leave, and moving around the desk to escort her to the front door. "I hope you'll come to the opening-day barbecue, Carolyn. Please consider yourself personally invited. I'd love to have you here."

There was no doubting his sincerity. Carolyn smiled automatically, murmured something inaudible and hurried down the walk to her car, her mind still whirling, her face pale as she climbed in, drove out the gate and headed rapidly toward the town of Crystal Creek.

"HI, BETTY," Carolyn said, keeping her voice deliberately casual as she stepped into Vernon Trent's cluttered real estate office and smiled at his secretary. "Is Vern around?"

Betty frowned at her computer screen and waved a cheerful greeting over her shoulder. "Damn thing's eaten *another* document," she muttered. "I hate this monster. Hi, Carolyn,'' she added. ''He's gone over to the Longhorn for coffee.''

''Oh, right,'' Carolyn said, hesitating in the doorway and attempting a smile. ''I guess it's coffee time, isn't it?''

''Actually,'' Betty said, studying a bank of floppy disks on a shelf beside her, ''I think it's doughnut time, Carolyn. Vern said he'd had a real light breakfast, and he was just starving by ten o'clock. Suffering a massive snack attack, poor thing.''

''I'll just bet,'' Carolyn said bitterly, then smiled to soften her tone as the secretary cast an inquiring glance at her. ''Thanks, Betty. See you later.''

She left the secretary still muttering curses at her computer monitor, went back out into the sunlight and crossed Crystal Creek's shady town square toward the Longhorn Motel and Coffee Shop. By the front door she met Bubba Gibson and Billie Jo Dumont on their way out, giggling together, followed by Martin Avery, Wayne Jackson and Manny Hernandez. They all paused to greet her, exchanged some cheerful banter and small talk, then went their separate ways.

Carolyn drew a deep breath, opened the door and peered into the pleasant interior of the coffee shop, cool and dim after the brilliant morning sunlight. As always, she had a sensation of time warp, as if she were suddenly seventeen again.

The Longhorn hadn't changed as long as she could remember. The red gingham curtains at the door, the smell of grease and frying onions, even the juke-boxes, the napkin holders and the red-checked cloths on the tables seemed to have been there forever, as if all the changes in the outside world had somehow bypassed this place altogether.

Carolyn normally found this timelessness comforting, but not today. Right at this moment, she could barely control the raging tumult of her emotions as she stood and gazed at the stocky man seated alone at a table near the back, working his way steadily through a big plate of home fries smothered in gravy.

Vernon hadn't noticed her yet. Carolyn studied him for a moment longer, painfully aware of her conflicting feelings.

Part of her thrilled and shivered at the sight of him and the sweet sexual memories of the previous night, and longed to go over and stroke his thick shining hair, touch his tanned cheek, run a hand over his shoulders and chest.

But another part of her, much more insistent, wanted to pick up one of the heavy old-fashioned steel napkin holders and lob it right at his head. She let the door close softly behind her and approached his table while Dottie popped her head around the kitchen partition and waved. Carolyn waved back, indicating that she didn't need anything at the moment, and Dottie nodded cheerfully and withdrew.

Vernon caught Dottie's nod and turned to look over his shoulder. When he saw Carolyn his face lighted and his brown eyes sparkled with joy, then with a quick flash of guilt as he looked down at the greasy plate of food in front of him.

But the happiness triumphed. He sprang to his feet, unashamedly delighted at her unexpected arrival.

"Caro!" he murmured. "What a surprise. Darling, it's so good to see you. Sit down and…"

Carolyn sank into the chair opposite him, staring at him. His voice trailed off and he began to look uneasy.

"Caro?" he said hesitantly. "Is something…"

"I've been to see Scott Harris," she said coldly. "He'd been out all morning, just got your message while I was there, Vern. I guess you were trying really hard to get hold of him, weren't you?"

"I was just—"

"You were just trying to warn him that I was coming, right, Vern?" Carolyn continued in that same quiet toneless voice. "You wanted to make sure that your lies didn't get all crossed up, and that I'd just keep looking like an idiot."

"I never lied to you, Caro," Vernon said, stung by her tone and her cold angry expression. "I just didn't tell you the whole truth. That's not lying."

"You deceived me," Carolyn said, leaning forward, her blue eyes flashing with rage. "It's the same thing, Vern. Why'd you do it? Why pretend last night that you...cared about me, when all the time you were busy making me look foolish?"

"Pretend!" he echoed, staring at her in disbelief. "Goddamnit, Carolyn, if you think I was *pretending* last night, then you sure as hell don't know much about anything."

"I know enough to understand a cheat when I see one!" she whispered. "Why'd you do it, Vern? You had to realize I'd find out sometime, didn't you?"

"Oh, God," he said wearily, spreading his hands in defeat. "I knew how upset you were about the dude ranch, Caro. I guess I just hoped that if I could stall until the thing got started, until you'd had a chance to meet Scott and realize there weren't going to be any big problems, it might be easier for everybody. I just didn't want you mad at me," he ended with a tone of almost childlike appeal.

"Well," she said bitterly, "you sure messed up there, didn't you, Vern? Fact is, I can't remember when I've ever been so mad at anybody. Especially after...after last night..."

Carolyn's voice broke and she couldn't continue. She sat rigid in her chair, staring down at her clasped hands, but pulled away when Vernon made a tentative move toward her.

"Caro," he whispered, gazing at her in agony. "Look, it doesn't have to make any difference to us. I'm sorry I didn't tell you right away. I know it was stupid of me, but I just wanted so desperately not to let anything put distance between us when we were finally starting to get a little closer. It doesn't change what happened last night," he urged, leaning toward her, his rugged face taut with emotion. "Caro, we can still—"

"No, we can't," she said abruptly. "Never again, Vern."

His face drained of color and he stared at her, stricken by her words. "What are you saying, Carolyn?" he whispered.

"I'm saying that I can't trust you," she said bitterly. "And I want nothing more to do with you."

"You know that's not true!" he protested. "Dammit, you *know* you can trust me with your life, Carolyn. You always could. Just because I didn't tell you something pertaining to my own business, that doesn't mean I'm somehow not trustworthy."

"It's not just that, Vern," Carolyn said wearily, looking up to meet his eyes. Her anger was slowly draining away, to be replaced by a vast aching misery that chilled her to the depths.

"What, then?" he asked. "What's the problem?"

She looked at his plate, at the sodden golden fries swimming in rich gravy.

Vernon followed her glance and stiffened defensively. "I was...I got real hungry this morning," he said, trying to keep his voice light. "Just couldn't make it all the way to lunch."

"Betty said you were going out to get some doughnuts."

"I did. But the doughnuts just didn't quite hit the spot, somehow."

"Oh, Vern," Carolyn said sadly. "You'll never change, will you? And you claim that I can trust you," she added with growing bitterness. "How can I trust you? You're busy killing yourself, Vern. What's the point in getting all tied up with a man like you?"

He gazed at her, his dark eyes puzzled. "What's going on, Caro?" he asked abruptly. "Are you mad at me over selling the dude ranch, or over the *food* I'm eating, for God's sake?"

"I'm mad at you for making me care about you, Vern," Carolyn said grimly, getting to her feet and pushing her chair back into position. "It was a real bad mistake, letting you into my bed, and it'll never happen again, believe me. Never!"

"Because you found me eating a plate of fries?" he asked in disbelief.

Carolyn's blue eyes darkened with emotion. "Yes," she said, leaning close to him and forming her words clearly. "Yes, Vern. Because you have no control over your habits and no concern for your health. Because you're twenty pounds overweight and badly out of shape and you don't give a damn. Because any poor woman who gets involved with you is inviting the kind of heartache that I just don't need at this point in my life. *That's* why, Vern.''

He sat thunderstruck, gazing at her openmouthed while she turned on her heel, marched though the door and vanished in the harsh morning sunlight.

FOR A LONG TIME after Carolyn disappeared, Vernon sat gazing at the window, frowning as if the force of his concentration might somehow cause her to materialize again.

But he knew it was futile. Carolyn Townsend was a woman who meant what she said. And she'd said, ''Never again''. His heart ached within him, a slow burning ache that was physical as well as emotional. Vernon rubbed his chest thoughtfully.

Maybe Carolyn was right. Maybe he really was killing himself with this kind of diet and life-style. But then, if he couldn't have the woman he loved, he might as well just keep on eating. What did it matter, any of it, if he had to live without her?

''You sit there any longer, Vern,'' Dottie Jones said cheerfully at his elbow, ''you might just as well order your lunch, get a jump on the crowd.''

Vernon stared up at her blankly, trying to take in her words.

Dottie returned his glance in calm silence. If she'd caught any of his exchange with Carolyn, she certainly wasn't letting on. Dottie knew every secret in town, but she always minded her own business just the same.

"Special today's chicken-fried steak or barbecued brisket with grits an' fries an' peach cobbler. Ice cream's extra," Dottie added, holding her order pad at the ready.

Vernon hesitated. For once in his life, the thought of all that rich food didn't tempt him at all. He couldn't forget Carolyn's pale face or her dark tragic eyes.

But she was gone, and she wouldn't be back, and he had to go on living. Somehow, after that one night of wild sweetness, after the inexpressible joy of holding her in his arms and pouring his love into her, he had to find a way to subdue his longings and cope with the empty loneliness of his life.

He stared at Dottie's pleasant face. At last he shook his head in regret.

"Sorry, Dottie," he said, getting to his feet and pushing away the unfinished plate of greasy fries. "I guess I'm just not very hungry today after all."

He smiled automatically, dropped a few bills on the table, then squared his shoulders and strode off without a backward glance.

CHAPTER NINE

"IT'S GONNA RAIN," Hank Travis said with gloomy satisfaction. "It's fixin' to be a real ol'-fashioned gully-washer. I kin feel it in my bones."

"Really?" Cynthia McKinney said, resting her knitting in her lap for a moment and squinting dubiously at the cloudless blue sky. "How can you tell? It doesn't look like rain to me."

"I *said*, I kin feel it in my bones," Hank repeated, giving her a disdainful glance and setting his rocking chair into rapid motion again.

"You mean literally?" Cynthia persisted. "Like, your bones are actually physically hurting, so you know it's going to rain? Is that medically possible?"

Before Hank could open his mouth to reply, his grandson interjected himself hastily into the conversation, obviously fearful of what the old man's next words might be.

"You know, he's usually right, honey," J. T. McKinney told his young wife. "I know it sounds incredible, but when Grandpa predicts a big rain, even if it's a clear blue sky and a fair calm day, I go out and make sure the calves have some shelter.''

''No, you don't,'' Cynthia said, smiling at him cheerfully and applying herself to her knitting again. ''You tell Ken, and *he* goes out to check the calves. Right?''

''Right,'' J.T. said, his hands tugging impatiently at the warm blanket that covered his knees.

''Just for another month or so, J.T.,'' Carolyn said gently, feeling a deep welling of sympathy for him. ''Just till Nate says the worst danger's passed, and you can go in for the angioplasty. Then you'll be able to be out and about again just like you always were.''

''Gonna rain for weeks. Claro's prob'ly gonna flood. All them silly little summer cottages along the river washed away like matchsticks,'' Hank added. ''People dyin' like flies. I seen it happen before.''

''Not for years and years, Grandpa,'' J.T. protested. ''The Claro hasn't flooded like that as long as I can remember. I think there's too much irrigation now for it to get that high.''

''Nothin's stronger than nature,'' Hank said darkly, his old face set and stubborn. ''I feel a big rain comin' in the next coupla weeks.''

J.T. gazed at the lazy, sparkling river winding its way past his ranch, his dark eyes troubled. Cynthia gave old Hank a quick glance of irritation, then reached over and grasped her husband's hand.

"Don't you worry, J.T.," she whispered. "Don't worry about anything, dear. That riverbank's so high, the water could never threaten us. We're all safe as can be, and there's not a thing for you to fret about."

J.T. smiled and patted his wife's cheek, then turned to Carolyn.

"Have you talked to Vern at all lately, Carolyn?"

Carolyn gave a guilty start and flushed uncomfortably. "Vern? Why, not for…not for a couple of weeks, I guess," she faltered. "I…ran into him at the Longhorn one day around the beginning of the month, and I've seen him around town a couple of times since, but I haven't really talked with him."

Cynthia's wide brown eyes rested on the other woman's face for a moment but she said nothing.

"Yeah. Neither has anybody else," J.T. said with a brief frown. "Everybody says he seems to have dropped out of sight. People are getting a little worried, the way I hear it."

Carolyn stared at the other rancher, her face draining of color. "What do you mean, J.T.?" she asked abruptly. "Has Vern gone away somewhere, or what?"

"I seen the Claro turn into a wall of water forty feet high," old Hank said with considerable relish. "Throwin' cattle up in the air like bits of fluff, carryin' houses along an' droppin' 'em twenty miles downstream, people drownin' who never knew what hit 'em.''

Carolyn shivered, chilled by the old man's words. She turned back to J.T., suddenly anxious to hear his answer.

"Well, no," J.T. said slowly. "He hasn't gone away, exactly, but he's sort of disappeared just the same. I mean, apparently he still sleeps at his house and he goes to the office sometimes, but he is not doing much work at all and he never goes into the Longhorn anymore, or out to Zack's in the evening. He kind of slips around town and doesn't talk much to anybody. Nobody knows what he's doing.''

"Oh, I don't believe *that*," Carolyn said, trying to smile though her heart was suddenly chilled with fear. "In this town, there's always somebody who knows what you're doing. Maybe he's just working real hard on a deal in the city, something big and top secret, and he'll be around again when he gets it all tied up.''

J.T. shook his head, his dark eyes still worried. "Betty says he's not working. She says he seems to be going out to Brock Munroe's place a lot, but it's not business. She doesn't have any idea what he's doing out there. She's real upset about him.''

"Ol' Jim Kendall, next to the Townsend place, he was crossin' the river once with a herd of mares, swimmin' 'em across when the high water hit just like a freight train,'' Hank was saying. ''Washed them mares into the next county. Sixteen good brood mares, wiped out in just a coupla minutes. Ol' Jim, he got pulled outta the saddle an' hung onto a tree till the boys got there with a rope an' snagged him.''

Carolyn shuddered again, wishing Hank would find another topic to dwell on. She thought of the Kendall ranch, so close to her own, and the awesome power of the shallow sleepy river they all took so much for granted these days. But J.T. was right. A flood like that on the Claro couldn't happen anymore, hadn't happened for decades.

She shrugged off the concern and returned to thoughts of Vernon Trent, whom, as she'd just told J.T., she hadn't talked with since that miserable scene in the Longhorn a couple of weeks ago.

She remembered Vernon's anguished face, his baffled confusion when he asked her what exactly she was upset about, the dude ranch or his own eating habits.

And he had a right to his bewilderment, Carolyn thought miserably. At the time she hadn't even realized herself why she felt so angry, and it had taken her a lot of introspection to figure it out. Now, as she sat with her neighbors on the shady patio at the Double C, she analyzed her feelings.

She'd been furious when she learned that Vernon

Trent had been instrumental in selling the property for the dude ranch, not because of his part in the business deal but because of his secrecy. Taking a man into her bed was the most intimate expression of trust that Carolyn Townsend could visualize. Vernon, she'd felt, had betrayed that trust.

And she'd been furious, too, about his life-style, his flamboyant and careless disregard for the rules of healthy living that sensible people took seriously.

But that was his own business, wasn't it, and none of hers?

Carolyn frowned, watching a pair of shiny bay colts nickering and playing within the white rail fence of the pasture, half-listening to Hank as the old man horrified Cynthia with more stories of hideous natural disasters.

The extent of Carolyn's anger with Vernon Trent, she understood now, was in direct proportion to the intensity of her feelings for him. Back when she'd found him just mildly attractive, she was just mildly irritated by his small quirks.

But now that she adored the man...

Carolyn shifted awkwardly on her wicker patio chair. This was a brand-new kind of honesty for her, the private admission that she loved Vernon Trent. A few months ago, she would have scoffed at the possibility. But not anymore. Not after that night in her bed, and the wondrous amazing sweetness of his lovemaking...

Carolyn moved again in the chair, her cheeks flushing a delicate pink as she remembered his hands on her body, his lips, his tongue, the whispered endearments, the hot passion and surprising gaiety.

I want him again, she thought desperately. *Oh God, I want him right now! Vern, where are you? Why don't you call, dammit? I didn't mean half the things I said, surely you must know that....*

There was this naked longing in her, this yearning for his touch, for the feel of his arms around her and his body above and inside hers, as close as a man and woman could get. And there was the loneliness, the constant need to talk to him, to tell him things, to ask what he was thinking, to laugh with him and share all the little joys and problems of life.

If that wasn't love, then Carolyn Townsend had never experienced the emotion.

But blended right in with all that yearning, scattered through the warm feelings like a crop of weeds in a flower garden, was the fear. Loving meant putting yourself in such terrible danger. If you loved somebody, you could lose them, and Carolyn knew well enough how it felt to lose people.

She was shaken and terrified by the strength of her feelings for Vernon Trent. How could she bear to give herself to him, throw her life in with his, lose herself in the kind of pleasure they had together and then lose *him* to his own life-style choices?

But what was the alternative? She couldn't change him. Nobody could. People had to change themselves. Did that mean she had to cut him out of her life, doom herself forever to this agony of loneliness, this sleepless aching hunger for his body and his laughter?

Carolyn moaned inadvertently, a small helpless sound that startled both herself and Cynthia, who turned to her with a quick troubled glance.

"Carolyn? Is something the matter?"

Carolyn shook her head, feeling awkward and embarrassed as J.T., too, shifted in his chair to look over at her with concern.

"No," she said hastily. "Nothing. I just…" Her mind dashed around in frantic circles, searching for some excuse that would satisfy them. "I just remembered that I forgot to shut off the pump at the well before I left and Karl doesn't know I turned it on. If nobody notices, the trough will overflow and there'll be water running all over the ground. I'd better get on home and tend to that pump."

She could feel their eyes still on her as she stood, gathered up her handbag and the stock certificates she'd brought to show J.T. and prepared to leave.

"It's okay," she said. "Don't anybody get up. I guess after all these years, I can find my own way out. Bye, Grandpa," she added, dropping a kiss on the old man's cheek and giving him a quick fierce hug. "You behave yourself, hear?"

Hank pulled away from her embrace with an indignant snort and continued his stories.

"I recall once back in the thirties," he said, "there was a tornado touched down near Pearsall, picked up a house with an ol' lady in it, just a-settin' in her rocker. Put that house down at Charlotte, more'n thirty miles away, an' there she was, still knittin'. Hadn't missed a stitch."

Cynthia gazed at him a moment, then looked down ruefully at her own inexpert length of knitting. "Words can't tell you," she said cheerfully, "how much I loathe the woman in that story. Carolyn, are you sure you're all right? You look a little pale."

"I'm fine," Carolyn said, pausing on her way through the kitchen door. "See y'all later. Look after each other, okay?"

J.T. grinned wryly. "Count on it, Carolyn. We're looking after each other so well, nobody lets anybody do a thing around here. And you check up on Vern if you get a chance, would you?" he added. "I'm a little worried about that boy."

"Me, too," Carolyn said, trying to keep her voice cheerful. "Sounds like he's up to no good, doesn't it? Maybe I'll call him tonight and find out what he's doing."

"Promise," J.T. said, giving her a keen glance.

"Okay," Carolyn said with a helpless wave of her hand. "I promise."

BUT LATER that evening, long after she'd tended to her chores and visited Bluebonnet, cooked herself a light supper and tidied the dishes, Carolyn hadn't been able to keep her promise. Several times she actually crossed the kitchen and stared at the telephone, willing herself to pick it up and dial his number, but something always held her back.

She thought about J.T.'s description of Vernon's odd behavior, and the few times that she herself had seen him around town since their argument. She knew that he'd deliberately avoided her, ducking into the drugstore or the library when he'd seen her coming, vanishing around corners like a hurried furtive ghost.

He'd even looked different, Carolyn thought, not at all his usual neat, well-dressed self. The times she'd seen him he'd been wearing tattered baggy jeans and a bulky old corduroy jacket too hot for the day, and he'd huddled anxiously into his clothes like a man trying to hide from the world.

Well, maybe he was, Carolyn reflected miserably. Maybe he wanted nothing more to do with her or anybody else after the cruel things she'd said to him, the way she'd behaved.

But surely, she argued with herself, a lifetime of friendship still meant something, didn't it? Aside from their recent intimacy and all their conflicts, she certainly had every right to check up on an old friend and see how he was doing.

So she reached for the phone again, her hands trembling with nervous excitement. But something still kept her from dialing the familiar number, and she knew it was her own fear.

If she called him now they'd start all over again, but this time it would be on his terms. She'd have to leave him free to live as he pleased, and those terms were terrifying to her. The thought of bringing Vernon back into her life, sharing and opening and softening to him and then losing him, was enough to drive the breath from her body, to send her into a dry-mouthed panicky whirl of bitter dread.

"Oh, God," Carolyn whispered aloud, gazing at the telephone. "Oh, God, Vern, why won't you just—"

The telephone rang.

Carolyn jumped, badly startled, then stared at the phone in alarm. It shrilled again and she picked it up, feeling a little shaky.

"Hello?"

"Could I speak to Carolyn, please?"

"It's...it's me," Carolyn whispered, her heart beating crazily.

"Carolyn," Vernon said quietly at the other end of the line. "Didn't sound like you. I thought it was Lori."

"No, she's...she's with a client tonight. How are you?"

"Just fine," he said.

But he didn't sound fine. He sounded strange, rather distant and cautious, not at all the laughing cheerful man she'd always known, or the passionate lover of recent times.

"I saw you in town a couple of days ago," Carolyn ventured in a small voice. "I guess you didn't notice me, though. You were just going into the library."

"I guess so," he agreed, apparently not interested. "Actually, I just called you about the barbecue, Carolyn."

"The barbecue?"

"The opening-day celebration at the Hole in the Wall. I wondered if you'd like to go with me. It's two weeks from today."

"I know when it is. I just wasn't sure if I..."

"Okay," he said instantly. "If you don't want to, that's fine. I just thought you might be—"

"No!" Carolyn said hastily. "No, Vern, I wasn't saying that. I was just...all right," she added, feeling a surge of pleasurable excitement. "I'll go with you. What time?"

"Apparently Scott's got a lot of demonstrations and things planned, and a big horseshoe tournament, so there'll be stuff going on all day. How about if I pick you up around two o'clock?"

"Well, all right," Carolyn said again. "Sure, that'll be..."

"Good," Vernon said briskly, his voice as cool and formal as if they were strangers arranging a business luncheon. "I'll see you then."

"Vern, I—"

"Sorry, Carolyn," he interrupted. "I have to go now. See you in a couple of weeks."

"Goodbye, Vern," she murmured tonelessly and hung up the phone, staring at it in stunned disbelief. No chatting or jokes or cheerful gossip, no inquiries about her life or Bluebonnet's welfare, no news about himself or what he was doing.

If he was going to be so brusque, why had he bothered to call at all? Was he just trying to show her that he didn't care anymore, that he'd gotten over all his feelings for her and was able to be merely a casual acquaintance?

Carolyn glared at the telephone, trying to recapture her old energizing feelings of anger. But she couldn't. Her body was still singing from the pure excitement of hearing his voice, and her heart was doing flip-flops. She wanted him so much, ached for him, hungered for the man with every fiber of her being.

Two weeks, Carolyn thought. She had to wait two weeks to see him again, and then she had to try somehow to overcome his wary hurt feelings before they could learn to be close again.

And what about your own terror? she asked herself cruelly. *What about that, girl? Maybe you can talk him back into your world. But can you talk yourself into accepting him, or is the same thing just going to happen all over again?*

It was a question to which she had no answer.

A WEEK PASSED, dragging by on leaden feet even though the world was still bursting with spring, still celebrating its newness and freshness and glorious rebirth.

Carolyn spent hours trying on outfits for the barbecue, mocking herself all the while for her ridiculous adolescent behavior. But no matter how she tried to discipline herself, she still shivered with excitement when she remembered Vernon's voice on the phone, and warmed with sexual yearnings every time she recalled their night together.

Maybe things would be different after the barbecue. Maybe he just needed some time to himself right now, and after they had a chance to talk and relax with each other again, get that angry scene behind them, then they could...

Carolyn frowned and gazed across the hay meadow at the shimmering hazy sky, already heavy with the promise of afternoon heat though it was still quite early in the morning.

"Good morning, Carolyn," Karl said, approaching from the barn with a pail of crushed oats in one hand and a mass of coiled twine in the other. "Looks like another scorcher, don't it?"

"Hi, Karl," Carolyn said, smiling at the young foreman. "It sure does. But I smell a thunderstorm, too."

"Well, it's the time for 'em," Karl said, pausing beside her and leaning his arms on the top rail of the fence. "An' it's gettin' hot so early this year, I guess we gotta expect the odd thunderstorm."

Carolyn glanced at his boyish profile, tempted once more to ask him about his relationship with Rosa Martinez. She'd seen their shy friendship, and she wanted to let Karl know how much she approved. But until one of them confided in her, it was their business and she'd best keep out of it.

"Old Hank Travis says it's going to rain real hard. He's predicting floods and all kind of problems," Carolyn said, a trace of nervousness in her voice.

Karl looked over at his employer with quick concern. "I never known ol' Hank to be wrong about the weather," he said. "When's he figger it's comin'?"

"This week, I guess. But we don't have to be concerned, do we, Karl? I mean, even a big flood wouldn't affect us much anymore, would it? Not the way we have the ranch laid out now."

"I don't think so," Karl said. "We got all the buildin's above the floodplain now, an' the hay crop wouldn't suffer too much at this stage. An' the riverbank's real high an' mostly reinforced all along. We should maybe move all them cows an' calves outta the stubble an' up into the north pasture, though, if Hank Travis is callin' for high water."

Carolyn nodded. "Okay, I think I'd feel better if we did that. Could you send somebody out this afternoon to gather the cows, Karl?"

"I'll go," he said at once. "I'll take Rosa to help me," he added casually, but his face reddened a little. "She's workin' that high-headed sorrel gelding, an' he sure needs a good long ride."

Again Carolyn was tempted to say something, but Karl was already moving away, hurrying to get his chores done.

Her thoughts were interrupted by the arrival of a car that pulled up behind her in small cloud of dust. Carolyn turned and glanced with an absent smile at Beverly and Lori, who were in the front seat.

"Good morning, girls. Where's everybody going?" Carolyn asked.

"We're heading over to the Double C," Beverly answered. "I have some photographs and fabric samples that Amanda wanted me to show Cynthia."

"And I'm working with Ruth and Tyler on some financial projections for the winery," Lori added.

Carolyn smiled at them a little wistfully. They both looked so happy and full of energy, so directed and purposeful and busy with their plans. She, on the other hand, wasn't doing a thing but waiting. Waiting for the minutes and hours and days to pass until next weekend, until Vernon Trent would finally stand in front of her and she'd say...

"See you later, Mama," Beverly said. "Oh, by the way," she added casually, rolling her window down farther so she could converse more easily, "I was talking to Scott yesterday, and he said—"

"Scott?" Carolyn interrupted with a teasing grin. "My, aren't we getting friendly?"

Beverly ignored her. "And he's interested in making you an offer on that little piece of rocky land down next to the highway. You remember how Daddy always said he wished he could find somebody dumb enough to take that property off his hands?"

Carolyn nodded.

"Well, Scott wants it for something, I forget what.

Maybe RV parking, or something. He said you should call him, Mama.''

Carolyn nodded again, and watched as the car vanished down the drive.

Then she resumed her walk up to the house, frowning thoughtfully.

She had no objection to selling Scott Harris the land in question, a useless little piece of rock and cactus that had been cut off from the rest of their property years ago when the highway went through. As a matter of fact, she found herself much less opposed to the dude ranch altogether now that she'd actually seen the operation and met its new owner. If Scott wanted the land, she might as well just...

Carolyn stopped abruptly, struck by a sudden thought.

She'd need a realtor to close the deal, wouldn't she? She could hardly be expected to handle the sale of that land all by herself. It was a perfect excuse to call Vernon Trent without looking as if she was just longing to hear his voice again. Quickening her pace, smiling with sudden excitement, Carolyn hurried into her kitchen and dialled Vernon's office number.

''Sorry, Carolyn,'' Betty said. ''Vern's not in the office ''

Carolyn's smile faded and her heart, still beating madly in anticipation, began to slow. ''My goodness, is it coffee time already?'' she asked, trying to hide her disappointment and keep her voice light. "Is that man over at the Longhorn at this hour of the morning?"

Betty's voice over the telephone sounded worried, and Carolyn tensed as she listened.

"No, he's not at the Longhorn either, Carolyn. He was in real early, about six o'clock, I guess, doing a bunch of paperwork, but he left before I even got here. I hardly see him at all anymore. He's not taking on any new business right now," Betty went on, her voice rising a little in her concern, "and he said I should refer any calls to the agency in the city until the end of the month. It's real strange, Carolyn. I'm getting worried."

Carolyn was worried, too, knowing what a cheerful workaholic the man was, and how out of character this behavior appeared. But she said casually, "Maybe he's gone fishing, Betty. Maybe he's decided it's time he had a holiday."

"Either that," Betty said darkly, "or he's got a girlfriend stashed somewhere and he's spending every minute with her."

Carolyn shuddered at the picture of another woman savoring those kisses, being caressed by those gentle hands, laughing and whispering and lying beneath the body that Carolyn hungered for.

With a heroic effort she kept her voice cheerful and casual. "Well, there you go. That's probably what's happening, Betty," she said, "and more power to him. Poor Vern's been lonely for a long time. I guess he's entitled to some happiness."

They exchanged a few more casual pleasantries and then Carolyn hung up, turning gloomily to contemplate the spacious kitchen that usually brought her such pleasure.

But the beautiful room was no comfort to her this morning. The day stretched ahead of her, an endless aching void that needed to be filled somehow, with meaningless activities that served only to pass the interminable moments stretching between her and next weekend.

Maybe she'd go through the livestock book and update the pedigree information on all the purebred cattle. That was a painstaking tedious chore, one that she always hated, and it would take all day.

With sudden decision, Carolyn placed the dishes into the sink and marched into her office. Her stride was brisk and purposeful but her face was strained, her blue eyes dark with fear.

Where in hell *was* the man, and what exactly was he doing?

CHAPTER TEN

VERNON TRENT SQUINTED over his shoulder at the darkening skyline, his breath coming in noisy ragged gasps as he ran.

Storm clouds had gathered, building ominously above the western hills. The sultry air contained a strangely metallic scent. Lightning split the sky, followed by a distant rumble of thunder.

"Looks like it's gonna pour, Alvin," Vernon said, panting as he glanced down at the small ugly Australian blue heeler who was trotting along the rutted path beside him. "If I get caught out here in quicksand or something, will you be like Lassie and go for help?"

The dog ignored him and continued to race grimly for the shelter of the distant ranch buildings, his ragged mottled sides heaving with effort.

"Maybe not," Vernon said with a brief grin, and stumbled on a twisted root snaking across the path.

"You didn't have to come, you know," he told the dog.

Alvin wasn't a real sparkling conversationalist,

Vernon mused, but he was the best available at the moment.

"Fact, I told you to stay behind, remember?" Vernon continued in a gasping voice. "I told you it'd be too rough for you. But would you listen? Oh, no, not ol' Alvin. You had to prove how macho you were, right? You had to…"

Eventually Vernon fell silent out of pure necessity. It was taking every ounce of strength he had just to maintain this pace, and try to keep ahead of the storm sweeping in at their heels.

Another vivid spear of lightning split the sky from zenith to horizon. Thunder sounded almost simultaneously, a deafening booming roar that made the buildings shake, just as Vernon and his frantic companion reached the shelter of a tumbledown unpainted barn. Side by side they bolted through the sagging door into the dusty interior, which was illuminated by a single bulb on a long dusty cord.

Vernon threw himself full-length onto a pile of loose hay covered with canvas, while Alvin whimpered in terror and scurried underneath a rusty wheelbarrow, compressing himself into a tight furry ball.

"Poor ol' Alvin," Brock Munroe commented with a grin from his seat on an upended pail. "He just hates thunderstorms. These days I find him in bed with me about half the time."

Vernon grimaced and rolled over onto his back,

gasping, his chest heaving painfully. "I can think…" he began jerkily, and then paused for breath, "of lots more…appealing bed partners…than Alvin."

"Me, too," Brock agreed wistfully. "Say, you look a little tuckered, Vern."

Vernon glared at the younger man with as much dignity as he could muster.

"How'd I do?" he panted.

Brock consulted his watch. "Best yet. Just over twenty-two minutes. You're almost runnin' seven-minute miles, Vern. Pretty soon I'll be able to enter you in the Texas Relay. With the odds I could get on you," he added, "I'd likely win a million bucks."

Vernon sat up, and grinned at Brock. "Not bad for an old guy, right?" he said.

Brock nodded, then got up to haul Alvin out from under the wheelbarrow and cradle the shivering animal in his arms, caressing his ears and nuzzling him fondly. Vernon watched, touched by the big man's tenderness with the terrified dog.

Brock Munroe was about ten years younger than Vernon Trent. Throughout the past decade the two of them had enjoyed a warm casual friendship based on nothing more substantial than a sense of humor and a shared interest in sports cars.

Brock was a tall, lean, handsome man with thick dark hair, laughing brown eyes and an appealing disheveled look that women apparently found irresistible. They flocked around him every time he went to town, but Brock never seemed to have much time for a love life. He was too busy building up the ranch that his lazy gambling father had almost run into the ground before he died.

"Twenty-two minutes, hey?" Vernon repeated with satisfaction. "I'm real pleased with that, Brock. You know, I think old Alvin could have made it in ten," he added, "if the thunderstorm had blown up a little sooner."

Brock chuckled and set the dog gently under the wheelbarrow again, then turned to pull a small pile of gleaming chrome bars into the center of the barn. Whistling cheerfully, he started to fasten a series of weights to various bars.

Vernon watched and groaned. "Come on, Brock, not today," he pleaded. "Let's not bother with the weights today. Not after such a good run, and all those calisthenics."

"The whole routine," Brock said implacably. "We worked this out together, an' you told me you wanted to do the whole routine, every day. You made me promise I wouldn't let you weasel your way out of any of it."

Vernon exchanged an eloquent glance with Alvin, who was huddled under the wheelbarrow, whimpering as the thunder rumbled and rain hammered against the weathered roof of the barn. "That poor little sucker looks as miserable as I feel,'' Vernon told Brock. ''Can't you have some pity on us both just this once? How about if we all go up to the house and eat cookies?''

''Nope,'' Brock said. ''Strip,'' he added laconically. ''These things are all ready.''

Sighing and muttering, Vernon tugged off his damp shirt and singlet and stepped out of his jogging pants, finally standing naked except for his running shoes and boxer shorts.

Brock examined the other man's body with an air of detachment, as if he were some likely specimen of livestock.

''Not bad,'' he said grudgingly. ''Getting a *little* better.''

Vernon looked down at his own torso, smiling in spite of himself. ''Like hell,'' he said cheerfully. ''It's great. I haven't been in such good shape since boot camp.''

It was true, he thought. In the weeks since he'd put himself on a rigid diet and started coming out to Brock's place for this regimen of heavy physical training, he'd dropped fourteen pounds and gained masses of hard flat muscle along his upper body.

His stomach was getting so firm that the ribs showed faintly above his ridged abdomen, and his legs looked lean and strong. He was warmly tanned from hours of running half-naked out in the blazing sun on Brock's sprawling acres, and best of all, he could push himself a lot further now than he would have believed possible just a month ago.

"We'll start with arm curls," Brock said, approaching his charge with a couple of short weighted bars. "Twenty-five each arm. Real slow an' easy for maximum extension. Then sit-ups."

"Oh, no. Not *sit-ups,*" Vernon groaned. "Please, Brock."

"Fifty of 'em," Brock said, unmoved. "An' if you can push yourself to do ten more, you get an extra helping of salad tonight."

"God, you're a brutal man," Vernon complained, taking the weights and bracing his legs, preparing to count off the arm curls. "You remind me of someone, Brock, you know that?"

Brock merely nodded, frowning critically as he watched Vernon's technique. Vernon hefted the weights automatically, his biceps bulging and flexing. He was only dimly aware of what he was doing. He was thinking about Carolyn, about her sternness over his diet and her disapproval of his life-style.

She was going to be so surprised and happy when she saw him. Vernon grinned in anticipation, dreaming about her eyes, her body, her arms and lips and soft golden skin....

"Slow down, man," Brock complained. "You're

pumping away like a madman. That won't do you any good.''

"Sorry," Vernon said, embarrassed by his own thoughts.

He adjusted his arm curls to the slow steady pace that Brock demanded, and returned to his wistful thoughts of Carolyn.

He found it such agony, this self-imposed time away from her, this constant longing to see her and touch her and hear her voice. Last week when he'd called her, it had been all he could do not to break down, beg to see her. He'd had to hold himself in so tightly that he probably ended up sounding like an idiot, but at least she'd agreed to go to the barbecue with him.

And now the barbecue was only a few days away. Soon he'd see her again, dazzle her with his surprise.

Vernon knew his secret was safe, that nobody in town suspected what he was doing. Brock Munroe was nothing if not discreet. Even Betty, though she tended to gossip a lot more than Brock, hadn't gotten a close enough look at her employer lately to suspect anything. Vernon had even taken care to wear baggy clothes around town so nobody would get wind of his activities and start talking before he was ready to display what he'd accomplished.

All this secrecy was important to Vernon, because he wanted Carolyn to be the first to know. This new look and new life-style was his gift to her. It was his apology for hurting her and his earnest promise that as far as he was able, he intended to make her future safe and happy.

God, he loved her so much! It made him weak as a kitten, just thinking about her, remembering her in his arms.

Vernon frowned, battered suddenly by all the old doubts. What if she really didn't care for him at all anymore, and had just agreed to go to the barbecue out of neighborly courtesy? What if his weight loss and new physical conditioning just left her cold, and they'd never have the chance to...

"Okay," Brock was saying disgustedly. "If you're gonna keep pumping at those things like you're Hulk Hogan or something, we might as well just start on the sit-ups. Get down on the canvas, Vern. Alvin, come sit on his feet."

Alvin slunk reluctantly out from under the wheelbarrow, tail and ears drooping, and cast Brock a bitter sidelong glance that made Vernon forget his worries and smile.

For a brief merciful time, all thoughts of Carolyn fled from his mind. He concentrated on the gritty agony of performing fifty sit-ups to Brock's exacting specifications, while Alvin lay warm and solid on his shaking extended legs.

"HI, CAROLYN. Wet enough for you?" Manny Hernandez asked cheerfully, stepping into the warm lighted interior of the Townsend barn and shaking moisture from his cap, his long raincoat, his boots and gloves.

"Oh, it's certainly getting there," Carolyn said dryly, greeting him in the doorway. "I've never seen our river so high. Or at least, not for years."

"Any danger?" Manny asked quickly, concern in his voice.

Carolyn shook her head. "We prepared for this, Manny, years ago before Frank died. We still run one herd down on the floodplain but Karl moved them to higher ground a few days ago." Manny nodded. "Most everybody says the same thing. I guess we don't have to worry a lot about flood damage. It's sure raining, though, isn't it? God, seems like the skies will never empty."

"I wonder what's going to happen to the barbecue over at the Hole in the Wall?" Carolyn said, trying not to show her anxiety about that particular social event. "It's scheduled for the day after tomorrow. Will Scott cancel it if the rain doesn't stop?"

"Hell, no," Manny said cheerfully. "He's got enough room out there to shelter the whole community under one roof if he needs to. Besides, the forecast is for clearing. It's supposed to break tomorrow and we might even have sunshine by Saturday. You know Texas weather, Carolyn…it could be hot and dry by then.''

Carolyn relaxed and smiled.

''Oh, by the way,'' Manny said, ''I saw Vern this morning, told him you were looking for him to talk about selling that little piece of land to Scott Harris.''

Carolyn's heart leaped and thudded, but she kept her voice casual. ''Oh, good. What did he say, Manny? I haven't been able to get hold of him at all.''

''Neither has anybody else. He just said that sounded fine, and he'd talk to you about it soon. Said he was real glad you'd gotten over being upset about the dude ranch, and that Scott Harris was likely going to be a good neighbor to you.''

''How did he…how did he look? I mean, was he…'' her voice trailed off and she made aimless circles with her rubber boot on the muddy floor of the barn.

''He looked all right, I guess. He was in his car, and he didn't get out. Just the same, it was the closest I've been to Vern for about a month. He's gotten to be a real mystery man, ol' Vern has.''

''He certainly has,'' Carolyn agreed. ''Well, let's have a look at this little fella, okay, Manny? I'm interested in hearing your opinion.''

Manny followed her across the barn, bent over and

examined Bluebonnet, who thumped his tail at the touch of those familiar brown hands.

"Well, well," Manny said thoughtfully. "I think you're right, Carolyn. I think maybe today might be the day."

"Shh," Carolyn hissed urgently, and drew the young man closer to her. "It's Teresa," she whispered, in answer to his inquiring glance. "She hides in here somewhere and listens all the time. She probably won't be around when it's pouring rain like this, but if by any chance she is, I don't want her getting her hopes up until we're really sure."

Manny, who knew about Bluebonnet's little guardian angel, nodded. "Good idea," he whispered back. "But it looks pretty good, Carolyn. He's still weak, but the fever's finally dropping and his eyes and mucous membranes look clearer than before. We could see a real dramatic improvement from now on."

Carolyn nodded and looked at the terrier. Manny had removed the cast a few days earlier and the injured dog now made feeble attempts to stand up, though he was still weak from his long bout with fever.

The knowledge that Bluebonnet was going to be all right should have made her happy, but it didn't. She stared into the little dog's bright dark eyes and understood at last what Vernon had been trying to tell her all this time.

Nothing was connected, and there were no guarantees when it came to life.

Bluebonnet might recover and thrive, but that
didn't make J.T. any safer or ensure that the other
people Carolyn loved couldn't be harmed. Life was
too terrifying, she thought wearily. It was all so
damned sad and scary, all of it....

"Carolyn?" Manny asked, looking at her in alarm.

Carolyn met his eyes with a small wintry smile of
apology, and turned quietly away from the little dog.
She pulled her raincoat collar up, tugged an old canvas hat over her hair and walked beside the young
veterinarian into the rain.

TERESA LAY plastered against the floor up in the dark
loft, her eyes fixed to the knothole in the plank floor,
her thin little body rigid with terror.

She'd hardly been able to hear anything they said
with the rain pounding on the bare roof just over her
head, and part of the time they'd been whispering,
too.

But Teresa had heard and seen enough.

She'd heard Manny say today was the day. She'd
seen how Gloriana hushed him quickly and whispered to him and then turned to stare at Bluebonnet,
her beautiful face looking so sad.

They were giving up.

They were tired of looking after the little dog, and

now they were going to put him to sleep. Bluebonnet would never have the chance to run and play like other dogs, to dig holes in the garden and hide bones in them or to sneak into Teresa's room at night to sleep at the foot of her bed. He'd be dead, cold and stiff and rotting under the ground like the little colt that had died last week when the coyotes got it.

Tears welled up in the child's eyes. She dashed a dirty hand across her eyes, swallowed hard and then sat up hugging her knees.

Of course, it hadn't come as a complete surprise to Teresa. She'd long since made plans in case Bluebonnet's safety was ever threatened. But she hadn't counted on this rain, which made everything a lot more complicated.

Frowning, Teresa crept over to the small ventilation slit and peered out. The whole ranch yard was under water, and the trees bowed under the driving force of the rain.

But Teresa had heard Manny say the sun might shine tomorrow.

She and Bluebonnet couldn't wait till tomorrow. People were going to kill Bluebonnet today, and she had to save him before that happened. She had to take him to the secret place she'd prepared for him. She had food hidden away there, supplies, everything they needed. It wouldn't be nearly as nice with this rain pouring down, but they'd help each other through it, and then when the sun started shining again they'd be on their own, free from everybody, free to laugh and play and love each other....

Teresa sighed blissfully. Then, galvanized with sudden energy, she hurried across the loft, slipped down the ladder and ran over to the manger where Bluebonnet lay waiting for her, his tail thumping, his dark eyes bright with adoration.

CAROLYN CAST a rueful glance at the pile of clothes on her bed. She couldn't decide what to wear to the barbecue at the dude ranch, day after tomorrow. Every time she settled on an outfit and felt a surge of relief at having reached a decision, doubts would start to nag at her again.

This white dress and the turquoise necklace, for instance. What if it looked too girlish for a woman in her mid-forties? What if Vernon got the impression that she was just trying to snare him by dressing this way? Or worse, that she was showing off, flaunting her expensive jewelry? Maybe she should just wear her denim skirt and a T-shirt. After all, lots of people would be dressed casually....

"Mama?" Beverly said, popping her golden head around the door. "You in here?"

"In my bathroom," Carolyn called.

Beverly strolled into the room, blue eyes widening

as she saw the heap of discarded clothes on the bed. "Goodness sakes, Mama. What's all this?"

Carolyn came out of the bathroom, tying her hair back with a blue cotton scarf and looking a little abashed.

"I'm just... I'm sorting through some of my things," she said hastily. "Trying to decide what I should get rid of before I let Amanda take over my wardrobe."

Beverly's eyes brightened. She loved these earnest discussions about fashion and makeup, but was seldom able to get her mother interested. "Can I help?" she said. "Maybe we can trade a few things," she added cozily, riffling through the pile. "I've always loved this pink shirt, Mama, but you never wear it."

"Sure," Carolyn said. "Whatever. Amanda says I shouldn't wear pink, anyhow."

"She's right," Beverly said. "Your best colours are...oh, I forgot," she added, holding a denim jumpsuit against her slender body and frowning at herself in the mirror. "Rosa's in the kitchen. She wants to talk to you."

"Rosa?" Carolyn asked blankly. "What would she want at this time of night?"

Beverly shrugged. "I don't know. She sure seems upset about something, though. Say, Mama, can I try on this green—"

"Whatever," Carolyn repeated, feeling a flicker of

concern. "Just take what you want, dear, and hang the rest back in the closet."

She hurried down the hall and into the kitchen, where Rosa Martinez stood by the door in a dripping raincoat.

"Rosa?" Carolyn asked. "What's the matter?"

"It's Teresa," the woman whispered. "She's gone."

"Gone?" Carolyn repeated. "What do you mean, Rosa?"

"She didn't come home for supper," Rosa said, twisting the edge of her rain hat with thin brown fingers. Her knuckles were white and her body trembled.

"Does she always come home at supper time?" Carolyn asked.

"Always," Rosa said. "There's a nature program on television at five o'clock and she never misses it. And then it's one of her chores to help me serve the food and do the dishes after the men eat. She's really good about it."

Carolyn glanced at her watch. "It's almost nine o'clock now, Rosa. Where do you think she might be? Where would she go in this weather?"

Rosa shrugged helplessly. "She could be anywhere. But with all the rain, I'm really starting to worry. I haven't seen her since lunch, and it's getting so cold, and the river..."

Rosa's fear began to infect Carolyn, with a slow creeping sense of alarm.

"What about Bluebonnet?" Carolyn asked suddenly.

"He's gone, too," Rosa said, her face twisting with pain. "That's what really scares me, Mrs. Townsend. She loves that little dog, and she takes real good care of him, always. She wouldn't take him out in this weather unless she was...she was..."

"We'll find her," Carolyn said, feeling less confident than she sounded. She saw Beverly come into the kitchen carrying an armful of clothes. The girl stopped abruptly in the doorway and gazed from her mother to Rosa.

"It's Teresa," Carolyn told her. "She hasn't come home all day, and Rosa says Bluebonnet is missing, too."

"This time of night?" Beverly said, frowning. "But, Mama, she wouldn't take Bluebonnet out in this rain unless..."

"We already figured that out," Carolyn said.

"How late is she?" Beverly asked Rosa.

"At least four hours. No matter what she's doing, she always comes home before five o'clock," Rosa said. "Karl, he's been out looking for her since before supper, all her usual hiding places, and he can't find her anywhere. He even checked the hayloft in the barn. That's likely where she's been spying on you these past weeks, Mrs. Townsend,'' Rosa added, glancing over at Carolyn. ''Karl figured out tonight that she must have been hiding up there all along. He went right away to look, but she's not up there now.''

Beverly stood thinking a moment longer, then turned to her mother. ''We'd better get some more help,'' she told Carolyn with sudden decision. ''The sooner the better. She's probably all right, just hidden away in a building somewhere, but in this kind of weather with the river so high we can't take any chances. I'll call the Double C and ask J.T. to send some of their men over here, and the Hole in the Wall, too. Scott has quite a few men who can help. You and Rosa get our people organized, all right? And somebody should stay here in the house and coordinate things....''

Suiting actions to words, Beverly dropped the pile of clothes on an oak bench by the wall and hurried across the room to the telephone, punching buttons rapidly as she spoke.

Carolyn watched in amazement as her daughter suddenly became a crisp competent organizer, a whirl of efficiency with no thought for anything but the welfare of a little girl whom none of them really knew.

TERESA HUDDLED in the darkness of the big crate, gripping Bluebonnet tightly in her arms. He struggled to get free and she set him gently in her lap, holding him in place with her hands. Her flagging spirits were cheered somewhat by the feeling of his warm wriggling body and his damp pink tongue licking her fingers. Suddenly he pulled away from her restraining hands and stood upright in her lap, little paws braced against her thin chest, happily licking her face.

"Bluebonnet," Teresa whispered. "Bluebonnet, you're standing up! You never did that before! You must be feeling lots better. Lots and lots better, aren't you?" she crooned, cuddling him fiercely.

And they would have killed him, she thought bitterly. They thought he was still sick, and they would have put him to sleep forever if she hadn't rescued him.

The child shifted on the hard wooden surface, her faltering courage bolstered by this grim thought. No matter how hard and scary this was, no matter how much she felt like crying, it was worth everything to protect Bluebonnet. Just the two of them against the world, that was what it was, and they had to stick together.

What if it was lonely and a little frightening out here now that the darkness had closed in on them? They had each other, and that was what mattered.

"Don't we, Bluebonnet?" she whispered over the

roar of the rain. "We have each other, don't we? I love you so much, Bluebonnet. I love you so much."

As if he understood, the little dog settled in her lap again, turning around a few times and brushing his furry tail across her arm before he curled against her in a warm comforting ball and fell asleep.

Teresa cradled him a moment longer, then tucked him down in a corner, covered him carefully with burlap, and eased open the lid of the big wooden box.

When she'd first thought of this plan it had seemed like such a wonderful idea to hide overnight with Bluebonnet in the heavy crate she'd hauled out to the island. They were so small, she and Bluebonnet, that there was lots of room for both of them inside the crate.

"I guess I won't be able to fall asleep," she murmured, speaking out loud because it was really starting to get dark and scary outside and the sound of her voice gave her courage. "If I fall asleep, we might suffocate in here, Bluebonnet. And I can't leave the lid off or we'll get soaked. So I just have to open it every now and then, just a little, but I won't let you get wet."

She flipped the switch on her battered old flashlight and shone it briefly across the furry head resting against the dry warm sacks, assuring herself once more that Bluebonnet was safe. Then she moved the lid aside, leaving the cover over the dog's half of the

box and wincing as the rain slashed into her eyes and
cascaded onto her shoulders.

Teresa hunched herself up against the driving onslaught and shone her flashlight into the darkness.
Puzzled, she stood up and squinted, blinking the
moisture from her eyelashes.

Everything looked so weird. Nothing was where it
should be.

The bushes that ringed the little rocky island
seemed to be much smaller now, shorter than they'd
been just a few hours earlier. Even the island itself
looked smaller. It was like some kind of evil magic
was afoot, as if the night had turned into a hungry
monster that was nibbling at the edges of everything,
gobbling up the world.

Standing in the box, gazing in bewilderment at the
fierce storm that raged all around her, Teresa felt
dampness at her feet and looked down quickly, shining her flashlight onto the ground. She recoiled in
horror as she saw the oozing water that pooled at the
base of the box, creeping into the lower seams.

Slowly her mind began to grasp what was happening.

There was water everywhere. The box was standing in water, the bushes were swimming in it, even
the gnarled old tree roots were covered, the bottom
of the tree trunks hidden by the swirling surface of
the river. And the shoreline, usually so close and

comforting, was no longer visible at all. There was just water churning and frothing everywhere, a whole black world of water. Teresa frowned, trying to recall what the river had been like when she crossed over earlier that afternoon with Bluebonnet in her arms.

There had been more water than usual. She remembered that because the big stepping stones had been mostly covered and very slippery, and she'd had to be so careful not to fall. But she hadn't seen anything to make her think that her little island wouldn't be safe.

But now, all that had changed. The river had become a roaring thundering demon that threatened everything. Huge waves slashed and pounded against the rocks, sending a cold white spray up over her head. Tree branches and other debris swirled past in the darkness, sometimes getting caught in the bushes on the island, sometimes even brushing against the sides of the box. The rain continued to hammer on the surface of the river and the noise was deafening, so loud that even if Teresa screamed at the top of her lungs, nobody would ever be able to hear.

She gulped and swallowed a sob of terror, trying to think what to do. Maybe if they just stayed here, they'd be safe. The box was leaking a little, but it wouldn't fill up with water, she was fairly certain of that. And even if the water did start to come in, she could hold Bluebonnet up high and use her cup to bail out the bottom so they'd stay dry.

The child brightened a little, hunching down into the crate and pulling the lid carefully over their heads again. She comforted herself by picturing their heavy box as a kind of little boat.

But what if..?

Bluebonnet began to whimper and moved toward her, climbing onto her leg. All at once the box rocked. Teresa clutched the dog to her chest as more water trickled in about her legs.

Hastily, she unzipped her waterproof jacket and tucked Bluebonnet inside against her chest. Then she pushed the box lid carefully to one side and stood up, climbing out onto the sodden grass, holding on to the box frantically to keep from being swept away in the swirling flood. The flashlight was ripped from her hand and she was forced to operate by feeling alone, pushing the lid of the crate back into place and climbing up on top of it, gazing fearfully down at the water that licked and tore at the sides of the box. The wooden crate was still wedged solidly among a circle of big rocks, safe for the moment, though it rocked alarmingly with each fresh wave.

Teresa moaned with terror as their makeshift raft bucked and shifted. The river was like some cruel fiend, stalking them, drawing nearer and nearer, ready to devour them....

Teresa screamed aloud. "Help! Oh, please, somebody help me! Mama, I'm here, I'm on the island, help me...."

But her words were torn from her mouth and thrown away by the wind, and all her screaming made a sound so small and frail that it was no more than a breath, drowned instantly in the rushing mighty tons of water.

Teresa clutched Bluebonnet to her chest and thought with fierce longing about all the people in her life, about Rosalind and Sir Galahad, about Gloriana and Vernon and about the other ranch hands who sometimes frightened her. Now, she'd give anything in the world just to see any one of them. She couldn't even remember why she'd always been so afraid of them.

Tonight, this minute, Teresa knew only that she loved all of them. And she desperately wanted somebody, anybody to come for her and Bluebonnet, to hold them and hug them, to kiss them and tuck them away in her warm safe bed with a light on and soft pillows and her books nearby, with big strong walls and windows to keep out the water that wanted to tear and ravage her....

"Help me, Mama," she sobbed. "Please, Mama, I'm so scared. Please..."

But her voice was just a whimper now and the storm was raging full force, a thunderous roaring howling inferno of water. And the river was getting closer all the time. It was edging nearer in the darkness, tugging at the sides of the box. Like a horrible hungry monster with jaws agape, the river was waiting for the chance to get her and Bluebonnet, to creep up and snatch them from the last place of safety in the whole world.

CHAPTER ELEVEN

CYNTHIA MCKINNEY RETURNED to the living room and sank into her chair by the fireplace, picking up her knitting and staring at it blankly. Her hands were unsteady but she squared her shoulders and tried to smile at her husband, who sat opposite her.

"That was Tyler on the phone," she said in response to J.T.'s questioning glance. "He asked if we could send Lettie Mae and Virginia over to help in the kitchen. He says they've got dozens of people there now, with more joining the search all the time, and they need extra hands to help make coffee and sandwiches."

"Did you tell him they're already on their way?" J.T. asked.

"I didn't have to. They arrived before he hung up. It sounds like a real madhouse over there," she added, struggling hard to keep her voice even.

"Any progress?" J.T. asked his wife.

Cynthia shook her head. "Not yet, I guess. Ty says that one of the ranch hands saw her in the upper pasture this morning, out by the old limestone formations, so they're concentrating the search over there. They think she might be hiding in one of the caves.''

''God,'' J.T muttered gloomily, staring into the flickering warmth of the fire, ''I'd give anything to be able to help, Cynthia. I feel so goddamn useless, just sitting here while they're all—''

''Don't say that!'' Cynthia interrupted passionately. ''How can you say you're not helping? You've sent seven people, five vehicles and a ton of equipment over there already. If that's not a substantial help, I don't know what is. And we've told Carolyn we'll do whatever we can to help with the rescue workers, put people up if they need to stay overnight, supply her with all the food and coffee they need, anything.''

''It's not the same,'' J.T. said morosely. ''It's not like being out there, hunting along with them. That's what they need more than anything.''

''I know, dear,'' Cynthia whispered, reaching across to squeeze her husband's hand. ''I know how hard it is for you. But you're getting better every day. If we're just patient a few more months, you'll be your old self again. Please, darling, please try not to fret so much.''

J. T. McKinney looked at his young wife and his dark restless face softened with affection. ''I love you,'' he said unexpectedly, his voice tender.

Cynthia smiled back at him, then blinked away her tears and returned to her knitting. Silence fell in the room. They could hear the rain pounding on the tall darkened windows, the howl of the wind and the ominous rumble of the swollen river.

Old Hank Travis sat with eyes half-closed, watching and listening.

They were talking love again, he thought. Seemed like that was happening a lot these days. The woman looked sweeter and softer, too, now that she was in foal. She'd lost that gaunt Boston elegance, developed a glowing rosy softness that flattered her a lot more, at least in Hank's opinion.

There was no doubt that J.T. noticed the change, Hank mused. The boy looked at her all the time with his heart in his eyes. In fact, Hank was pretty certain that J.T. was getting as much exercise up in the big master bedroom these days as he was in his slow careful walks around the ranch yard.

But that was the way it should be, Hank thought, letting his eyes drop shut and setting his chair rocking gently again. Love and sex and babies, that was what life was about when you were young. That was the way of the world.

But tragedy was the way of the world, too, he thought, frowning to himself. Like tonight, when fear and disaster hung dark and heavy in the nighttime air. Somebody was lost, out in the storm, some little kid that everybody was looking for.

Hank's eyes drooped shut, his head nodded onto his chest and the rocker stilled. He drowsed, warm and cozy by the fire, lulled by the gentle drumming of the rain and the distant roar of the storm.

Then all at once, with horrifying swiftness, the texture of the world changed. Dark wings rose and beat around Hank's ears and the cold began to suck at his legs, dragging at him, trying to pull him down into the cruel void. Water churned all around him, black and violent. The old man felt dizzy, light-headed, terrified by the relentless downward force of all those tons of power.

He flailed and fought and shouted, struggling to keep himself clear of the black rushing onslaught, and all the time he was thinking, *so this is it. This is how it feels to die.*

With every ounce of his strength he resisted, battled the cruel clutching darkness, strained to hold himself above the relentless flood, tried to keep from giving in to the dreadful bone-numbing terror that left him shaking and breathless with panic.

At last, mercifully, his eyes opened again and he sat gripping the padded arms of his rocker, blinking at the warm comfortable room, the bright leaping flames on the grate and the frightened gaze of the two people who were nearby.

It wasn't him, Hank realized slowly, limp with relief. It wasn't him, after all, who was threatened by
that dark monster.

He must have made some noise or movement in
his panicky struggles because the boy and his wife
were both staring at him.

Hank drew a deep shaking breath. "Tell 'em," he
said hoarsely, "that the little kid is on a high rocky
place somewhere, barely hangin' on. There's water
all around her. In front, behind, both sides, all
around. It's almost washin' her away, and she can't
hold on much longer."

The old man sagged back in his chair, trembling
and exhausted, while the others continued to stare at
him with blank faces. "But, Grandpa…" Cynthia began, her voice low and hesitant.

"*Tell 'em!*" Hank shouted fiercely.

Cynthia nodded and set her knitting aside with
shaking hands. Then, without another word, she got
up and ran out of the room and down the hall to the
telephone.

CAROLYN HUNG UP the phone and looked around.
Her kitchen was full of people, some making sandwiches and coffee, some packing plates of food to
be passed around in the big living room. That room,
warmed by a roaring fire in the vast stone fireplace,
had been turned into a temporary comfort station for

searchers who straggled in for a few minutes of rest, coffee and food before setting out again.

Carolyn moved back to her place by the table, buttering bread automatically and thinking about the telephone call she'd received from Cynthia McKinney.

Old Hank had apparently experienced one of his ''seein's,'' something Carolyn would have scoffed at and dismissed instantly if it had been anybody else.

But coming from Hank Travis...

Carolyn frowned and gazed off into the distance, pondering.

A high rocky place, with water all around her, front, back and sides, pulling at her...that certainly couldn't be the limestone caves. The water would never rise high enough out there to feel that close. And *pulling* at her...that sounded more like a current, like a river or a creek. But where would the water be on all sides, unless she was on some kind of island...?

Carolyn uttered a sudden little cry of shock and dropped the knife. She covered her hand with her mouth and gazed out the window, her eyes wide with terror.

The *island!* Why hadn't she thought of it before?

Of course a child like Teresa would have discovered the little island. It had been one of Carolyn's own favorite hiding places when she was a little girl,

with its feeling of high rocky fastness and the de-
lightfully scary access over that slippery row of boulders. But Carolyn had stopped going there by the
time she was ten years old, and she hadn't really
thought about the place since.

She'd never even shared the secret with her sister.
And Beverly had never discovered the island as a
child, either, being the sort of little girl who didn't
like the bugs and creeping things that lived near the
river. In fact, children living on the ranch were dis-
couraged from playing near the river at all, because
of the dangerous snakes that were said to inhabit the
bank. Copperheads and rattlesnakes and water moccasins had all been sighted there at one time or another.

But Teresa certainly wasn't the kind of child to be
frightened by such warnings. And she had already
explored the ranch so thoroughly, found so many of
the secret hiding places.

Carolyn shook her head, still gazing out the window at the darkness, thinking hard. What if the child
had gone out there earlier in the day, before the river
rose...

"Mama?" Beverly asked, whirling by with a clipboard on which she'd attached a list of various areas
of the ranch along with penciled notations of who
was searching in each zone. "Mama, what's
wrong?"

"Oh, God, Beverly," her mother whispered. "I just thought of the most awful thing."

Beverly's eyes widened in alarm at her mother's white face and strangled voice. But before the younger woman could reply, the kitchen door was flung open and Brock Monroe and Vernon Trent stepped into the shelter of the room, pulling off their wet caps.

Carolyn gazed at Vernon, whose square pleasant features looked different tonight, somehow. Maybe it was just because he was so tense and pale with concern, or because it seemed like such a miserably long time since she'd seen him last.

Her heart thudded and she felt a sudden flood of pleasure at seeing that beloved face. Everything she'd ever said to him, any disagreements they'd had or criticisms she'd expressed were wiped completely from her mind. All she wanted to do was fling herself upon him and feel the loving warmth and safety of his arms around her.

But he was standing so quietly, avoiding her eyes, and now certainly wasn't the time....

"Sorry, Carolyn," Brock was saying earnestly. "Vern and I were...busy, sort of, out at my place, didn't even hear about this until Betty called us a half hour ago. What can we do to help?"

"Have you got your truck?" Carolyn asked him,

moving quickly across the room to stand close to the two men. "The big four-wheel drive?"

Brock nodded.

Keeping her voice low so as not to cause a general alarm, she told them about Hank's vision, and her idea that Teresa might be on the little island.

"I was just thinking," she faltered, "that the water always seems highest and fastest in that narrow portion. For some reason, it seems to flow twice as hard there when the river's in flood."

Brock nodded. "The Venturi effect," he said.

Carolyn and Vernon both stared at him.

"The velocity of water through an aperture increases in direct proportion to the narrowing of the channel," Brock quoted, and then looked a little embarrassed. "I just tend to remember stuff like that," he said awkwardly. "I don't know why."

Carolyn continued to stare at the young rancher, but Vernon was already tugging on his cap and firing rapid questions.

"How wide?" he asked Carolyn.

"Wide?"

"The channel. What's the distance from the shore to the nearest solid purchase on the island?"

"Depends how high the water is. Fifteen, maybe twenty feet, I guess."

"Carolyn, do you have a long aluminum extension ladder? Thirty feet or more?" Vernon asked.

Carolyn nodded. "In the barn," she said and pulled on her oilskin slicker and rubber boots. "Come on, I'll show you. Hurry!"

Beverly came over, clipboard at the ready, giving them an inquiring glance. Carolyn hesitated, reluctant to cause a panic by voicing her fears, especially since Rosa was waiting all alone in the little cottage for news of her child.

If Teresa had really gone out to the island, the chances for her survival were poor at best. And in that case, Carolyn wanted to be the one to break the news to the child's mother.

"We're just checking some supplies down in the barn," Carolyn told Beverly finally, giving the two men a quick warning glance. "We'll be back soon," she added.

They stopped at the barn to load the big aluminum ladder in the back of Brock's truck, added a heavy-duty lantern and all the coils of nylon rope they could find, then bumped across the water-logged alfalfa fields to the river's edge.

Carolyn rode between the two men, conscious of the nearness of Vernon in the passenger seat. Though part of her still yearned to nestle close to him, her mind was on the task at hand.

"Down here," she muttered, gazing anxiously out the front window at the swirling muddy fields. "It's hard to see the trail anymore, but I think it branches off right here. If we park at the edge, we can shine the headlights right onto the island.''

Brock obeyed, wheeling the big truck around with grim expertise.

"Not too close!" Carolyn warned urgently. "The bank isn't all that secure.''

Brock nodded, his handsome face taut with concentration, and skidded to a splashing halt near the furious torrent of water.

Carolyn clambered out of the truck behind Vernon and clung to the door, battered by fierce wind-driven gusts of water. She peered into the flowing darkness, where long glittering needles of rain were illuminated faintly by the headlights of the truck.

The river was so high that there was no longer any visible channel, just a wild tumbling expanse of water. The few stunted trees on the island were faintly discernible through the storm, swaying and whipping in the wind, but the three people along the bank couldn't make out any other details. They shouted frantically, but it was impossible to hear anything over the roar of the water.

"What d'you think, Vern?" Brock asked, gazing dubiously at the older man. "Is it possible she's out there?''

Vernon frowned and stared at the dark churning river. "There's just no way to know," he said finally. "If she was there earlier, I doubt she could still be hanging on. But we have to try," he added. "Let's see if we can get the ladder down. Brock, you hold this end, and I'll..."

All three of them struggled with the heavy length of aluminum, battling the wind and rain as they tried to position the unwieldy ladder so that it stretched between the riverbank and the island.

After a number of unsuccessful attempts, they finally got the ladder into place and wedged against the rocks at the edge of the island to hold it in position.

"Is it solid, d'you think?" Brock shouted over the roar of the water, wrestling with the heaving end of the ladder as the floods buffeted it. "Have we got it wedged tight enough?"

"I can't tell," Vernon shouted back, peering into the thundering blackness. "I don't even know what it's hooked against out there. We just have to trust that it'll hold."

Carolyn shuddered, watching as Brock lashed the near end of the ladder to the bumper of his truck and then crawled onto it, testing his long body against the springy length of aluminum.

"Not too solid," he panted, stepping off, "but it's our best shot, I guess."

Vernon nodded tightly, pulled his cap down firmly onto his head and climbed out onto the ladder himself, his heavy rubberized slicker falling all around his body like a tent as he crouched on hands and knees, looking like a big dark bear crawling slowly out over the rushing current.

Brock moved back and braced his weight against the end of the ladder, trying to steady it while Vernon crept farther along its extended length.

Carolyn watched, her eyes widening in horror as she realized what they were doing.

"But..." she protested wildly, "but, why is *Vern* climbing out there? Brock, you're so much younger and thinner than he is. Maybe you should do the..."

"I can't swim," Brock said.

Carolyn stared at him blankly, absorbing his words.

She knew that Vernon could swim. In fact, he'd been county champion during their high school years. But what did swimming have to do with any of this nightmare? There was no swimming involved here, just strength, endurance and agility.

And Vernon Trent didn't have much of those, Carolyn thought in panic. He was forty-five years old, flabby and overweight and out of shape. How could he possibly be expected to...

She watched, her hands covering her mouth, moaning in terror as Vernon's bulky black form continued to inch out along the ladder into the dark raging night. Already the slippery length of aluminum was bending well below the surface of the water so only the slick oilskin over his rounded back was still visible, shining dully in the glare of the headlights, bobbing out across the rushing current with agonizing slowness.

Soon he vanished altogether, disappearing from sight in the foamy sprays of water that caught the muted glare from the headlights and flung them back into her eyes in a stinging curtain.

Carolyn blinked and trembled, her heart breaking with love and fear, her whole body concentrated in a single frenzied prayer for the man she loved...for his safety, his protection, his deliverance from the black flood that had swallowed him.

VERNON CURSED frantically as a sudden crash of muddy water pounded the ladder and nearly washed him away. He steadied himself, gripping the metal rungs beneath the surface of the water with hands that felt like clumsy lumps of ice.

This whole journey couldn't be much more than twenty or thirty feet, he thought, but it seemed like miles. He had to go so slowly to keep the ladder from springing and bucking, throwing him off just by the force of his body's movements. And the water sucked and tore at him, the current surging so powerfully that it required all his strength just to withstand its force.

He groaned under his breath, pausing to steady the

ladder, trying not to think about a helpless little child somewhere in this raging abyss. What chance would she have of surviving, if it took all his masculine strength and will just to hang on?

She's probably not here at all, he told himself, inching forward again. He winced with pain as his knee slipped harshly on the corrugated edge of a ladder rung, tearing the fabric of his jeans and scouring the flesh beneath. *More likely she's up in one of the limestone caves, scared as hell but warm and safe....*

Another wave crashed past him, grasping his body like a piece of straw and tearing him off the ladder. Vernon felt himself falling, dropping through the rushing void, his breath torn from him in one long gasp. But when he broke the churning surface, spitting and rubbing muddy bits of debris from his eyes, he was amazed to find that he still clutched one edge of the ladder with a numbed hand.

Frantically he kicked and paddled, treading water while he gripped the long shaft of slippery aluminum. Then, slowly and carefully, he pulled himself back into place, balancing delicately and distributing his weight on the swaying ladder with more brute strength and dexterity than he'd ever dreamed he had.

While he eased himself back into position he gave fervent thanks for all the training and working out he'd forced on himself during the past month. Even in this kind of dreadful nightmare it felt good to be in command of his body, to be able to force his muscles and limbs to do what was required of them.

He heard frantic muffled shouts in the distance, coming from behind, and understood that Carolyn and Brock had felt him falling off the ladder, then sensed the weight shift as he struggled to climb back on. There was no way to reassure them of his safety, because even at this small distance the roar of the river drowned out their voices. Doggedly Vernon began to creep forward again, forcing his chilled bruised hands to grip the edges of the rungs, placing his feet with infinite care as he moved on into the void.

"Dear God," he muttered aloud, gritting his teeth in agony. "How much farther can it be? I feel like I've been on this damned thing all my life."

But even as he spoke he sensed a difference in the ladder's sway, a wonderful new feeling of tautness that told him he was nearing the other end. Buoyed with sudden optimism, his weary muscles charged with fresh strength, Vernon surged forward and collapsed among the ragged rocks at the edge of the little island, gasping with relief, oblivious to the sharp jutting surfaces and the whipping branches that tore at his face.

After a few long ragged breaths he drew himself upright again and struggled forward across the sodden surface of the tiny island, clinging to the stunted trees for support while the water tore past him, waist high in places.

The night was so dark and the storm so fierce that he almost stumbled into the big crate before he saw it, a square bulking shape in the night, rocking and swaying with each new surge of the current. On the storm-tossed box a black shape was huddled, clinging to the edge of the crate with one hand and a nearby tree branch with another.

Vernon's heart gave a great leap when he saw her, then settled and steadied as a deep calm took hold of him, a sense that nothing in his life had ever been as important as this one moment.

He waded around and gathered the child in his arms, conscious of the pitiful thinness of her soaked body, her tiny fragile bones, her white terrified face in the darkness.

She sobbed and clung to him, and he felt a soft bulk in the front of her waterproof jacket, a small wriggling shape.

"Is that Bluebonnet?" he shouted close to her ear. "Is he inside your jacket?"

The child nodded, still clinging to him in the darkness, her dark cloud of wet hair whipping into his eyes and mouth as he held her.

"Good girl," he shouted again. "You look after him, and I'll look after you, okay?"

She was still sobbing too hard to answer, but Vernon sensed that she heard and understood. He shifted and braced himself against a tree trunk, deeply protective of the exhausted child in his arms, grimly conscious of the fact that she would have to cooperate if they were both to make it back to the safety of the riverbank where help was waiting.

"Teresa," he shouted, "do you know how to ride a horse?"

Again she nodded, a jerky bobbing movement of her head beneath his chin.

"Good," Vernon said. "We're going to play a little game, you and me. I'm going to be the horse, and you and Bluebonnet are going to ride me back across the river, okay? All you have to do is bend down and hang on real, real tight, and I'll do all the rest. Can you do that, sweetheart?"

Again the vigorous jerky nod.

Bless the kid, Vernon thought, hugging her tight, hot tears stinging his eyes at her courage. Bless her for being so brave, for hanging on longer already than any little kid should ever be expected to....

"Okay," he shouted aloud. "Here's the plan, kid. I'm going to carry you to the magic railroad over there, and then I'm going to crawl across on my hands and knees, and you two are going to ride on my back. Here we go."

Just as he started away the current caught the big

wooden crate beside them, flung it five feet in the air and carried it off, bouncing on the crest of the waves like a child's toy block. The little girl lifted her head and stared at the black bobbing shape, then looked up at Vernon. He caught another brief impression of a white terrified face, of big glittering eyes in the darkness. Again tears stung his eyes, and he had to swallow hard before he could speak.

"Well, it looks like we missed that boat," he forced himself to shout cheerfully. "Now our only choice is to go home on the train, I guess. Come on, sweetheart, let's take you home. Your mama's getting worried."

Vernon carried the little girl to the place where the ladder end was wedged among the rocks. Carefully he set her down, bracing her against his legs for a moment while he rolled some heavy boulders across the length of aluminum to weight it more securely. Then he lowered himself onto all fours and crept out onto the first rungs, drawing the child close beside him, praying that her courage wouldn't falter now.

"Hop on, kiddo," he shouted in her ear. "And be careful of that damned dog. I don't want him peeing on me and getting me all wet."

Miraculously, she giggled at that, a warm gust of breath against his face. Vernon laughed with her, feeling on top of the world all of a sudden, full of hope and suffused with the strength of ten men. He hugged her and kissed her icy wet cheek, then waited while she clambered onto his back, reaching up over his shoulder to make sure she was securely anchored.

Teresa bent forward, protecting the dog lodged firmly within the front of her jacket, gripping Vernon's muscular shoulders with both hands and locking her thin legs tightly around his midsection.

He waited until he was confident that she was in place, clinging to his back like a little wet limpet. Then he drew a deep shaking breath and started out on the long return journey, creeping along the flexible strip of aluminum that bent alarmingly even with the child's small added weight.

Vernon couldn't feel anything now, hardly knew where his hands and feet were or what they were doing. He was operating mostly on instinct and a grim will to survive, driven by the strength of his own resolve and little else. With each move forward the ladder dipped and plunged his head below the surface of the water, forcing him to strain upward and gasp for air when he surfaced again.

But the child and the dog, up on his back, rode mostly above the water. Teresa slipped sideways and almost fell several times, battered cruelly by the current, but she hung on to the man's body with grim determination. The storm raged around them and pulled at them as they inched along, their whole world now compressed into nothing more than a double beam of light, glimmering faintly ahead of them through the driving rain.

CHAPTER TWELVE

CAROLYN and the two men stood in the kitchen of Rosa's small clean cottage, their heavy oilskins dripping onto the pads of newspaper that covered the floor.

Carolyn shivered in the harsh overhead light, her hair hanging in wild wet tangles around her pale face. She was chilled through and almost sick with exhaustion. Vernon stood close beside her with one arm around her shoulders, holding her firmly against his side. She trembled again, fearful that if he moved away she might tumble in a heap on the soaked newspapers.

He, too, was shivering, his body racked by occasional deep spasms. Carolyn glanced up at him, but he seemed unaware of her. His face was distant and withdrawn, white with tension as he gazed fixedly down the narrow hallway.

Karl Walters, also in a long slicker, stood by the kitchen counter talking quietly with Brock.

Carolyn felt Vernon's body shift, and looked up

to see Rosa Martinez approaching down the darkened hallway.

Carolyn's mouth went dry and her throat tightened as she stared at the woman, then relaxed in a flood of relief when she saw the glow on Rosa's face, the shining happiness in her dark tear-filled eyes. "She's fine," Rosa whispered, smiling at the three visitors and going over to stand by Karl, who put an arm around her and drew her close to him.

Rosa smiled up at the young ranch foreman with a look of love and trust that brought another lump to Carolyn's throat.

"Thank you so much, Vern," Rosa whispered brokenly. "How can I ever thank you enough? What you did tonight...it was..."

"Forget it, Rosa," Vernon said, his voice husky. Carolyn felt his hand tremble on her shoulder, then grip with sudden fierceness as he composed himself. "Anybody would have done the same thing. How is she? Is she really all right?"

Rosa nodded again. "It's like a miracle," she murmured. "All she has are a few bruises, and of course she was real cold and wet, but her body temperature's normal now. Thank God."

Brock cleared his throat awkwardly after a brief hushed silence. "How's the little dog?" he asked.

Rosa smiled again and exchanged another warm glance with Karl. "Oh, he's fine. She kept him pretty dry inside her jacket, I guess, and he looks real good. Better than he ever has, actually.''

The young woman was silent a moment. Then she turned shyly to Carolyn.

''That's why she did it, Mrs. Townsend,'' Rosa said. ''Why she ran away, I mean. She heard you talking with Manny this morning and she thought you were planning to have the dog put down. She thought she was saving his life by taking him away and hiding on the island with him.''

Carolyn stared at the younger woman, her mind moving sluggishly, trying to remember.

Was it just this morning that she'd talked to Manny about Bluebonnet? It seemed like another century, another life....

Slowly the memory came back to her. She heard Manny announcing that today was the day, and herself hushing him, then whispering urgently to him. Carolyn realized with a great lurch of pain just how easily Teresa could have misread that whole scene, and how much agony the child had endured as a result.

''Oh, Rosa,'' Carolyn whispered in anguish. ''I'm so sorry.... That wasn't what we were saying at all. We'd just decided that the little dog was probably going to make it after all, and I was planning to find a way to give him to Teresa for her very own, with your permission. Oh, Rosa, I'm sorry. I just don't know how to—''

Rosa waved her hand in dismissal. ''Don't worry, Mrs. Townsend,'' she said. ''It's fine. You didn't do nothing wrong, and everything's going to be fine now. Just having her back safe again after all those awful hours is so wonderful...''

Rosa's voice broke and Karl drew her tenderly into her arms, holding her and patting her back, gazing down at her dark shining hair with quiet intensity.

Finally Rosa regained some of her composure, dashed a hand across her eyes and turned back toward Carolyn, trying to smile.

''Do you think you could talk to her for just a minute, Mrs. Townsend?'' Rosa asked. ''Could you maybe tell her that the dog is safe, and nothing's going to happen to him? I think she probably won't believe it until she hears it from you.''

''Of course,'' Carolyn murmured, her own weariness forgotten in her concern for the little girl. ''I'll go talk to her right now. Is she awake?''

Rosa nodded and watched as Carolyn pulled off her heavy raincoat, hung it by the door and faltered down the hall to the child's room, where a partly opened door cast a thin slice of pale golden light across the bare walls and ceiling of the hallway.

''Teresa?'' Carolyn murmured, opening the door

wide and stepping inside, then pulling it quietly shut behind her. "Are you awake, dear?"

She approached the bed, blinking to adjust her eyes to the dim glow of the night-light on the little bedside table.

Two pairs of big dark eyes gazed up at her, side by side, and she realized that Bluebonnet was snuggled on the pillow beside the little girl's face, his silky gray fur freshly dried and fluffed, his topknot tied back with a narrow ribbon.

Carolyn tried to smile, but her throat was tight with tears and it was all she could do to keep her voice steady.

"My goodness, he looks comfy there, doesn't he? I think there's just no doubt that you take real good care of that little dog, Teresa."

The child gazed up at Carolyn, her face white and pinched, her dark eyes enormous. Carolyn realized that she'd never been this close to Teresa Martinez, never once heard her speak.

"Can he stay?" Teresa asked, her voice hoarse and awkward, as if rusty from lack of use. "Mrs. Townsend, can he please stay with me? I'm sorry about all the trouble I caused, but please, please don't let them put Bluebonnet to sleep."

"Of course not, Teresa," Carolyn said, reaching down a gentle hand to touch the child's springing mass of black hair. "You misunderstood what you heard this morning. The veterinarian was telling me that Bluebonnet was going to be getting better from now on, and then we started whispering because I wanted to keep it a secret from you, just until I had the chance to make a little deal with you.''

''A deal?'' Teresa asked cautiously, reaching up a thin pajama-clad arm to pull the drowsy dog closer to her cheek. ''What kind of deal?''

''Well,'' Carolyn began awkwardly, seating herself at the side of the bed and gazing intently down at the girl, ''I thought maybe I'd give you Bluebonnet to keep for your own and look after. But that's a very important job,'' she added hastily, seeing how the child's eyes lighted with sudden joy. ''Anybody who's looking after a sensitive little dog like this has to be a very reliable and responsible kind of person. There are some things I'd want to be sure of before I let Bluebonnet come to live with you.''

''Like what?'' Teresa asked.

Carolyn drew a deep breath, wondering if this was the right time to broach the subject after the dreadful trauma the little girl had just endured. Finally she continued, reluctant to pass up such an obvious opportunity.

''Well,'' she began carefully, ''I'd want to be sure that you were going back to school and learning all the things you need to know, dear. I thought maybe that could be our deal, just between you and me. You go back to school, be a good girl and go every day like your mama wants you to, and I'll give Bluebonnet to you for your very own. How's that sound?''

There was a moment of tense silence while Teresa considered. Then she nodded and gave Carolyn a small ghost of a smile.

"Okay," she said. "I wouldn't mind going back to school, Mrs. Townsend. It's kind of funny, but I think after what happened tonight, I won't be so scared of stuff anymore," she added simply.

Carolyn leaned forward and hugged the girl, feeling her eyes fill with tears again. "Well, *I* think," she said, choking a little, "that you and your mother are going to be living here a long, long time, Teresa. And I think you'd both better start calling me Carolyn like all the others do."

"I always call you Gloriana," the little girl said shyly, and then paused, wide-eyed and frightened, obviously alarmed by what she'd just revealed.

"Gloriana?" Carolyn echoed.

"Like the ladies in the castles," Teresa explained in a soft faltering voice, hesitant at first but gaining courage as she spoke. "That's what you look like, a beautiful lady in a castle with silk and jewels, and a tall fancy headdress and white swans swimming in the moat."

"I do?" Carolyn asked, glancing ruefully at her muddy sodden jeans, her stained socks and tangled hair and dirty chilled hands that were scraped raw and bloody in places from tugging on the jagged rungs of the aluminum ladder.

Teresa nodded sleepily, her dark eyes dropping shut. "And Mama's Rosalind," she whispered, "and Karl's Sir Galahad, and Beverly is the lovely Lady Guinevere, and..."

Carolyn smiled tenderly at the two small faces on the pillow, one so pale and delicate, one furry and quizzical. She pulled the covers up gently and tucked them under the child's small chin, then dropped a kiss on her cheek and stood up, moving toward the door.

"Gloriana?" A sleepy voice sounded behind her in the stillness.

"Yes, dear?" Carolyn murmured, turning.

"I love you," Teresa said.

"Oh, sweetheart, I love you, too," Carolyn whispered, gazing back at the child in the dim glow of the night-light. But Teresa was already asleep, her thin chest rising and falling steadily, her face peaceful, rosy lips curved in a half smile while the little dog curled drowsily against her shoulder.

Tears flowed unheeded down Carolyn's face. She swallowed her choking sobs and crept out into the darkened hallway, leaning against the door. This was what people lived for, she thought. The only thing that really made life worth living. These rare brief moments of perfect love…between a man and a woman, between a child and a dog, between a frightened little girl and a lonely widow…these moments comprised the true meaning of life. They were what gave wonder and purpose to the whole difficult, baffling, unpredictable journey.

She'd been so wrong all this time, Carolyn thought. She'd wasted her time railing at fate, demanding absolute guarantees, punishing herself and others by her cold refusal to commit her love because of her fear it might be taken from her.

She knew that she could never have all the security she craved, never provide total safety and protection for the people she loved. But she could enjoy their smiles, welcome another morning, lift her face to the sun, smell the perfume of the flowers and the sage and know that every single day was a gift to be treasured.

And I will, she thought with sudden purpose. *So help me God, I will, starting this very minute.*

Suddenly Carolyn remembered Vernon Trent, standing wearily out in the kitchen. Her throat tightened as she recalled his quiet courage during the rescue of the child. She thought about the man, about his sweetness and generosity and the overwhelming goodness and loyal strength of his long, long love for her, a love she'd almost thrown away because of her cowardice and bitterness.

Carolyn's heart swelled and trembled. She had to restrain herself from rushing into the other room, throwing herself on her knees in front of him and begging his forgiveness.

When she entered the kitchen he was making polite conversation with Rosa and Karl. He carefully avoided Carolyn's eyes.

Carolyn drew on her cold slicker, said goodbye to the young couple and walked out of the cottage beside Vernon, pausing in the chill night air to look around.

"Where's Brock? Did he go back down to try and get his truck out?" Carolyn asked, peering into the darkened lane where they'd left Brock's big truck mired axle-deep in mud.

Vernon shook his head, his features only faintly discernible in the darkness.

"He and Karl decided to wait till morning," Vernon said. "They're going to need a tractor to haul it out. I think," he added, "that Brock's probably already joined the party."

"Party?" Carolyn echoed, walking slowly beside Vernon toward her house.

He gestured at the big ranch house where lights blazed into the dripping blackness from every window and a loud raucous burst of music could be heard each time a door opened.

"I guess they're celebrating," Vernon said. "Release of tension,'' he added. ''People were pretty scared there for a while.''

Carolyn nodded her understanding. She'd seen it before, this kind of spontaneous jubilant celebration that often sprang up when the danger was past. But tonight, a party was the last thing she wanted.

What she really wanted was... She glanced sidelong at the man walking silently beside her, but it was impossible to read anything on his face. He gazed upward, his handsome profile remote, looking at the sky.

''Look, Carolyn,'' he said quietly. ''The weather's breaking.''

She followed his uplifted hand and saw the rift in the clouds, a ragged bit of lace edged with silver from the hidden moon. The rain had stopped, she realized suddenly, and only occasional drops could be heard splattering from the soaked tree branches and dripping off the eaves of buildings.

''Thank God,'' Carolyn murmured fervently. ''I've seen enough rain to last me a good long time.''

As she gazed up at the silvered sky, she felt strength begin to flow into her again. The chill exhaustion slipped gradually from her as if she were shedding a cold wet garment, and she was conscious of a new stirring of optimism.

''Likely,'' she added with sudden awkwardness, trying to draw him into conversation, ''they'll have real good weather now for the barbecue over at the Hole in the Wall.''

Vernon didn't reply, just went on walking, taking her arm to help her over the muddy rutted tracks near the house. Carolyn thrilled at his touch, but felt a wave of unhappiness when she realized how little feeling there was in the gesture. He was just being courteous and considerate as always, nothing more.

Maybe he'd even forgotten about inviting her to the barbecue, she thought with a surge of panic. Maybe he didn't intend to take her at all, and had gotten so angry with her for her cruel rejection of him that his love had died completely. Maybe...

"Actually, it looks like the barbecue at the Hole in the Wall has just gotten an early start," Vernon commented, interrupting her panicky thoughts. "I think most everybody who'll be going to the dude ranch opening is here already, partying up a storm."

Carolyn grimaced, following him through the gate and gazing at the vibrant lighted expanse of the ranch house.

"Vern," she began hesitantly, "you can go in there and mingle if you like, but I truly don't feel up to it right now. I'm going to just avoid them all and slip into my room through the patio doors."

He gazed down at her in silence, his face still obscured by the darkness.

"Or you could...you could come with me, if you

like,'' Carolyn offered shyly, her heart hammering thunderously in her chest. ''You can clean up a little before you go over there and start dancing. I'll just toss your clothes in the dryer, and…''

''Sure,'' he said in that same flat expressionless voice, his face still guarded and distant. ''That'll be nice. Thanks, Carolyn.''

Together they crept around the side of the house to Carolyn's rooms, the only bank of windows in the whole sprawling house that weren't blazing a cheerful welcome. Carolyn slipped open the unlocked patio door, stepped inside and switched on the lamp, sighing with pleasure at the familiar quiet warmth and comfort.

''It seems like a year since I last saw this place, Vern,'' she said with an awkward little laugh as she tugged off her slicker and boots. ''It looks so damned good to me right now.''

Vernon was standing by the patio doors, twisting his cap in his hands, staring at the heap of clothes on the wide bed.

Carolyn followed his gaze and then blushed like a girl. ''I was…I was just trying some things on earlier tonight,'' she explained hurriedly, snatching up the clothes and tossing them out of sight on a bench in her closet. ''I was…trying to decide what to wear to the…the barbecue.''

The old Vernon would have made some cheerful

teasing remark about that, she thought miserably. But tonight he said nothing, just moved wearily aside to pull off his boots and fumble with the muddy fastenings on his slicker.

"Oh, God, Vern, look at you. You're chilled through," Carolyn murmured, forgetting her own nervousness in a flood of concern. "Look, I'll run a tub for you, and you just hop in and soak till you're warm." Carolyn hurried over to the Jacuzzi, which was hidden behind a screen of plants in a corner of the bedroom. She turned on the taps and poured in a reckless amount of bubble bath. "Leave your clothes here by the tub," she added, "and I'll go down to the laundry room with them."

He hesitated, still in the bulky oilskin coat, gazing at her with an unfathomable expression when she straightened and turned to him after switching on the faucets by the sunken tub.

"I'll just...I'll go into the bathroom here and give you a little privacy," Carolyn muttered awkwardly, her face flaming.

She grabbed a fleecy pale blue jogging suit from a shelf in her closet and hurried into the bathroom without a backward glance, wondering how everything had gotten so terribly complicated between them. Just a month ago they'd bathed cheerfully together in this very room, delighting in each other's nakedness. Now, he held himself cautiously aloof and she felt that she had to vanish before he could comfortably undress.

Just when I'm finally ready to love him, she thought with crushing desolation, gazing at her face in the mirror while she hastily soaped her hair and scrubbed her shivering body. *Now, when I've realized how foolish I've been and I'm anxious to make it all up to him, he's so far away I'm not sure I'll be able to touch him again.*

She moaned softly under her breath, devastated by the misery of it all, by the faulty timing and the myriad little cruel ironies of fate that kept people from getting together, condemning them to long wasted years of loneliness.

Moving in quick nervous spurts, painfully conscious of the man in the next room lying naked in her sunken tub, Carolyn dried herself and ran a comb through her wet hair, slicking it back behind her ears. Then she pulled on the pants and sweatshirt she'd brought with her, giving a small involuntary sigh as she felt the cozy fabric nestle against her weary body.

She tugged on a pair of fleecy blue socks, paused and took a deep breath, then opened the door and stepped out into the main room.

"Here I come," she warned, trying to keep her voice light. "I sure hope you're decent."

Wistfully she waited for Vernon to make some droll comment about his own decency or lack of it, but he was silent, lying back in the frothy tub with his eyes closed and the bubbles heaped around his shoulders so only his face was visible. Carolyn stole a surreptitious glance at that beloved face, worrying over the drawn tense look of it. Again she thought that he looked different somehow, though she still couldn't decide what the change was. He was pale and ashen with cold but he seemed to have gotten quite a tan somewhere since she'd seen him last. At least, he looked…

His eyes fluttered open and encountered her intent gaze. Carolyn colored in embarrassment and shifted uneasily on her feet, then dropped her eyes and bent swiftly to gather up the pile of sodden muddy clothes he'd left neatly folded by the edge of the tub.

"I'll just…I'll run down to the laundry room with these," she murmured, "and see if I can find something for you to wear while they're drying."

He nodded silently, his dark eyes still resting on her with an unfathomable expression.

Carolyn felt her heart swelling and breaking with love, with an emotion so intense that it amazed her. She'd never thought it was possible for her to feel this way about anyone, to experience such an overwhelming flood of tenderness and desire that she could scarcely contain the feelings raging through her body.

More than anything in the world, she yearned to

strip off her clothes and step into the cloud of bubbles with him, lose herself in his arms and mouth
and warm solid body.

But his gaze was so quiet and steady, his face so
unrevealing....

After a moment's hesitation, Carolyn turned and
left the bedroom, moving quietly down the hall to
the main floor laundry off the kitchen. The little room
was filled at the moment with a bewildering assort-
ment of emergency supplies...flashlights, life jackets, coils of rope, rubber slickers, cartons of milk and
coffee tins and plastic-wrapped loaves of bread.

Noise from the impromptu party came swirling in
through the louvered doors—laughter, loud conversation and music pounding with an urgent elemental
beat.

The doors opened to admit a fresh blast of sound
and the slim radiant figure of Beverly, who stopped
short in astonishment when she saw her mother.

"Mama!" the girl exclaimed. "We were all wondering where you'd got to. Did you just get back
from Rosa's place?"

Carolyn nodded and tossed Vernon's soiled
clothes in the washing machine, adding a scoop of
detergent and punching the knob while Beverly
watched in silence.

"How is she, Mama?" Beverly asked gently. "Is

she going to be all right? Was it all terribly traumatic for her?"

"She seems fine," Carolyn said with a brief far-away smile, remembering the small child tucked cozily in bed with her dog. "Actually, I think we're going to see a different Teresa from now on. She feels real good about having looked after Bluebonnet. Maybe now she can put the past behind her and get on with her life."

"Really?" Beverly asked, wide-eyed.

Carolyn nodded again. "I made her a deal," she said. "I told her she could have Bluebonnet for her very own if she'd settle down and go back to school."

"And she agreed?" Beverly asked in amazement.

"Almost instantly. She's very bright, you know," Carolyn said. "You should hear some of the things she says, Beverly. I'm really looking forward to getting better acquainted with that little girl."

Beverly hesitated by the door, frowning thoughtfully. "It won't be that easy, you know, Mama," she warned. "She may seem fine now, but likely she'll still need a lot of counseling and help to work through all the things that've happened to her."

"I know, dear," Carolyn said gently. "But at least now, I think she'll allow herself to be helped, if only for the sake of the dog. And that's the main thing."

Beverly looked up at her mother, her eyes shining

with tears. Carolyn gazed back at the young woman in thoughtful silence, pleased to see that her lovely sophisticated daughter could actually be moved to tears of happiness on a child's behalf.

"So," Carolyn said dryly as the moment lengthened and grew awkward, "I gather you're doing a bit of entertaining, my girl."

Immediately Beverly brightened and flashed her old beauty-queen smile. "Oh, Mama," she said gaily, "I just couldn't stop them. They took things right over. I was powerless."

"Well, keep it down," Carolyn said, trying to be stern though her mouth was twitching with laughter. "And don't you let this mob get out of hand. How many are here, anyhow?"

"Not as many as it sounds like," Beverly assured her. "Most of them went home when they knew Teresa was safe. There's just about twenty or so left of the younger people."

"Twenty or so, making all that noise?" Carolyn asked in disbelief.

"Oh, Mama, it's so much fun. Most of them are from the Hole in the Wall, and they're just having a good time. Why don't you join us? Everybody would love to see you."

"Oh, I bet they would," Carolyn said ruefully. "That's sure what they need, all right, a cold cranky middle-aged woman to throw a wet blanket all over their fun.''

"Where's Vern?'' Beverly asked, gazing around curiously. "I wanted to congratulate him, Mama. Vern's a real hero now, you know. Brock told everybody what he did.''

Carolyn blushed and shifted awkwardly under her daughter's frank clear gaze. "Vern's chilled and worn out,'' she said abruptly. "I don't think he wants a lot of attention tonight, Beverly. I've got him soaking in a hot tub, and then I'm going to get some warm food into him and send him home. By the way,'' she added thoughtfully, "those are his clothes in the washer. Have we got anything around here that he could wear while they're drying?''

Beverly frowned briefly, then brightened and moved over to a closet on the far wall. "Tyler keeps an old jogging suit in here,'' she called over her shoulder. "He wears it sometimes when he comes down to play tennis or go running with us. It's pretty loose on Ty,'' she added, her head and shoulders disappearing into the depths of the closet, her voice muffled, "so it should probably fit Vern. Now where…oh, here it is,'' she said, hauling out a pile of faded navy-blue fleece and handing it to Carolyn.

"Thanks, dear,'' Carolyn said, hugging the soft fabric to her chest and smiling at her daughter. "That's just perfect. You have a good time, now, and don't let them climb the walls. If those animals break any of my Delft china, I'll shoot 'em on sight."

"Don't worry a bit, Mama. Everything is under control."

Carolyn snorted and watched her daughter's bright figure whirl off down the hall again.

Suddenly Beverly paused and turned back. "By the way, Mama," she said curiously, "what made you think about looking out on that island, anyhow? Nobody else gave it a single thought."

Carolyn opened her mouth slowly, wondering how much to tell about old Hank's vision.

"I asked Brock," Beverly was saying, "but he didn't know. He said the idea just sort of came to you, so you asked them to check it out with you."

Carolyn hesitated, struck by the young rancher's tact and thoughtfulness. Brock was right to keep silent, she decided. Hank Travis would detest having the whole countryside gossiping about him, discussing his psychic exploits as if he were a fortune-teller at the county fair.

"That's right," Carolyn said finally. "I just remembered how much I was fascinated by that same island when I was a little girl, and thought it might be worth checking."

Beverly shuddered. "I don't know how you

could,'' she said. ''Just thinking about being out there with the river so high gives me the shivers.''

''Me, too,'' Carolyn said, feeling the remembered trickle of cold fear snaking along her spine as she spoke. ''Me, too, darling.''

Carolyn stood watching as Beverly vanished into the noisy depths of the house. Finally she sighed deeply, then turned and wandered down the darkened hall to her room.

CHAPTER THIRTEEN

VERNON LAY in the steaming froth of bubbles, his weary arms resting on the shallow ledge, his bruised tired body luxuriating in the healing warmth.

He should have been in seventh heaven, lost in blissful reverie, delighting in the release of tension, in the little girl's safety and the warmth and comfort of this beautiful room after the howling dark nightmare they'd just survived.

But he couldn't feel happiness. His whole being was gripped with a fear so deep and intense that his body still trembled, despite the warmth of the gentle steaming water.

He stirred restlessly beneath the cloud of bubbles, gripping the washcloth in nerveless hands, frowning at the door through which Carolyn had just disappeared with his muddy clothes.

She'd looked so lovely in that soft pale blue outfit, with her wet hair slicked back to show the classic structure of her face, the high cheekbones and fine-drawn brow and chin. Vernon Trent, who'd spent a whole wistful lifetime gazing at her, couldn't remember her ever looking so utterly beautiful and desirable.

Tonight's the night, Vernon thought. Tonight he would learn what his future was going to be. He couldn't delay any longer. He'd worked so hard to make himself acceptable to her, but he was still the same man, with all his own weaknesses and frailties. What if his best wasn't good enough? What if...?

Vernon had never been so frightened in his life. The raging black river he'd just crossed, the old nightmare of sniper fire in the jungles of Vietnam, none of that was anything compared with the cold heart-stopping terror he felt now.

For a brief frantic moment he even considered escape. He could dry himself off, wrap up in a couple of those big towels, slip out the sliding doors....

And go where?

Vernon grinned, a bleak humorless smile that vanished as soon as it came.

There's no escape this time, my boy, he told himself grimly. *This time you've just got to face the music, and no matter what she says, you'd better be prepared to take it like a man.*

Just as he framed this thought, the door opened and Carolyn stepped back into the room, lingering in the shadowed alcove so he couldn't see her face.

"Well," she said, clearing her throat with a nervous little cough, "I've got your clothes washing,

Vern. I can just toss them in the dryer after the wash cycle, and they should be good as new inside an hour or so. Meantime,'' she added in that same bright forced voice, ''I rustled up something for you to wear. These are actually…''

She moved stiffly toward him, holding out some kind of navy-blue fabric that Vernon looked at without even seeing.

''Carolyn,'' he said gently.

''They're actually Tyler's,'' Carolyn continued as if she hadn't heard him, ''but Beverly thinks they should fit you, Vern. I'll just…''

''Carolyn,'' he said again, bracing his arms on the ledge behind him and preparing to heave himself out of the tub.

''Yes, Vern?'' she whispered, moving close and bending toward him.

Vernon gazed up at her and caught his breath. Her blue eyes glowed, shining with a radiance that illuminated her whole face. Her expression was soft and tender, her lips parted gently, her face alight with warmth and passion.

''Caro,'' he whispered in awe, sinking back into the water again.

''There's something I have to tell you, Vern,'' she said, ''and I can't put it off any longer.''

She drew a deep breath, staring down at the floor

as if summoning all her courage, then turned to him with mute appeal.

"I love you, Vern," she said, gazing at him steadily, kneeling closer to the edge of the tub so she could look into his eyes. "I know I've been awful to you," she went on, the words coming in a rush now that she'd started, "and I probably have no right to even say it, and I certainly have no right to expect you to respond at all, but I wanted to tell you. I love you," she repeated, as if saying the words brought her some kind of fierce deep pleasure. "I love you with my whole heart and I always will, and I'm so sorry for hurting you."

"But, Caro…" he floundered, searching for words while his battered spirit stirred, lifted, began to soar. "Caro, darling, what about all those things you—"

"Don't, Vern," she whispered, leaning over to touch his lips with an urgent trembling hand. "Don't say it. All those things I said came from my own cowardice, that's all. I was just so terribly afraid."

"And now you're not?" he asked, looking up at her in wonder.

She shook her head, smiling at him tenderly. "Now I'm not. I'm like Teresa. After tonight, Vern, I think I won't be so scared of stuff anymore."

Vernon continued to gaze up at her, his tired body singing with joy. He knew that she was waiting, her beautiful eyes anxious and frightened, wanting some kind of response from him.

But he couldn't speak. Instead he moved on the seat, bracing himself against the edge of the tub. Then he slowly pulled himself clear of the froth of bubbles and climbed the ledge to stand dripping on the tiles in front of her.

Carolyn's face tinted pink at his sudden nakedness, so fully and calmly exposed. All at once her eyes widened and she stared at him, gazed the length of his body and then back at his face.

"But, Vern," she whispered, her hand to her mouth, her eyes still wide with shock. "But, Vern, what on earth..?"

"I did it for you, Caro," he said huskily. "I love you so much, and I wanted to show you that I was willing to respect your wishes and make life less frightening for you. I wanted you to know how much I..."

He couldn't go on because she was in his arms, pressing joyously against him, heedless of his wet body that soaked her clothes. Her hair was in his mouth, her lips moving over his chest and neck and mouth, her hands dreamily exploring his ribs, his back, his hard-muscled thighs and hips and shoulders.

"Vern," she whispered against his mouth. "Oh, Vern..."

He tugged gently at her sweatshirt and she moved to help him, pulling the soft garment over her head and tossing it aside. Then she stood silent and quivering while he knelt on the dampened tiles to pull her jogging pants down. He lifted them carefully free of her feet as she stepped out of them, then he eased her panties down over her legs, pausing to gather her into his arms and kiss her flat stomach, her slender hips and thighs. He buried his face reverently against her, savouring the pure rich essence of womanhood that breathed from her.

At last he stood up and released her, kissed her lips with great tenderness and led her into the tub, then turned to draw her gently down beside him in the foaming heated water. She came into his arms like a blessing, like a wondrous gift from some rare and distant place that only existed in his dreams. He gazed into her eyes, stunned and humbled by the love that shone there for him alone, a love so vast and endless that it filled his soul with a sweet soaring rapture.

Vernon held her slender body close, knowing that he would hold her like this for the rest of their lives, that he would cherish her endlessly for all the days and years to come.

"Caro," he whispered in her ear. "I love you, my sweet darling. I love you so much...."

Don't miss After the Lights Go Out, *available next month*.

READER SERVICE™

The best romantic fiction direct to your door

Our guarantee to you...

The Reader Service involves you in no obligation
to purchase, and is truly a service to you!

There are many extra benefits including a free
monthly Newsletter with author interviews,
book previews and much more.

Your books are sent direct to your door
on 14 days no obligation home approval.

We offer huge discounts on selected books
exclusively for subscribers.

Plus, we have a dedicated Customer Care team
on hand to answer all your queries on
(UK) 020 8288 2888
(Ireland) 01 278 2062.

GEN/GU/1

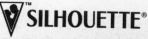